"David Howell is a consummate storyteller. He brings to the task a generative memory, an ear for how real people talk to each other, and an eye to clearly see the quotidian realities of sex, alcohol, God, college, football, cars and, as of late, conspiracy theories. The outcome of his imagination is a story that smacks of specificity, but that at the same time reiterates the recurring realities of intimate human community. You will want to hear this tale of faith, honesty, and human frailty."

—Walter Brueggemann, professor emeritus of Old Testament, Columbia Theological Seminary

"*All Saved Great and Small* is imaginative, theological, and explores life's mysteries: love, betrayal, death, and redemption. You won't be disappointed."

—Jewell-Ann Parton, pastor, Westminster Presbyterian Church

"David Howell is grateful for, critical of, and so revealing about his Appalachian roots. In this book, Howell uses his considerable narrative skills to bring us from Appalachia of the distant and near past, taking us right up to present day realities. Part memoir, part mystery thriller along with theological reflection, David Howell sure knows how to tell a well-wrought tale."

—Will Willimon, professor of the practice of Christian ministry, Duke University

"*All Saved Great and Small* will grab you from the start with multi-layered characters and a setting and plot made so real by the author's experience of the context in which the story is told. In the arsenals of those who hope to leave the world better than we found it, our most powerful tools are stories that leave us changed; this is one of them."

—Amy K. Butler, author of *Beautiful and Terrible Things*

"David Howell tells stories that will intrigue, delight, fascinate, and haunt you. In *All Saved Great and Small*, he weaves together AI, climate change, a Chesapeake cult, conspiracy theories, religion, and the FBI. It's a narrative cocktail that could too easily appear in tomorrow's headlines!"

—Brian D. McLaren, author of *Faith after Doubt*

"Paradox and surprise are two special qualities of good storytelling. With characters as different as two feet in different worlds, they manage to come together as a unified body to make reading David Howell's latest book a pleasurable reward."

—Donald Davis, featured storyteller
at the annual National Storytelling Festival

"David Howell knows how to tell a story, and this book is ample evidence thereof. As most of his books, *All Saved Great and Small* grows out of his experience as a product of Appalachia. But the sweep of this story reaches well beyond the hills and hollers of his home to gather up law enforcement, religious phenomenology, and even science fiction. Told with Howell's near-breathless present tense narrative style, his sentences keep you turning pages, wondering whether you've anticipated the next turn of events or about to be surprised. More often the latter than the former."

—Paul Hooker, retired associate dean,
Austin Presbyterian Theological Seminary

"David Howell's creative storytelling delivers a moral fiction narrative, *All Saved Great and Small*, which will keep you enticed, fascinated, and absorbed. This work provides an exciting read to everyone interested in the struggles and tragedies humans endure and the triumphs humans experience."

—Grace Ji-Sun Kim, professor of theology, Earlham School of Religion

"I have known David Howell as both a preacher and instructor of preaching. Now, in this intriguing novel, he takes readers on a fascinating journey from the hills of Appalachia to the corridors of power, introducing us to a cast of memorable characters, and a cult leader's disturbing scheme to remake the world."

—Michael B. Curry, XXVII Presiding Bishop of The Episcopal Church

All Saved Great and Small

All Saved Great and Small

SURVIVING A CHESAPEAKE CULT AND AN APPALACHIAN APOCALYPSE

DAVID BROWN HOWELL

RESOURCE *Publications* · Eugene, Oregon

ALL SAVED GREAT AND SMALL
Surviving a Chesapeake Cult and an Appalachian Apocalypse

Resource Publications
An Imprint of Wipf and Stock Publishers
199 W. 8th Ave., Suite 3
Eugene, OR 97401

www.wipfandstock.com

PAPERBACK ISBN: 979-8-3852-2531-6
HARDCOVER ISBN: 979-8-3852-2532-3
EBOOK ISBN: 979-8-3852-2533-0

For my parents, Lena and Jack who did everything they could for me
Siblings: Larry, Carolyn
Nephews: Jeff, Brent, Matthew
Children: Wendy, Shannon, Meredith, Morgan, and their spouses
Mary, Nathan, Jake
Grandchildren: Zina, Aidan, Reese, Nolan, Maddox, Abby
Great granddaughters: Capri, Calia
My favorite theologian, Mary Ann Howell

"Once we deeply trust that we ourselves are precious in God's eyes, we are able to realize the preciousness of others and their unique place in God's heart."

—Henri Nouwen

"The universe is made of stories, not atoms."

—Muriel Rukeyser

Preface

An intentional multi-genre work, *All Saved Great and Small* begins as a Conspiracy Thriller (chapter one is the crisis). Chapter two flashes back as Appalachian Noir to explain the childhood background of the two protagonists in a remote, impoverished, and dangerous area in the Appalachian Mountains. The book returns to the Conspiracy Thriller genre as a brilliant, radical scientist risks the fate of civilization to save the planet from the climate crisis. Our protagonists discover the plot and how the scientist sees himself as a descendant of Mary, the mother of Jesus. Moral Fiction genre wraps the entire work as the protagonists struggle with situational depravity, tragedy, personal identities, and internal battles with shame and honor. Written from a reality perspective (no dragons or ghosts), the events of *All Saved Great and Small* could happen. The characters are all fictitious and a product of the author's imagination. No part of this book is AI-generated.

In her Pulitzer winning novel *Demon Copperhead*, Barbara Kingsolver uses the term Melungeon. If you are not familiar with Melungeon, you might want to read Appendix A in the back of this book. Appendix B will help you be more familiar with the 1960s and 1970s in the Appalachian mountains where our protagonists begin their journeys.

Thanks to
Janet Ferrell
Norb McKinney
Darlene M. Davis
Lisa Fox Davis
Claudette Wilson Childs
Kristi Anzivino
Marilyn Howell
Dennis L. Howell
Mary Ann Howell

TITLES BY DAVID BROWN HOWELL

Tethered to an Appalachian Curse: A Surprise Calling

Buried Dreamer

ONE

"Finn, we've called you out of retirement for one last undercover operation. It's a situation that has us very worried. We've received substantial threats against the government. You're uniquely qualified for this assignment," Associate Director Carla F. Johnson of the Bureau's Counter Terrorism Unit explains in the deep raspy voice of a life-long chain smoker as she mashes her cigarette butt in the ashtray on her desk.

"Sorry, I shouldn't smoke in here, but the stress of what I am about to tell you has caused me to pick up the nicotine again."

The nerves of the Bureau's top brass couldn't be more edgy.

"I've accepted every assignment in my career. I guess I can do one more, but this is it. I'm well past FBI retirement age," Finn Boone says as he puts his closed hand near his mouth and coughs in the smoke-filled room.

"Your age is going to be your cover. In the setting you're going into, you'll be less suspicious than a younger agent," Johnson says.

"Good to know that growing older has some benefits," Finn chuckles.

"Finn, this could be bigger than 9-11, much bigger," Johnson explains as she leans forward, her eyes radiating. "We knew the day would come when a person with extensive AI ability might try something. You don't need an army to control the world anymore. One brilliant scientist can defeat an army. A genius-like person with AI expertise who can stay one step ahead of everyone else can have the world at his mercy. Finn, you've had experience as an undercover agent, experience with domestic counterterrorism and cyberterrorism. We want you to infiltrate a cult near Irvington, Virginia. I don't know if you've heard of Irvington, but it's near the Chesapeake Bay. This person has powerful quantum computers and software. You'll find out for us exactly what is going on."

"Will I be working alone?" Finn asks while he thinks Carla's voice sounds like throat cancer in the making.

"Yes, at first," Johnson says as she puts her finger on her glasses and pushes them up her nose. "I'll be your main contact. If it's important and you can't reach me, you're going to have direct access to the Director. This is big. John L. Maetson in the Richmond field office and Sara M. Burnes at Quantico will be aware of what's going on as well. This is Top Secret Classified. Nothing slips through the cracks on this one."

When Finn hears TSC, he knows what that means, a situation that could cause exceptionally grave damage to national security.

Johnson clears her throat from the smoke irritation and leans back. "I remember now why I quit smoking. Stuff irritates my throat. I should know better. Back to your assignment. We'll set you up with a fake identity. You're going to be the Reverend Jonah Crow from Elkhart, Indiana. You're frustrated with your church there. You want them to be more active on the political right and a friend to the white supremacy movement. But some in the church, although they like the idea, worry it might be going too far and get the church in trouble. You've resigned your position and moved to an RV campground on the Rappahannock River near Irvington. You're looking for like-minded right-wing extremists on the Virginia coast. Through another government agency that can't be traced, we've rented a warehouse for you near Kilmarnock, just a few miles from Irvington. You're gonna start a new church. Name it what you want, but we like Tabernacle of Deliverance. Nice ring to it. You want to offer people hope of a new world order through new spiritual knowledge. You'll preach coming change when the righteous will rule. Maybe, you'll preach that the seven signs of deliverance are being revealed to you. You know, the secrets to escape the coming judgment or some such crap as that. The cult will hear about this, and hopefully you can get your foot in the door."

Finn shifts nervously, "For heaven's sake, I don't know how to preach."

"Don't worry. You're going to have some good coaching. A theology professor at a seminary in Richmond who's an expert on cults will get you up to speed. We're already working on flyers and newspaper ads for your new church."

"You've put a lot of thought into this. What's this group trying to do?" Finn asks as he releases a deep breath.

"Well, from what we are hearing, it's as serious as anything we've ever dealt with, maybe worse, a lot worse. The leader of this cult, whoever it is, knows what he's doing. I said he, but it could be a woman. We don't know. We do suspect the person is an unhappy and disgruntled employee of a high-tech area of the government or military or maybe even of some big corporation? We know these corporations have been working on some amazing projects, using AI to possibly regenerate the brains and vital organs of their top executives, so that they can essentially live forever."

"Why not just move on the cult in Irvington? Arrest them?" Finn asks.

"I wish that'd solve the problem, but the leader is not on site. There's a small crew there, and the leader directs the operation by secret code we've not been able to decipher or trace. The leader is incredibly talented, maybe one of the best minds on the planet. He bounces things off proxy servers all over the world, making it impossible to track him down."

"Sounds like quite a challenge," Finn sighs. "Why're they in Irvington, Virginia?"

"At the start of World War II, the Navy was concerned Germany might invade the United States. If we had lost the war in the Atlantic, that could have happened. So, the Navy dredged the creeks in Irvington that flow into the Chesapeake Bay. With the deeper water, they could bring small ships up into the creeks and hide them there. The Navy dug underground bunkers near the creeks for staff and equipment. Our military won the battle of the Atlantic and forgot about the bunkers. Through a series of shell-companies, an individual bought a series of bunkers. That's what you must penetrate and let us know what's going on.

"We think you're the man for this challenge. Let your hair and beard grow out. We'll get you some up-to-date training on cult thinking and language before you go in, and you'll learn how to preach from a theology professor," Johnson says, and then adds, "Finn, I can't overstate how important this is. The last message we received said, 'Minotaur Will Destroy This Government.' The fate of the country, maybe of civilization, is at stake."

"I'll do my very best."

TWO

On a sticky hot August morning in 1962, yellow jackets swarm outside while water drips from a leaky kitchen faucet in Tinnie Wilson's house. The smell of drifting smoke from elderly widow Tinnie Wilson's wood stove moves through the air. Tinnie's mother died in childbirth. They lived in Tennessee at the time. Her father named her, Tennessee, after the state. In her late eighties, Tinnie refuses electricity, saying it's of the Devil, and cooks all her meals on a wood cookstove she inherited from her mother.

Tinnie always wears unbuckled galoshes that jingle as she walks. Since Tinnie has been 'on the cane' for several years, she sits in her rocking chair most of the day with her cheek full of Navy brand snuff. A homemade spittoon, her constant companion, made from an empty Maxwell House coffee-can stuffed with tissue now soaked with dark brown snuff spit, sits at her side. On this unusually hot day in the mountains of North Carolina, Tinnie pulls up her long dress to stay cool. Her legs look like roadmaps with bluish-red varicose veins running in all directions.

Whack! Whack! Screams!

Familiar sounds come from Reuben Boone's house, the next house up the hill from Tinnie's and just past Tinnie's ancient, sagging barn covered by old growth vines with one barn door already off its hinges. Underneath the vines, expired automobile license plates of different colors paste one side of the barn. Tinnie's husband kept the house and barn repaired, but he died nearly twenty years ago .

"He's gonna kill one of those boys one day," Tinnie thinks to herself as she smacks a fly with a swatter she always keeps by her side.

"Oh! Please don't hit me again!" Seth Daniel Boone screams.

The oldest boy, Seth, got his middle name from Daniel Boone, the explorer and Reuben's ancestor. Fiona, the mother and of Irish descent, insisted on the next boy, Finn, having an Irish name as well. Mickey is the youngest boy, and both younger boys' middle names are Daniel.

TWO

"Come here, you lil' brat!" Reuben, smelling of sweat and cheap beer, roars. Seth pulls away from his angry father's grasp, but there is no escape, only momentary hope.

"Got you!" Reuben, a wild ass of a man, roars in smirking pleasure. His strong forearms show beneath his rolled-up sleeves.

"Stop! It hurts! I won't do it again!" Seth begs.

"Whack!" "Whack!" "Whack!" Finn hears the heavy leather belt strike his brother's rump and legs. Reuben bought the genuine leather, bullwhip-like belt at the reservation in Cherokee.

"I won't do it again!" Seth promises in a crying scream.

"You boys gotta stop stealin' food out of my refrigerator. Times are hard. We feed you boys two good meals a day. More than some young'uns get these days!" Reuben barks, nostrils flaring.

"I promise! I promise!" Seth cries.

"I know how to raise boys, like my daddy did. Fathers gotta whoop their children when they disobey. It's in that Bible your mama reads in church. Moses beat the shit out of those lil' Hebrew brats when they needed it."

"Whomp!" Finn knows Seth just got 'the kick.' Father swings his size fourteen shoe into Seth's rear. The kick always comes after the belt blows.

Finn hates waiting. He knows his father comes for him next. But if he doesn't get his beating first, Finn can hope for a knock on the door from a neighbor or a customer, and father stops the beatings.

Knowing his father comes for him any minute, Finn's dread intensifies. It's gonna hurt bad. He waits, his breathing heavy.

Fiona goes outside when her husband beats the boys. She hates Reuben as much as she could hate anything, she thinks. When she can, she reassures the boys they'll be better men than their father.

The door opens. "Finn, get your sorry ass in here! Damn you boys. You're troublemakers!"

As Finn enters, Reuben swings his left arm around and grabs Finn's right arm. Finn tries to pull away, but his father's grip is too strong.

"Oh!" Finn screams as the first blow lands.

Another blow stings. Then another and another. His father drops the belt, but only to wipe the sweat from his forehead.

Lucky for the brothers, these are morning beatings. Reuben doesn't get drunk until mid-afternoon. When drunk, Reuben is dangerous. He often goes into Burnsville hoping to get into a fistfight in the pool hall or at Burnsville's hamburger joint.

"You're the worst boy I got!" Reuben declares as the blows resume. Finn feels his backside rise until he is almost on his tiptoes as the size fourteen boot lands.

Tears run down Finn's cheeks as he leaves the room. Anger flushes through his face. He swears to himself he'll get revenge someday. At this moment, he doesn't care about being a better man than his father.

Mickey cries and trembles as he listens to his brothers' beatings. Red patches spot the whites of his eyes. He holds his breath.

"Tell the Little Doll to go crawl under his mother's apron," Reuben shouts. He won't whip Finn's little brother this time. Mickey is frail, sickly. Reuben calls him a little sissy and says he will never be a man. Reuben does not hide his scorn for the little boy he calls "Little Doll."

Twenty minutes later when the boys are outside, the boys hear the usual argument following every beating.

"You don't have to whip those boys so hard!" Fiona pleads. "You're gonna regret this someday!"

"What do you know, ole woman!" Reuben laughs. "Your father was no good and what did you have, three mothers? Or was it four? All damn sickly."

Fiona Dunnegan Boone knows she will be fortunate if she escapes a beating. And Tinnie Wilson knows this as well as she rocks, spits, sighs, and says to herself, "Those poor boys and that poor woman." A tear flows down her cheek.

By the time Reuben Roy Boone was thirteen, he stood toe to toe with his father Silas Boone and held his own during fist fights with his father. At sixteen, Reuben towered over his father and every man in the county. He was a chiseled six foot and five inches. He could make a fist almost as big as a bowling ball, and a handshake felt like being in a vice.

Reuben's violence respects no one. Locally renowned, he fights anyone who crosses his path and always wins. He brags the only way he can be beaten is with a bullet, but he'll crush the skull of the first man who pulls a gun on him.

Reuben makes his living as a bootlegger. He pokes fun at the other men in the community who work for minimum wage in the mines or in the factories. "Them corporations from up north who put their factories here for cheap labor keep all the money they make. You fools are making them rich."

Yancey County in the Appalachian Mountains of North Carolina is a dry county to this day. In 2010, Burnsville citizens voted for alcohol sales within the town limits of Burnsville. It was a Reuben Boone bootlegger's paradise with any public sale of alcohol illegal. Reuben's house sits on a bank overlooking the South Toe River. Mitchell County, another dry county, is just a few miles away. Reuben supplies good times to people in two counties.

Once a week or so, Reuben drives to Buncombe County where public sale of alcohol is allowed. Asheville sits in the middle of Buncombe County, but Reuben needs to go no further than Flat Creek to fill his pickup bed with Pabst Blue Ribbon, Schlitz, and Budweiser. For the holidays, Reuben stocks Wild Turkey. For the supervisors and foremen who get paid more than minimum wage in the factories and mines, Reuben keeps a supply of Mateus Rose, and for the budget wine drinker, he stocks Thunderbird. Reuben marks up each product two hundred percent or more. It's a fine living for Reuben.

Customers simply drive up to Reuben's house, park, and knock on the door. They tell Reuben what they want and hand over the money. On Friday afternoons when the men finish their week of work, Reuben sits on his front porch with coolers full of ice-cold beer. An elderly feeble customer might blow the car horn, and Reuben happily takes their order. Once a month for legal protection, Reuben meets a local official on an isolated dead-end road and hands the man ten percent of the monthly sales.

THREE

The second of sixteen children, Fiona Dunnegan grew up on the North Toe River in Mitchell County. Her daddy, a miner, made her quit school in the third grade, stay home, and help with the babies being born every nine or ten months. Fiona's mother died giving birth to her little brother. Her father quickly married Sophronia Sparks who was at once with a child. Sophronia died giving birth to her fifth baby. Nate Dunnegan brought in a third wife who bore him more children. Fourteen children survived, with one dying in childbirth and another falling into the fireplace as a toddler.

Sixteen-year-old Fiona and two friends approach a swimming hole just north of the one lane bridge that crosses the North Toe River and connects Mitchell and Yancey counties. They hear voices and splashes from the water as they make their way along the crooked path in the dense thicket of laurel and rhododendron bushes that leads to everybody's favorite swimming hole. They expect to see a young family with kids splashing wildly in the water.

Instead, Fiona and her friends see the Boone brothers taking turns swinging from a rope tied to a huge limb of a giant oak tree sitting high above the river. Screaming all the way down, they make monster splashes when they hit the pool of water below. Reuben has his three younger brothers with him. All the boys have biblical names: Jacob, Jeremiah, and Elijah. Reuben, as he always does, runs the show, and the younger brothers dare not challenge him.

Reuben eyed Fiona before at Maude Gurley's little store in Micaville. As a teenager, Reuben is already perhaps the tallest man in the county, and Fiona, tall as well, stands nearly five feet and nine inches tall. Thin as a rail, Fiona weighs a mere one hundred and ten pounds. She's somewhat malnourished as the family food must be shared with two adults and fourteen children. Kids tease her that she is "wormy." But it is not a parasite, just a lack of good nutrition. Still, she is a "looker" with red-auburn hair, robin-egg blue eyes, and enough fatty tissue in all the right places.

THREE

Reuben dropped out of school in the ninth grade to work on a logging crew. Even then, his strength wowed the other men on the crew. A huge log fell on a co-worker. The man's legs were caught under the log. He would bleed to death if he didn't get medical attention soon. Two men could not move the log. Reuben told the men to stand aside and, like a bulldozer at full throttle, rolled the log just enough so that the other men could pull the injured man to safety. The legend of Reuben Boone is born.

Fiona and Reuben eye each other on that warm summer afternoon. Reuben makes his way over, "If you want to hold on to that rope, I'll give you a big push."

"Well, that sounds like fun!" Fiona says.

Later, they sit on the riverbank.

"I heard you quit school a long time ago," Reuben says.

"Yep, I had to help at home. I've got a lot of younger brothers and sisters," Fiona says.

"Well, I quit school too. I like having a piece of money in my pocket, and school didn't pay nuttin," Reuben says.

"I wonder what kind of job I can ever get without no education? I've missed out on a lot of book learning," Fiona says.

"The hosiery mill in Burnsville will put you on. You look like you are in your twenties. Just don't tell them your real age," Reuben says.

"I'm a wondering if I might come up to your house on Saturday night? I got a real good tabletop radio. We can listen to the Grand Ole Opry. It comes on 650 AM, WSM radio out of Nashville, Tennessee," Reuben says, trying to impress Fiona with his knowledge.

"Where did you get a tabletop radio? Only people with money have those," Fiona asks.

"You might say I borrowed it," Reuben rolls his eyes.

"My daddy won't let me . . ."

Before Fiona can finish, Reuben makes up a lie, "I'm gonna give it back. Ole man Silvers been in the hospital, down with the gout. He ain't needed it, anyway."

Thus begins the courtship between Fiona Dunnegan and Reuben Boone.

World War II winds down. Reuben avoids the Army as he has not turned eighteen. Reuben's first cousin was killed at the Battle of the Bulge. Another cousin returned from the war with a limp so severe he had to use both arms to move his right leg.

Dating Fiona, Reuben struts about as happy as a bird with a french-fry. Reuben takes Fiona to the picture-show in Spruce Pine every weekend. After cheeseburgers and onion rings at a drive-in restaurant, they go parking. Ole man Todd Burleson's farm hasn't operated for over two years, and nobody lives there while the children fight over the ownership in the slow-as-molasses Mitchell County Court.

Reuben borrows a black 1942 Chevrolet from his uncle for courting. The uncle makes big money in a mica mine and bought one of the last vehicles made until the war was over. The government prohibits the automobile industry from making cars after the 1942 model. Factories convert to manufacture military vehicles.

Reuben pulls the shiny Chevy behind the Burleson barn. Stars shine brightly through the clear sky.

Although she desires Reuben, Fiona doesn't want to have sex. During earlier episodes in the Chevy, Fiona resisted Reuben's advances. But this night is different. Without any artificial light in the area, the full moon glows over the old barn. Tree-frogs chirp down by the pond, making for a beautiful October evening, all the windows down in the Chevy and the crisp mountain air perfect.

"Let's get in the backseat, honey," Reuben says.

Fiona realizes this is probably the time. Reuben comes around and opens the passenger door for her. He opens the rear door and gives her perfect buttocks a gentle tap when she bends over.

Once both are on the backseat, Reuben moves his head toward hers. They look at each other's lips. Lips meet. Heavy breathing follows. Reuben runs his hand up her blouse and, reaching down with his other hand, pulls her skirt up. His hands move to the hooks on her bra. Her bra falls away. His hands move toward her breasts.

Fiona realizes they are reaching the point of no return. She doesn't know what to do. Could mean a big change in her life. Possible pregnancy. A baby. What would she do?

Reuben's hands make their way across her stomach. One hand slips up her thigh. Fiona wants to please him but is so scared.

Blue lights! A low roar pulls beside them. The gravel rattles as the deputy sheriff's car comes to a halt. A flashlight beams across their near nude bodies.

"You kids having fun? This is private property, you know," Deputy Sheriff Blevins asks.

THREE

Reuben rises, stone-faced. The flashlight illuminates his face.

"Reuben Boone! I didn't know that was you. I thought you drove your daddy's pickup?"

"My uncle lets me borrow this Chevy, you know, when I got a pretty girl."

"That's a pretty one for sure! Honey, what's your name?"

"Fiona Dunnegan," Fiona says as she holds her shirt over her breasts.

"Where you live?"

"Head of Rebel's Creek," a very polite Fiona says.

"Well, you kids don't do anything I wouldn't do," the deputy chuckles, steps into his police cruiser, pulls the steering lever down into drive, and pulls away.

Fiona did not want them to get into any kind of trouble, but she was hoping the deputy would make them leave.

Reuben smiles and moves back toward her. Hands touch her again. He pulls at her panties, and they are almost to her knees.

"Wait!" Fiona says. "Do you have a rubber?"

"No, but this train always pulls out of the station ahead of time. Ain't never got no girl pregnant before. Works every time," Reuben says.

Out of ways to stall the inevitable, Fiona wiggles her legs as Reuben slips her panties down her legs and off her feet.

FOUR

Fiona and Reuben marry six months later in Sawmill Holler Free Will Baptist Church. The preacher delivers a scorching sermon on the perils of the sinful life for the unsaved. Get saved or roast in hell for all eternity. Reuben watches a wasp buzz around the back of the church rather than pay attention to the preacher. Fiona listens intensely at the preacher's warning and wonders if she is saved, although she was baptized at twelve years of age. The preacher warns the couple of lust and adultery while from his pulpit perch above he admires Fiona's cleavage below.

They exchange cheap rings bought from the Dime Store in Spruce Pine. They embrace and kiss in front of the altar, and then the choir erupts in verses of "Jesus Saves."

Give the winds a mighty voice:
Jesus saves! Jesus saves!
Let the nations now rejoice:
Jesus saves! Jesus saves!
Shout salvation full and free:
Highest hills and deepest caves;
This our song of victory;
Jesus saves! Jesus saves!

The honeymooners travel to Marion, North Carolina. They eat dinner at the Fish Camp Restaurant on the Catawba River. The room at the roach infested Whispering Pines Motel on the Charlotte side of Marion costs Reuben ten dollars for their one-night stay. Reuben drinks a six-pack of Pabst Blue Ribbon and smokes half a pack of Marlboros, although Fiona asked him not to smoke in the room.

Figuring he has waited long enough, Reuben does not pull the train out of the station on time. Seth Daniel Boone was born nine months later in McDowell Hospital in Marion. Neither Burnsville nor Spruce Pine had a hospital at the time. In the maternity ward waiting room, Reuben chain smokes, unless he's out in the car drinking tall cans of Schlitz. Without insurance, the hospital agrees to send Reuben a bill that he never pays.

FOUR

Fiona will be in the hospital for a couple of days. Reuben stops at a Piggly-Wiggly on the way home and buys a box of Swisher Sweet Blunt cigars for his friends.

That evening, Reuben stops at the drive-in restaurant in Spruce Pine and pulls beside an old girlfriend, Geraldine, who sits in her new candy-apple red Ford Thunderbird she bought after landing a secretarial position with a minerals' corporation in Spruce Pine. Reuben asks to drive her new car. Geraldine and Reuben end up in the back seat of the Thunderbird at the end of the road at the county landfill on this dark night. Little does Fiona know, the rest of her life will be like walking barefoot on shattered glass.

Ten months later, Fiona gives birth to a healthy Finn Daniel Boone. After another eleven months, Mickey Daniel Boone is born prematurely. Mickey struggles with health issues, anemia, and asthma, throughout his childhood. He doesn't have the energy of the other children in the area. Most of the time, he plays with a small set of plastic cars and trucks on the brown linoleum floor in the living room.

Reuben quits his job with the logging operation after an altercation with the owner who refuses to make Reuben a partner. Reuben says he will start his own operation, but it will not be logging.

Fiona attends church services most every Sunday at Born Again Baptist Church. From time to time, she sings with the choir. The choir director begs her to join the choir permanently, telling Fiona she has the voice of an angel. She doesn't attend the adult Sunday School class at the earlier hour. She fears what people in the class might say about her since she is married to the most notorious man in the area.

At the close of the Sunday service of worship, Reverend Leroy blesses the congregants with a benediction. While the choir sings the postlude, he makes his way to the front porch of the church where he will shake the hands of each person who exits the church. He'll smile at each person and hug the older widows who are the largest contributors to the church due to their husbands' life insurance payouts. Children run by the preacher and begin playing in a grassy area behind the church.

John Alfred Towe, a member of the Board of Deacons and a farmer, asks Reverend Leroy to pray for rain the coming week. His crops are failing. Mildred McKinney asks Reverend Leroy to pray for her sister who is in the Asheville hospital suffering from a collapsed lung. Reverend Leroy asks

Tammy Butner how her sister is doing after the car accident two weeks ago. Reverend Leroy does his pastoral work.

Butch T. Buchanan, whose wife died of cancer three years ago, shakes the preacher's hand and heads for his new silver Cadillac Custom Convertible sitting in the far side of the parking lot. He pays for the car and his new brick rancher home with the considerable profits he makes as the area bootlegger. He parks well away from the other cars since he doesn't want anyone opening their car door and denting his shiny Cadillac, glistening in the noon day sun.

Butch notices a figure hunched on the other side of his car. As he approaches his car, he realizes it is Reuben Boone.

"Come on around here Butch. I need to talk to you about something," Reuben says. Butch walks around the other side of the car not knowing what is about to happen.

"Butch, we need to get something straight. This is my territory now. You're gonna quit selling," Reuben says with an intense stern look on his face.

"Listen friend, you just can't take over. I've been selling here for over twenty years. These people know I give them a good price on their liquor and beer."

"I'm not your friend. You better listen and do as I say," Reuben barks.

"Wham!" Butch's head jerks to the right as Reuben's massive right fist slams into the left side of Butch's face.

"You, son-of-a-bitch!" Butch screams. Everyone in the parking lot turns to see. Shocked, Fiona covers her mouth with her hand.

All the air explodes from Butch's lungs as Reuben's left fist drives into his stomach. Another right hook and Butch tumbles backwards, falling down a bank into a creek. When he is finally able to get on his feet with the creek water running around his ankles, he looks like a wet dog with drenched hair and clothes hanging from his skinny body.

"Butch, I think you understand now. My territory from now on. You best find another trade. You ain't selling here anymore. You sell anymore, and I'll hurt you real good next time. Go home and send anybody that's looking to buy to my house. You understand?" Reuben says looking down at the humiliated former bootlegger. The parishioners who were observing the beat-down hustle to their cars as lightning cracks and thunder rumbles in the western sky.

FOUR

"You didn't have to beat him at church!" Fiona protests. "Everybody in the area knows now."

"Well, that's good. Good for business. They know where to come now," Reuben chuckles.

The following Sunday Reverend Leroy makes this proclamation to his congregation: "Brothers and sisters, you saw the terrible thing that happened to Butch last Sunday. Reuben Boone has a dark soul. He and probably his entire family will be turned away from the gates of heaven. They are doomed, cursed, beyond redemption."

Reuben gets word about the preacher's pronouncement. The preacher gets a visit. Reuben sits in his car at the preacher's house. Reverend Leroy arrives from a hospital visit in Marion. Reverend Leroy's heart skips a beat when he sees his visitor. Reuben steps out of his car and leans against the hood while he finishes his Pall Mall cigarette. Reverend Leroy, pushing his hands down into the pockets of his pants, approaches in fear and trembling, his insides fluttering like a caged bird.

"I heard what you said about me on Sunday."

"Well, I uh...," Reverend Leroy struggles to find words.

"You were just doing your job. You're the preacher. I understand that. We all got jobs to do, right?"

"Yes, we do," Reverend Leroy releases held breath.

"Your job is to preach the very Word of God. Right?"

"Yes, it is. It's my calling."

"My calling is to provide the fine citizens of this community with the spirits they need to survive in these hard times. I hate busting a feller's head, but I must get what's rightfully mine," Reuben says.

Reverend Leroy begins to think maybe he will survive this encounter with the meanest man in the county, but he wonders if Reuben is toying with him, like a cat toys with a mouse before the kill.

"Get in the car with me," Reuben says. "I want to give you something."

Reverend Leroy gets in the passenger side. Reuben sits behind the wheel and reaches under the seat.

"I want you to have a drink with me," Reuben pulls out a fifth of Wild Turkey and two Dixie cups.

"I don't drink. I did, but my daddy and mother died of the cirrhosis. I found Jesus, got saved, and went into the ministry. I ain't touched a drop in over fifteen years."

"I'm just trying to be sociable here. Don't go and hurt my feelings," Reuben frowns. "Just one lil' drink ain't gonna hurt you none," Reuben says as he pours whisky into the Dixie cup and hands it to the preacher. "Just relax. I think we can be friends."

Reverend Leroy hands shake as he takes the cup. He opens his mouth and throws his head back, hoping to not taste the whiskey as it sails down his throat.

"That a boy!" Reuben yells as he slaps Reverend Leroy's back.

"Just one more shot, and I will be on my way. I know you have the Lord's work to do. But keep this bottle. It'll do you good. There's plenty more where this comes from. Meet me every other Wednesday at the head of Shoal Creek Road. It's a dead end and nobody lives up there. I'll be coming back from my run to Asheville. I'll have two fifths for you. Get you through the week and help you with your stress. And bring a little of that offering plate money to help me along. Okay? I don't want to hear no poor-mouthing."

Looking stricken, Reverend Leroy nods his head in submission.

"And remember to pray for me and my family. You hear?" Reuben concludes.

Fiona and Reuben set up house in a rental overlooking the South Toe River. Reuben's uncle dies, and they get his pots, pans, dishes, and utensils. The white board house has two stories, four bedrooms, and a working fireplace with a handsome red brick chimney. The back side of the house facing the north has some green mold spots. Reuben promises Fiona that he'll scrub it off, but he never gets around to it. They'll be renters until they can buy the place. The elderly widow, Tinnie Wilson, is their only neighbor. Reuben thinks he needs an isolated spot like this for his bootlegging operation. He doesn't think Tinnie will even know what's going on. He'll tell Tinnie he just has lots of friends who love to visit him.

Reuben's bootlegging business flourishes. Area residents need their alcohol to cope with their lives. Most of the area residents feel a kind of hopelessness. Their assembly line jobs in the local mines and factories are monotonous and boring. The thought of cold beer and liquor shots to numb their aches and pains when they get home gets them through the workday. Reuben expands his product line. He sells hunting knives, switchblade knives, used firearms, and even brass-knuckles for fist-fighting.

One day after selling beer, a switchblade, and a set of brass-knuckles to two teenagers, Fiona hears Reuben say to them, "You boys be good." Fiona tries to pretend it's not happening. She focuses on raising her boys and builds a psychological wall of denial.

When Fiona complains, Reuben always has something clever and sarcastic to say. "You know that time I went with you to church and Reverend Leroy talked about Jesus taking them loaves and fishes and multiplying them? Well, that's kind of what I'm doing. I'm giving these people something that eases their pain and suffering. You don't tell anybody this, but Reverend Leroy can't come here cause somebody might see him. But I meet him every two weeks up at the end of Shoal Creek Road, and he takes a good supply home with him. Don't you ever say a word about that! You understand?"

Fiona nods her head as Reuben opens the refrigerator door, pulls out a milk carton, and guzzles down several big mouthfuls, returning the milk carton to the refrigerator.

Reuben tells his customers, "Doctor gives you pain-pills and you don't take 'em all, I'll buy them. Bring 'em the next time you come." Reuben begins the area's first opioid pharmacy.

Making big money, Reuben's confidence grows into a malignant narcissism. He has the preacher and the county officials in his back pocket. He doesn't see any threats to his growing illegal empire.

One morning, Fiona sees a white Dodge truck sitting in the driveway. Reuben was out drinking with some buddies after an evening of listening to their dogs chase foxes on Humpback Mountain. After the chase, they go to Calvin Riddle's house for poker and whiskey.

"Whose truck is that?" Fiona asks as she looks out the window while stirring a pot of oatmeal on the electric burner white stove.

"That's our truck. I won it in a poker game last night."

"Looks like Calvin Riddle's truck," Fiona responds, still puzzled.

"Used to be his. It's ours now. We need a second car. I told Calvin he shouldn't bet his truck on a hand of poker but that's what he wanted to do."

What really happened started with lots of free whiskey, courtesy of Reuben, at the poker game at Calvin Riddle's house. The three other men never drank Blanton's Original Single Barrel Whiskey before, and they were thrilled with the smoothness, nothing like the cheap stuff they normally drink. Reuben had picked up several bottles during his last trip to Asheville. Calvin Riddle drank the smooth whiskey way too fast. Reuben kept pouring him refills and telling Calvin what a man he was, who could hold his liquor like that. Several glasses too many, and Calvin blacks out with his head on the card table.

Reuben makes a deal with the other two poker players. He'll give them fifty dollars each to go along with his story that Calvin bet his truck on the last hand, and how Reuben's four kings beat Calvin's flush. Reuben warns the other two players what his fists will do to them if they don't go along with his story.

Calvin complains to the authorities the next day when he finds out Reuben claims to have won his truck in the poker game.

"Reuben's got two witnesses who said you bet the truck on the last hand. What am I supposed to do?" The local official says as he blows his nose, looking down into his white handkerchief. "Sounds like Reuben won it fair and square. And sounds like you better cut back on your drinking before you lose your house and farm! You'll have to sign the title over to Reuben. I'll take it to him." For his trouble, Reuben delivers a case of Blanton's Whiskey to the official's house.

Reuben insists the family watch *Walt Disney* every Sunday evening. He likes the series about Davy Crockett and especially the series about Daniel Boone.

"That's your ancestor, boys!" Reuben brags.

Reuben goes to town and brings back coonskin caps and toy flintlock rifles for the boys. Reuben teases Mickey before he gives him his hat and rifle. "You ever gonna be man enough for a real rifle?" Fiona begs Reuben not to taunt the little boy.

"I'll show you how to be a man. Fiona, grab that box of kitchen matches. Your mama gonna burn the hair out of my ears."

"Reuben, I can do that with scissors."

"Strike a match and stick it in my ear. But you gotta be quick."

Fiona does as she is told.

"Ouch! Damn! Now do the other ear."

"Are you sure?"

"Yes!"

"Okay."

"Whew! That's how you be a man. I'm hot-blooded, too. Ain't no little match gonna hurt me much."

FIVE

The first Saturday in October is for hog killing. The cool air signals the beginning of cold weather. Preparations for another hard winter are going on. During August and September, Fiona cooks and cans vegetables from their garden. Potatoes, which the boys dug up two weeks ago, are stored in the cellar. While Seth's job is to feed the chickens every day, Finn slops the hog with table scraps and potato peelings.

Mickey is sick, but Reuben, Seth, and Finn get up early and start the fire outside. A tub of hot water boils. Reuben shoots the hog between the eyes with his rifle, and then slits the hog's throat. Finn is attached to the animal he calls Ben. Finn flinches when his friend is shot and looks the other way when the throat is cut.

Reuben throws a rope over an oak limb running parallel to the ground with one end of the rope tied around the hog's feet. Reuben pulls the massive animal off the ground while at other homes and farms entire families are needed to lift the behemoth creatures. More blood runs out of the hog's neck. Seth and Finn throw buckets of hot water on the hog. Then, they take butcher knives and scrape off the hair. Their job is finished. Reuben carefully removes large sections of meat. Fiona carefully wraps each piece in old newspaper, and the life sustaining meats are placed in the white chest-freezer.

Early evening, Fiona chops vegetables that will be boiled and served with fresh pork chops for supper. Biscuits bake in the oven.

The boys feast on the pork chops and biscuits while reluctantly chewing down a few vegetables. Sensing Reuben is not happy about something, the boys go outside and listen for a hoot-owl.

"You burned my god-damn pork chops!" Reuben shouts at Fiona. "I raised that hog and worked all morning trimming off the meat, and you burn my pork chops! Good pork chops are expensive and have gotten higher than a cat's back at the grocery store!"

Reuben walks to the cookstove, grabs the handle of the black cast-iron skillet still full of hot grease and slings the pan. The pan flies through the air and onto the floor in the living room. Hot grease strikes Fiona on the left side of her face. She screams in pain, grabs her face, but the hot grease burns her hands as well. The boys run into the house.

"Mama!" Seth screams. Mickey cries and shakes. Finn stares at his mother who is in great pain.

"She dropped the pan. Grease flew up into her face," Reuben explains. "I'll take her to the nurse's house."

Antionette Greene, a nurse at a local hospital during the week who lives about two miles away, hears the knock on the door. "Who is it?"

"Reuben Boone! Fiona's done burned herself, real bad!"

Antoinette opens the door, helps Fiona on to the sofa, and begins to clean and bandage Fiona's face.

"I'm gonna go outside to smoke," Reuben says.

When Fiona is convinced that Reuben is far enough away from the house, she says, "he threw the grease on me."

"I wondered about that," Antoinette says. "You're burned pretty bad. I'll take you to the hospital."

Antoinette tells Reuben to go home and put the boys to bed. She'll take Fiona to the hospital. Reuben smokes and drinks until there is a knock on the door just after midnight.

"They're gonna keep her overnight. She's gonna be alright but probably disfigured for life. Shame it happened to such a pretty face," Antionette says.

The hospital keeps Fiona for two nights. The doctor worries about infection, but so far Fiona has avoided any complications. Rueben brings her home to three worried boys. She assures them she will be fine. They stare at the large bandages on her face.

Two days later, a knock on the door. It's a local official. A soft wind has the wind chimes clinking on the porch. Reuben invites him in.

"Fiona, I'm sorry you got burned so bad. Nurse Greene told the hospital you said Reuben threw the grease on you. Is that true?"

Fiona does not speak.

"Listen, if he did, he probably didn't mean to. Sometimes, women get a lil' uppity, and a man does something he shouldn't do, but he's just trying to keep her in her place. You know, for her own good, in the long run. I'll take Reuben outside and have a little talk with him, and you just heal up as soon as you can. I promise you he won't do it again."

FIVE

Reuben and the man go outside and talk about the upcoming bear hunting season. They never speak about Fiona.

The boys are traumatized. Mickey doesn't speak for over two weeks and cries the first time he sees his mother's face without the bandages.

Outside and away from their father, Seth and Finn talk.

"I think daddy threw grease on mama," Seth says. "The pan was all the way into the living room. How did it get in there? He wasn't happy about something that night. Remember how he sent us outside?" Seth asks.

Finn nods his head.

"I'd like to kill him," Seth says.

"He's mean to her," Finn adds. "The authorities won't do anything. They're all big buds."

Fiona's face is blistered and crusty for weeks. The left side of her face will be scarred for the rest of her life. People stare at her when she goes to town. Finn cries when he thinks about her humiliation.

Reuben takes her disfigurement as an excuse to see other women. Fiona hears the rumors. She can live with that, better those women have him groping and crawling on them.

Mickey makes himself cornbread and milk one afternoon. He pours himself a glass of milk, leaving enough room for the crumbled cornbread. With a large spoon, he stirs the mixture together. When he places the spoon on the table, he knocks over the glass and the concoction washes across the table and drips on the floor. Reuben whips Mickey with the Cherokee belt. He screams in pain. Fiona puts her hands over her ears. Finn and Seth look at each other and then down to the floor.

Mickey has trouble breathing. Fiona rushes in with his inhaler and tears Mickey away from Reuben. He'll be alright, but Reuben has crossed a red line. Fiona wishes Reuben dead.

The boys grow taller by the day it seems, except Mickey. Seth and Finn might be as tall as their father in just a few years.

Down by Highway 80, Finn finds a beagle. Probably a rabbit hunting beagle, Finn figures since the old dog's ear is half torn away. A hunter, unhappy with the beagle for being old and not fast enough to hunt, tears the tags out of the dog's ear and abandons him on the side of the road. Finn brings the dog to the house and sitting on the porch steps starts pulling off blood-gorged ticks. Finn stops counting at one hundred.

"Find yourself a dog?" Reuben asks. "He's old and won't hunt. I'd just let him go."

"I wanna keep him. I'll take care of him, feed him, and all. I'll do some odd jobs for neighbors and buy his food."

"What're you gonna name him?" Seth asks.

"Blue! Ole Blue!"

Reuben takes a real job, except the work will be done by Seth and Finn. Since the boys are so big and strong, they'll be gravediggers. Reuben makes a deal with two cemetery associations to dig their graves as needed, but Reuben never touches a shovel.

When Reuben gets a call that a grave needs digging, he orders Seth and Finn into the truck. Arriving at the cemetery, Reuben shows the boys where to dig and places the template, a rectangle of 1x4's nailed together on the ground. Reuben's part finished, he goes back to the truck to drink beer. While the boys dig, empty Schlitz cans fly out the driver's side window.

Since people are buried in pine boxes, graves need to be six feet deep. Seth is over six feet. Reuben orders Seth to stand in the grave when he thinks it is deep enough. If Reuben barely sees Seth's head from his perch in the truck, Reuben pronounces the grave deep enough.

Before they leave, Reuben makes the boys pick up his beer cans and throw them into the bed of the truck.

Seth grows not only tall but thick and muscular. In the eighth grade while playing on the softball field at Micaville School, he hits a ball not only over the fence but across Micaville Creek. A feat never done before.

Young Finn, only an inch behind Seth in height, is very athletic and almost a head taller than the other boys in his class. Moreover, he is fast. The other boys can't catch him on the playground as he has speed to burn.

Finn picks up a ball and seems to know instinctively what to do with it. Baseball and basketball come easy to him. Everyone wants Finn on their team when they divide up to play. Sports like tennis, soccer, and lacrosse have not make their way into the mountains, but a football becomes magical in Finn's right hand. In the seventh grade, he throws a perfect spiral over forty yards.

All the youth sports association teams want Seth and Finn to join their teams. On the baseball team, Seth is the big, slugging first baseman while Finn plays any position, from pitcher to shortstop, very well. Playing centerfield on the baseball field, he runs downs any flyball that doesn't go over the fence. From the mound, Finn throws a scary fastball. Batters swing well after the ball pops in the catcher's mitt. Parents on the other team watch anxiously hoping the pitcher with the cannon-like arm doesn't accidentally hit their boy.

On a summer Thursday evening, the teams scheduled on the Burnsville baseball field receive quite a surprise. When they arrive, they see a large white tent on the field. Rows of folding metal chairs fill the tent. A choir finishes a rehearsal as cars start to fill up the parking lot. The two coaches are told a gospel revival will be held on the field this evening, and the coaches will have to reschedule their game.

Reuben storms through the kitchen door, cussing with every breath.

"What's wrong?" Fiona asks. "I thought there was a game."

"The damn mayor gave the field to a preacher," Reuben barks. "They said he was a traveling evangelist from Missouri, and he specializes in dental miracles. At the end of his sermon, people get in line, put money in a bucket, and the preacher lays his hands on their heads and any dental problems go away. The preacher says it might take up to two weeks for God's grace to bring the healing. Those fools putting money in the bucket tonight have got to realize that preacher gonna be long gone tomorrow, probably down in South Carolina gettin' money in a bucket."

It is one of the few times Reuben and Fiona agree on something.

The boys see their mother's scarred face every day and carry a load of anger at their father.

At supper one evening, Seth does the unthinkable. He is about to challenge his father. Seth pushes a glass of water closer and closer to the edge of the table. Reuben watches with his eyes glaring at Seth. Seth glares back, and it's like Seth is saying, "What are you going to do about it?"

Seth pushes the glass again, now only a couple of inches from the end of the table. Seth glares. Reuben takes a giant breath, like he is about to explode. He can't believe his own son is challenging him. Finn sees the drama taking place while Mickey plays with peas on his plate.

Seth pushes the glass to the very end of the table. One more nudge and the glass will crash into the floor. Reuben puts his hands on the table like he is about to stand. Fiona reaches and pulls the glass of water back beside Seth's plate.

The family just saw a preview of what is to come as the boys mature and begin to challenge their abusive father. Soon, the boys will be as big as Reuben, and they will have him outnumbered.

Finn's good looks catch the eyes of the girls beginning in elementary school. Clustering in small groups in the hall, the girls whisper to each other, "Here comes Finn. He's so cute." One of the girls might say though, "he's the son of a bootlegger." Most of the girls don't seem to mind though, as they continue their dreamy stares at Finn.

In the seventh grade, Sarah sits to the right of Finn in the classroom. When Finn looks her way, she winks. He smiles and looks away quickly, not sure what to do with the attention the girls are giving him. He'd rather be playing football or any kind of sport.

Grace Goins catches Finn's eye. Grace, also in the seventh grade, is one year older. Grace's dark brown hair looks slightly oily and like a bowl was on her head when her hair was trimmed. Her bright blue eyes flash quickly from side to side, like she is on high alert. Her clothes are baggy, looking like she is the second owner. Several times a week, she wears an odd pink dress that looks one size too large.

Grace's mother was deathly sick the year she was supposed to start school, and the trauma kept Grace at home. Very bright, school is a breeze for Grace. Grover, Grace's twin, is still not in school. His mother's death caused him deep emotional issues. When the school officials visited the home, Grover held on to the bedpost in his room and would not turn loose. Linda, Grace and Grover's aunt, was not married and stayed in the home taking care of her terminally ill sister. Linda always looked like an unmade bed since she never brushed her hair and wore baggy clothes.

Linda explains to the school officials that Grover has taught himself how to read. In the corner is a stack of books. Linda says, "He's read every one of them. I must get him seven or eight books a week from the library. He's reading stuff I read in high school."

Grover is six years old, extremely introverted, emotionally damaged, but apparently a budding genius. Endowed with extreme intelligence, he was not blessed with good eyesight. He wears glasses with lenses so thick his eyes are hidden. The school officials agree to let Grover delay school for another year, and then they forget about him. Grover never attends school. He read every book in the county library in the following years. He loves math and creates equations only he can solve. He flies through geometry and science books. Linda brings home a high school French textbook, and ten-year-old Grover teaches himself French in a matter of weeks. A traveling salesman drops by the house, and Linda buys a complete set of Encyclopedia Britannica. In less than a week, Grover has devoured every volume.

Grover refuses to talk to anyone except his aunt and his sister. In the mountains at the time, it was not unheard of for kids never to attend school.

In some cases, twelve-year-old boys might finally enter first grade, usually to drop out after a year or so. Kindergarten classes did not exist until decades later.

Throughout elementary school, Grace wears mittens to school, regardless of the outdoor temperature. Teachers ask her if it's necessary to wear gloves. Grace responds that she has a medical condition. Everyone just accepts that and gets used to the idea that Grace wears mittens.

Grace walks down the hall of the school one day. Billy Blevins sneaks up behind Grace, grabs one of her mittens off her hand, and runs down the hall. Grace quickly puts her hand under her sweater so no one can see. Finn happens to be on the other side of the hall. He chases Billy down the hall and into the boy's bathroom.

"Give me that glove!" Finn demands.

"I was just havin' some fun," Billy says.

"Give me the damn glove!"

"All right, here it is."

"You ever bother that girl again, I'll bust your head!"

Walking down the hall to return the glove to Grace, Finn thinks "I told Billy I'd bust his head. Sounds like something my daddy would say. Maybe, I'm going to be like him after all."

Grace thanks Finn for the glove but keeps her bare hand under her sweater.

"If he ever bothers you again, just let me know. I'll take care of him."

Buster and Loretta Goins live upriver on a small farm Buster inherited. His family lived in the area as long as people can remember with the same being true of Loretta's family. From their porch, they sit in their rocking chairs and listen to the roaring waters of the South Toe River. Buster and Loretta often walk down to the river in the cool of a summer evening, the only entertainment they can afford.

Buster works at the feldspar plant in Kona and dies in a mining accident just before twins Grace and Grover are born. Buster's bulldozer slides down a bank, turns over, crushing him.

Five years later, Grace and Grover's mother suffers a brain tumor. The physicians at the Asheville hospital tell the family there is nothing they can do. The family does not have health insurance, and the family suspects that is the reason she does not get further treatment. Loretta is sent home without any pain medicine because she cannot afford it.

Loretta languishes for months. Completely bedridden for months, she screams in pain. She loses her eyesight. She cannot sleep, screaming all night from the terrible headaches. Grace and Grover put pillows over their heads, but sleep is still episodic. Loretta Goins dies after eight months of continuous agony, witnessed and heard by Grace and Grover. Grace misses her first year of school while Grover is emotionally damaged for life.

SIX

Fiona goes to Lucille Johnson's house. Lucille has a beauty shop in a side room built on to the main house. Most of the women in the community get their hair done at Lucille's. Reuben arrives back home from a trip to Asheville to pick up booze. Coming into the kitchen, he notices Fiona's hair trim.

"Looks like you got yourself prettied up. Got you a new feller?" Reuben's irrational, narcissistic jealousy flares up.

"No, I don't have a feller. And this hairdo didn't cost you nothing. I traded two books of S&H Green Stamps for the hairstyling."

Ledford Brothers' Grocery in Burnsville gives S&H Green Stamps with the purchase of groceries. Fiona then pastes the stamps into a little booklet. When the booklet is full, it's five dollars off the next grocery purchase. Lucille trades a haircut for a booklet of stamps because she knows Reuben will not give Fiona the money for a trim.

"When a woman gets her hair fixed like that, she might be trying to attract a man," Reuben says suspiciously as he peels an apple with his ivory handled hunting knife. Fiona just ignores him, although she does harbor a secret.

Two weeks later, Reuben receives word his father's health rapidly deteriorates. On a cold, windy night in March, Silas Boone's family gathers in the family home on Rebels Creek with Ola Mae, Silas' wife. Reuben and the family enter through the front door that opens into the kitchen. An open loaf of Sunbeam white bread sits on the wobbly kitchen table. A jar of Duke's mayonnaise and a package of bologna on the table, family members know they are welcome to make a sandwich. Always hungry as wolves, Seth and Finn stop, spread mayo on slices of bread and add two slices of bologna. Mickey holds his mother's hand as she goes into the living room to greet the other family members. Reuben's brothers, sisters, and their spouses are gathered in the living room while kids are upstairs playing in one of the bedrooms.

When Seth and Finn enter the living room, they hear the wheezing and labored breathing of their grandfather Silas Boone whose hair and beard have long turned winter white. Silas is a retired miner suffering from silicosis that has badly damaged his lungs. Reuben makes the boys stay in the living room with the adults to show respect to their dying grandfather.

"He's passed," Reuben's sister, Clara, says at 2:00 A.M. when she comes out of the bedroom. Seth, Finn, Mickey, and two of Reuben's brothers sprawled across sofas and chairs must be stirred to hear the news.

"Open all the windows!" Ola Mae screams. "Yer daddy's soul leaving this earth. It has to get out!"

"And cover all the mirrors!" Clara shouts. "Soul sees itself in a mirror, and this place be haunted forever! And stop the clock on the hearth! Don't want his soul to get confused and think he's not dead."

Seth and Finn look at each other with raised eyebrows. Mickey cries. Reuben steps over and whispers to the boys, "Don't pay no attention. That's a bunch old timey horseshit."

"I'll get the cooling board ready," Ola Mae says. Silas's body will lay on the cooling board until the funeral. Passed down through the family since the early 1800s, the flat wooden board will have buckets of ice underneath to keep the body from decomposing too rapidly. With near zero temperatures at night, ice will not be hard to find.

"On funeral day, when you men take him out of the house, make sure he goes out feet first. You don't want him looking back in the house. He might want to take some of us with him," Reuben's sister declares.

"More horseshit," Reuben whispers to the boys.

"Maime Jones is still a sin-eater. I'll let her know she can come later tomorrow," Ola Mae says. Sin-eaters had high qualifications. The person needed to be the seventh child of a seventh child. A glass of grape juice and a morsel of bread will be left atop Silas. Ola Mae knows Silas has more sins than he could ever repent for. So, in the mountain tradition, Silas' sins will be attracted to the juice and bread and be trapped inside them. Maime will drink the juice and eat the bread. Maime will take a bath, a cold one this time of the year, in the river during the next full moon and all Silas' sins will be washed from her.

The next day in the cold wind with a heaviness in the sky, Seth and Finn dig their grandfather's grave while Reuben sits in the truck and downs Rolling Rock beer, a new brand selling in Asheville. He crushes each can in his massive hand and tosses it out the truck window.

SIX

Overnight, heavy snow falls from the sky. Twenty-four inches of white beauty cover the ground by early morning. When the family car pulls away from the house, Finn sees Ole Blue in the backyard sticking his nose in the snow and flinging snow into the air.

Silas Boone attended Sawmill Holler Free Will Baptist Church three times a week, Sunday morning and evening services, and Wednesday evening prayer meeting. All his children had to attend. Reuben and the other children once they learned how to read had to read the Bible for one hour each day. As a boy, Reuben hates reading the Bible, hates church, and hates his father for making him do all that.

At the funeral, the church is packed with family and neighbors. In the front corner of the church, a pot-belly stove roars with dry hickory firewood keeping the church warm. The casket stays open for the service.

"You children, be sure to touch his body. If ye don't, he might come back to haunt you," Clara says to her children.

In a black suit of clothes, Silas looks pale, even ghostly, as silicosis clogged his lungs and prevented a normal amount of oxygen from circulating in his body. The undertaker apologized to the family and explained he did his best to make Silas look normal.

Silas' youngest daughter, Arlene Boone, must be pulled away from the open casket. "My daddy can't be dead," she screams.

Clara Boone Briggs sings a favorite local hymn, "How Great Thou Art," and makes the family proud. The pastor simply delivers his stock hellfire and brimstone sermon, warning the attendees of the perils of an unsaved life. Silas' sons carry the casket to the hearse.

Several local farmers put blade attachments on the front of their farm tractors and open the road to the cemetery that sits on top of a hill overlooking Rebels Creek. Blowing off the mounds of snow, strong March wind has the windchill factor below zero at the graveside service. Standing around the grave, legs are numb from the cold. Frank Boone's hat blows off his head, flies across the cemetery, landing against a fence. The strong and steady wind kept it stuck halfway up the fence. Five-year-old Arby Jackson Boone says, "Mama, look, that hat on the fence! Is that a ghost?" His mother puts her index finger over her lips, "Shhh . . ."

Due to the cold wind, the pastor keeps the service brief. During the service, Finn spots Grace, Grover, and their aunt, Linda, in the freezing crowd.

After the preacher's fiery benediction, warning all sinners to repent, Finn heads to Grace.

"Thank you for coming," he says to the three.

"My family knew your grandfather, and Grace's father worked with him some," Linda says.

"Sorry it's so cold," Finn offers.

"You know what the Norwegians say?" Grover asks from behind his thick lensed glasses. The others lift their shoulders. "They say it never gets too cold, but it is possible to not be dressed properly. Good layering is necessary."

"Where does he get all this?" Finn asks.

"You know what they say . . . age is just a number, genius is a gift," Linda answers.

"You shouldn't say stuff like that," Grace says to her aunt with a hint of jealousy. "You'll give him the big-head."

"He's got a mind like a steel-trap," Finn says.

Family and friends pile in their cars and head to the Boone home-place. On the kitchen table and counter, friends and neighbors deposited serving plates heaped with fried chicken, country ham, potato salad, slaw, hot biscuits, and pitchers of iced tea. Reuben eats and leaves, always uncomfortable at social gatherings.

SEVEN

Disturbed by his father's death, Reuben goes on a "big drunk." In the mountains, a man's "big drunk" might last several days or even a week. Wives might not know where their husbands are but always trust they will return in a few days. As a way of dealing with anxiety or depression, the drinker throws down beer after beer, all day long. He drinks into the evening until he passes out. Sometimes, the drinker wakes up at a different place than home, having wandered up the road on foot or car. It doesn't matter, he starts drinking again and maybe wakes up the next day in an entirely different place with no memory of how he got there.

Reuben stumbles home after a two-day amnesic, alcoholic episode. He staggers into the kitchen and flops down in a chair at the kitchen table.

"Fiona! Give me a beer!" Fiona hands him a beer from the refrigerator. Five minutes later, Reuben demands another beer.

"Put me another beer on the table. Gonna take a piss and be right back," Reuben slurs as he slobbers on himself.

Reuben never makes it to the bathroom. When he stands up, a wave of alcohol infused dizziness sweeps over him. He takes two steps and collapses on the floor, face down, with arms and legs spread eagled across the living room floor. His large frame takes up most of the floor. The boys are asleep in their beds since tomorrow is a school day.

Reuben snores with drool running out the side of his mouth, and Fiona thinks it might be loud enough to not only wake the boys but Tinnie Wilson down the road as well. Fiona sees the right hand, palm to the ceiling, stretched out on the floor. She sees the hand that beats her boys, the hand that threw the painful grease on her face. Rage swells up in her, rage like she has never felt before.

Turning around, Fiona walks through the kitchen door and out to the woodshed. She returns at once and stands over Reuben. Tears run down her face. Her entire body shakes. She takes a deep breath and swings an axe toward Reuben's right wrist. She misses, with the tip of the axe-head going through the linoleum tile and into the wood below.

The jolt of the axe-head on the floor wakes Reuben. He looks up with one eye open. Fiona pulls on the axe handle, but it's stuck in the floor. Seth's bedroom door opens. He runs to his mother and helps her pull the axe out of the floor. Seth kicks his father in the stomach. Reuben's eyes close as his breath is forced from his body by the force of the kick.

"Wham!" Blood flies into the air, and Reuben's hand rolls to the side as Fiona severs his wrist.

"Son of a bitch! Got what he deserved!" Seth screams.

By this time, Finn and Mickey have entered the room. Mickey screams.

"Take Mickey back into the bedroom!" Fiona orders.

With Finn and Mickey in the bedroom, Fiona and Seth strategize. Fiona will try to stop the bleeding. She grabs a dishcloth from the kitchen sink and pushes hard against the end of the cut wrist. She feels his pulse through the cloth, and she slows the bleeding significantly.

Seth goes to the phone. They are on a party-line with Tinnie Wilson and two other families on the South Toe River. No one has a private line at this time. One of the party-liners' daughter is talking to a boyfriend.

"Get off the phone! My mama cut daddy's hand off! I got to call an ambulance!"

The line clicks. Seth doesn't realize he has told a potential witness his mother is responsible for the severed hand. Fiona and Seth can't make up an alternate account.

Reuben survives. Fiona does not visit him in the hospital. Four days later, a local official in a suit two sizes too big comes by to see Fiona.

"Fiona, can I come in?"

"Yes, of course, you can come in."

"They'll be bringing Reuben home tomorrow. Reuben's sister is going to come and take care of him for a while."

"I'll be here to take care of him," Fiona insists.

"Fiona, we know you cut his hand off. Look, I can see marks on your floor from the axe. And word has gotten around the area that you did it. Seems Seth told a neighbor."

Fiona is speechless. The man shifts in his seat like he is dreading what he is about to say.

"Before Reuben gets home, they're coming to take you down the country."

Fiona shivers. She knows what 'down the country' means. She is going to a regional psychiatric hospital. Former patients report abuse, harassment, and neglect. Few are fortunate enough to be released. Even though they might experience recovery, some patients spend the rest of their lives in the prison-like hospitals. The hospitals receive funding based on the number of patients, meaning the hospitals don't like vacancies.

The man sees Fiona's anxiety.

"Listen, we could take you to trial. Malicious wounding would probably get you ten to twenty years. With good behavior you might get out of the hospital in a few years. Sometimes, it's better to be crazy than guilty," the man chuckles.

When the boys get home from school, Fiona explains the situation. She's going to the hospital for a short stay. Mickey cries.

"Mama, are you sick?" Finn asks.

"No. It's what happened to your father. They want me to get some help. Learn how to deal with my frustrations better. I'll be home soon. Don't you worry. Your daddy is coming home tomorrow, and your aunt is coming to help."

"We'll come see you, Mama," Finn says as Mickey sobs.

"Listen, you boys are going to be good men. You're better than your father. You don't have to be like him. You understand?" Fiona pleads. The boys shake their heads.

The boys are off to school the next morning. Fiona waves as the bus pulls away and then bursts into tears, wondering when she will see her boys again. Finn and Seth have a game after school. Mickey will hang around and watch.

Midmorning, a white van pulls into the driveway. Fiona sits on the porch. She sees the van and picks up her small suitcase. Two men in white medical scrubs step out of the van, "Are you ready to go, Mrs. Boone?"

"Yes," Fiona says, wondering if she will ever see the light of day again.

Going down the steep road that leads to 'down the country', a slight smile rises on Fiona's face as she says to herself, 'Reuben can't beat my boys with just one hand'.

EIGHT

Freshman Seth starts at tight end at East Yancey High School and is the tallest player on the team. Although he is not fast like Finn, he'll have a fine high school career. Finn watches his brother practice with the football team. When practice is over and Seth showers, Finn goes out on the field and throws the football to another player's little brother. Finn zips the ball nearly fifty yards.

Impressed, the head coach still on the field says to Reuben, "Your boy be my starting quarterback next year. Never seen an eighth grader throw a football like that."

"Wait 'til you see him run," Reuben brags.

"I hear he runs like a scalded dog," coach says.

"Well, his ancestor's Daniel Boone. He must've been fast to outrun all those Cherokee," Reuben adds.

The next year as a freshman, Finn quarterbacks the East Yancey Panthers to a spectacular year. The only loss comes in the regional playoffs against Brevard. Finn limps through that game with a sprained ankle suffered in the previous game. As a freshman Finn is named second team all-conference. The first team quarterback is a senior at Harris High in Spruce Pine. Reuben says he is on the first team only because his daddy is a big banker in Spruce Pine.

Sophomore Seth has a solid year as a tight end on the football team. He is one inch taller than Finn at six-four but just doesn't have Finn's athleticism. Seth is the center for the basketball team and hauls down tons of rebounds. As a six-three freshman and the second tallest player on the team, Finn starts at shooting guard and finishes the season with the highest scoring average on the team, 15.3 points per game, and makes third string all-conference. Finn rains down long jump shots that settle in the net like a snowflake. Finn makes second team all-conference as a center fielder on the baseball team.

Tragedy falls upon the family once again in the spring. Reuben entertains women during the day. Some days, the boys come home from school to find Reuben in bed with a woman who might live just a few miles away while her husband works in the factory or mine. One afternoon, when the boys get home from school, they see a naked woman on the bed as Reuben emerges from the bedroom zipping up his pants and fastening his belt.

"Charlene is from over near Spruce Pine, and she won't tell if one of you boys want to get on her. She's a lot older, but she could teach you some things you need to know about pleasing a woman," Reuben offers.

Speechless, Seth and Finn shake their heads from side to side while Mickey cries.

"Oh, come on, lil' Mickey Doll, you want to be in bed with a man?" Reuben laughs.

The next day, Mickey rides the bus home while the boys go to baseball practice. Reuben travels to Asheville for liquor and gets home just before Seth and Finn arrive. When Seth and Finn are dropped off by the assistant baseball coach, Reuben screams as he walks back from the barn toward the house.

"That damn stupid boy! What's he done now! He never had no sense!"

Seth and Finn run to the barn.

"My God!" Seth screams.

The brothers see Mickey's eyes staring straight ahead. His body is motionless with his head pulled to one side by the rope around his neck. Mickey jumped from the barn loft with one end of the rope tied to a low hanging rafter and the other end around his neck.

Seth runs outside. "You caused him to do this! I'm gonna kill you!" Finn grabs his brother for he fears Seth might kill his father. Reuben calls the sheriff who summons an ambulance to come to the house. It's too late. The ambulance crew cuts the rope and places Mickey's body in the ambulance. They'll take him to Harper Brothers funeral home in Burnsville.

The next day, Reuben says, "You boys don't have to dig your brother's grave. I'll get somebody else to do that."

"We've already talked about it. We want to dig our brother's grave," Finn says. "You stay here. We don't want you up there drinking beer." Finn is surprised he has been so firm with his father but likes the feeling.

Two days later, Born Again Church has a different kind of funeral from Silas Boone's funeral at Sawmill Holler Free Will Baptist Church. Heavy grief fills the air. Unlike at Silas' funeral where folks felt relief that Silas' suffering was over, Mickey's death feels like such a waste of a young life.

The new preacher, The Reverend Robert Rufus Renfro, who received his 'theological education' and 'ordination' by way of a mail correspondence course, talks less about the perils of hell and more about how young people need to come to Jesus. He admonishes the young people in the pews to confess their sins and ask to be saved. He offers to talk to any of them after the service. Reverend Renfro, a physically delicate man, grew up near Marion in a little community called Stumpville. Some folks in Stumpville said he became a minister because he knew he was not cut out for the hard physical work in the mines and factories.

The hospital allows Fiona to attend. Her sister drives down and picks her up. Fiona has lost weight since her appetite diminished after entering the hospital. She sits between Finn and Seth with Reuben next to Seth. Fiona and Reuben do not speak. Fiona cries like her heart is being torn out of her. Finn and Seth cry for the first time in their lives. Reuben remains stoic.

After the church service as they wait for the hearse, Reuben lectures Finn, Seth, and their friends in attendance on the importance of talking about "yer stuff."

"You can't just hold yer stuff in," Reuben admonishes them. "You got to tell somebody about your problems. If you don't, it festers up in you, and you end up doing what Mickey did. Make space for what yer feeling," Seth and Finn look at each other with looks that say, 'We know who is responsible for this'.

"I mean you got to be yer own dog. You can't let other people get to you. Ignore the bastards who give you a hard time," Reuben declares.

Seth and Finn ignore their father. They know how their father taunted Mickey for being a sissy. "The lecture was just to make himself feel better cause he knows what he did to Mickey," Finn says.

They hug their mother as she gets in the car and watch the sister drive her away. Fiona has a time limit and cannot go to the graveside service. "I'm gonna get her out of there," Seth says.

After the committal service at Rebel's Creek cemetery, Reverend Renfro speaks to Reuben, "I'm sorry I didn't help Mickey more."

"What do you mean?" Reuben demands.

"You know, in the counseling."

"Mickey saw you for counseling?"

"Yeah, I thought Fiona told you."

EIGHT

"No!" Reuben fumes. "What fucking crazy ideas did you put in his head?! Some say you're a fag. You ain't got no wife! You try to make my boy a fag?"

"I don't know what you're talking about, Mr. Boone."

Seth and Finn observe the conversation and fear what their father might do. Would he slug the preacher? They go over, with each boy grabbing an arm, and pull Reuben away from the preacher.

Two weeks later when Deacon Roosevelt Fortner of Born Again Church goes to make a fire in the sanctuary potbelly stove early on Sunday morning, he beholds an awful sight. Reverend Rufus Renfro hangs by the neck, suspended by a rope tied around an exposed two by ten rafter. His feet dangle inches above the communion table spotted with pools of his urine. A note is taped to the side of the table. "I am a sinful man. I don't deserve to live." The note is signed "Pastor Rufus Renfro."

Church services are canceled, and word quickly spreads through the community that their pastor has died by suicide. When they get word, women wail in their homes. Some of the men outside Maude's store on Monday whisper to each other that the pastor committed suicide because he was a queer, and God had convicted him in his own heart. This rumor spreads like wildfire in the community, and word reaches Stumpville. The board of deacons of the church where Rufus Renfro grew up and made his confession of faith declares his funeral cannot be conducted in their sanctuary. He can be buried in their cemetery but only outside the chain-link fence that runs all the way around the other graves.

Seth and Finn have other suspicions, having seen the rage their father showed toward the preacher following the graveside service.

Another rumor sweeps through the community. Pastor Renfro had a sixty-watt light bulb up his rectum according to Mrs. Jones who works as a secretary for the local coroner.

On Monday evening following the pastor's suicide, the boys and Reuben make South Toe River milkshakes. Seth likes buttermilk, but Finn prefers sweet milk. They fill their glasses with milk and crumble cornbread into the milk and eat the thick blend with big spoons. They pass a bowl of pinto beans around the supper table, and all top their beans with chow-chow relish.

Reuben's sister knocks on the door. "I brought you boys some kettle greens, maters, and mashed taters to go with your pintos." Sitting the bowls on the table, she says, "I gotta run. Next time, I'm bringing some streaked meat, cornbread, and ramps with potatoes."

Seth says to his father, "You have anything to do with that preacher hanging himself?"

"Hell no! That fag took his own life. He knew he wasn't natural. He knew desiring other men, even boys, was wrong. Says it in the Good Book he preaches from, a man shall not lay with another man. He couldn't control himself and knew he would be found out sooner or later. So, he took the coward's way out. What I think. I think he got that bulb stuck in his ass, couldn't get it out, and hung himself."

Seth and Finn continue to have their suspicions. They figure their father made the preacher write the suicide note. They knew the local officials would never do anything to Reuben and lose all the bribe money Reuben sends their way.

A few days later Finn says to Seth, "I wonder if daddy is kind of relieved that Mickey is gone. That was going to be a big embarrassment for him when Mickey came out of the closet. He wants to project that manly man stuff."

"I've wondered about that, too."

NINE

Summer in the mountains means the men discard their shirts, but no man will be caught wearing sissy shorts. The standard attire for men in the summer is no shirt, long work pants, and boots. In hot weather, it's hard to find a man in the area wearing a shirt. Front porches are filled with bare chested men and women in long dresses. They watch their children play 'hide and seek.' The roads are traveled so lightly a passing car is a major thrill. It's no big deal if the car is recognizable, but if the car is from off somewhere, the people on the porch might even stand up in a kind of awe that anyone would be coming through.

The community spins into a tempest when Maude Gurley tells customers at her store that a man with New Jersey license plates stopped at her store. The traveler told Maude he was retracing the journeys of Daniel Boone through Virginia and North Carolina for a national magazine. Maude told him to talk to Reuben Boone since he was a direct descendant of Daniel. Reuben was on a liquor run to Asheville's ABC store and the boys were in school when the man came by. So Reuben never got to talk to the reporter and threw an empty Jim Beam bottle against a tree in anger. "Could have been my big chance to be famous!" Reuben lamented.

The shirtless men often gather in front of Maude Gurley's store, sit on wooden crates, and drink from six and one-half ounce "little" bottles of Coca Cola bought from Maude for a dime. A Coca Cola often called a "dope" since a local nurse warned some of the area residents not to drink too much Coca Cola because it was made from cocoa leaves that also produced illegal drugs in South America. Soon all carbonated drinks were routinely called dopes.

Summer youth baseball thrives in all the little communities. Fathers establish yearlong bragging rights if their boys are on the best team. Finn and Seth are invited to play on the Burnsville eighteen and under summer team. Although Finn is barely sixteen, he quickly becomes the best player on the team, chasing down fly balls in centerfield, and circling the bases after hitting home runs almost every game. Finn is so fast, he turns some doubles into inside-the-park home runs.

Seth's athletic career takes a pause. Siding falls off Tinnie Wilson's house. Reuben, Seth, and Finn take nails, hammers, and a saw to her house. Several pieces of siding need replacing. Seth cuts a new piece of siding to size but lets the saw run across his left index finger. The finger hangs by a shred of bone and skin.

"I thought I taught you better than that!" Reuben screams as he drives Seth to the hospital. They arrive at the hospital emergency room.

"Stay in the car just a minute," Reuben says.

Reuben goes to the bed of the truck and comes back with a pair of heavy-duty wire cutters.

"Stick that finger out the window!" Reuben demands.

When Seth extends his hand, Reuben snips off the end of Seth's finger.

"Ouch!" Seth screams in pain. "Why did you do that?"

"Make it simpler for the doctor. Now all he'll have to do is sew up your finger."

Truth was, Reuben figured it would cost him a lot less money for a few stiches as compared to the surgical expense of removing the end of the damaged finger. While the doctor stitches up Seth's finger, Reuben walks down the street and buys a pack of nabs and a grape Nehi.

Two days later Seth, his finger wrapped in white gauze, and Finn walk down their road toward Highway 80. Tinnie Wilson sits on her front porch with embroidering needles in each hand. She embroiders a sweater she wants to send to Fiona.

"You boys like to have a piece of cake?" Tinnie asks.

Never to turn down food, the boys say, "Yes!" They cross the yard and step up on the porch.

"Come on inside," Tinnie invites.

The house is furnace hot since Tinnie cooks on a wood stove. Windows, without screens, are open, but it still feels like the equator to the boys. They spy the cake on the table. It has white icing topped with lots of raisins.

"Terrible thing about your mother. I'm working on a sweater for her," Tinnie says as she approaches the cake with a knife and two plates. As she nears the cake, the raisins fly away.

"Mrs. Wilson, have you seen our dog, Ole Blue, the beagle?" Finn asks. "We ain't seen him for a couple of days."

NINE

"Well, I did see him a couple of days ago. This long-legged, elegant coon dog comes through the yard. She was a beauty. I thought to myself 'that's the Sophia Loren of dogs?' Your dog took off after her. Last I saw, they were headed around the curve."

Ole Blue returned home two days later and slept for another two days.

TEN

In the second grade, Grace Goins hands Finn Boone, who sits across from her, a note. "Do you like me? Check box: Yes or No." Finn is happy to check Yes.

Grace and Finn remain best friends through elementary school. Finn often leaves his house and walks up an old trail that follows the South Toe River and arrives at Grace's house in fifteen minutes.

During the summer between their seventh and eighth grades, Finn makes the trip up the trail and knocks on Grace's door one evening. She's never invited him inside, does not this time, but invites him to go up on the grassy ridge behind the house with her.

Darkness falls over the mountains, and Grace's eyes glow like a cat's in the dark. A brilliant sunset, the sun's rays shining up under a bed of clouds turning them red and orange, settles in the west.

"That's incredible!" Finn says.

"I come up here all the time," Grace says. "I come up here and think about my mama. I miss her so much."

"I remember her. She seemed like such a fine lady," Finn struggles to say since he is not used to talking about such matters.

"I don't know if Grover will ever get over it," Grace says. "All he wants to do is read. That's his escape, I guess."

"What does he read?"

"It used to be history, and then he read math books just for the fun of it. Ever heard of that? Now, he reads science all the time. Every book he can get his hands on. He tells me he can look at a page and pick out the verbs and nouns in seconds and that's all he needs."

"How come he doesn't come to school?"

"After mama died, they let him stay home for what should have been his first year and then they forgot about him. But now, he probably knows more than most of the teachers. He remembers everything he reads."

"Well, Grace, you're a straight A student. He can't be smarter than you."

"Oh, he is. My brother's a brain. He's a little weird but got a photographic memory or something."

"Look at those lightning bugs!" Finn says.

"Grover says people off the mountain call 'em fireflies. One night up here, he even told me the scientific name, just off the top of his head . . . it was something like Lampyridae from the family of Elateriod Beetles . . . I probably got it wrong but it's something like that."

"Grover's gonna be famous someday, maybe a scientist or something," Finn says.

"Sure smart enough. He's gotta come out of his shell though and get over all that anger over the way the hospital and doctors did mama," Grace says.

They sit in silence enjoying the fireflies in the night sky.

"I think they're God sparks," Grace says. "Little flickers of God in the world."

"You think about God a lot, don't you, Grace?"

"Yep, ever since mama died. I just can't help but wonder about all that, you know, heaven and hell. You think there's a heaven and a hell, Finn?"

"I guess so. I mean, if there is, my mama is going to heaven and my daddy to hell, for sure."

"I know what these preachers around here say, but I wonder how a loving God could send anybody to hell. Shouldn't God's love, in time, persuade any person, or soul, into an acceptable person?"

"Wow, Grace, you really do think about God a lot. You might be . . . . what do they call them?" Finn hesitates. "A theologian!"

"I might be. The Reverend Dr. Grace Goins! Wouldn't South Toe flip out? A woman preacher and a theologian at that!" They both laugh.

Finn says he better head home.

"You gonna be alright trekking through the woods after dark and all by yourself?"

"I'm one of Daniel Boone's descendants. I could get back with my eyes closed." They laugh again.

In the summer following their eighth grade, the Higgens brothers, Tommy and Jack, and Jimmy Penlands start talking to their friends about going to Grace Goins' house after dark. They sneak through a bushy area that leads to Grace's house, and at the edge of the bushes, they see directly into Grace's bedroom window.

"Oh, look at her," Tommy whispers. "She's bathing herself with that pan of water. I'd like to be that washcloth!"

"They're poor as mice, probably don't have running water," Jack says.

"Look at her titties. They stick straight out," Jimmy giggles.

"Her legs look like Hollywood legs," Tommy says.

Word gets back to Finn after the boys start telling their friends about peeping on Grace. They should have kept their mouths shut. Finn sees the Higgens boys go into Maude Gurley's store. The screen door slams behind them as they come out of the store.

"I hear what you been doin'," Finn barks as the boys step out into the parking lot.

"I don't know what you're talkin' about!" Tommy shrugs his shoulders.

"You damn straight know what I'm talkin' about!" Finn roars.

Tommy's face turns white.

"If you ever do that again, I'll bang your heads together so hard you'll see stars for a week! And tell Jimmy he's on my watch list too!"

The Higgens boys turn and walk away very quickly never to peep at Grace Goins again.

ELEVEN

Finn gravitates to other kids who are on the fringes. Early in elementary school, kids made fun of Finn for being the son of a bootlegger. Finn hangs out with other outsiders like Grace Goins and little Buster Blevins. Buster gets teased a lot because he is short with a face as flat as a pancake. In the fifth grade, he comes to school with bites all over his neck and arms. Turns out, his bed is infested with bed bugs. Kids seize the moment, and from that day forth, Buster is Bed Bug.

Bed Bug is one of the few circumcised boys in the rural area. Most parents could not afford the extra procedure at birth. Bed Bug has a unique ability the other boys say is because of the circumcision. He can urinate a stream that loops through the air and has been measured at sixteen feet and four inches. Bed Bug does not have much else going for him and is quite proud of his urinary skill.

When not at Grace's house, Finn hangs out at Bed Bug's house all he can to stay away from his father. A striking pair, Finn stands head and shoulders taller than Buster.

"What're you and Bed Bug doin' today?" Reuben asks as Finn heads out the door on a bright, sunny morning with a burlap sack over his shoulder.

"We're pickin' up dope bottles. Maude's offering three cents for Pepsi, Nehi, and RC's and two cents for little Coke bottles. We're gonna make us some spending money," Finn says. Since canned drinks are not yet on the market, soda bottles are refillable. Lots of people just throw the bottles out the window of their cars when finished. Young entrepreneurs like Finn and Bed Bug could make several dollars in an afternoon picking up the discarded bottles and selling them to Maude Gurley. She would give them to the drink-truck driver for a discount on the next delivery.

Maude sells true mountain delicacies. On her counter sit large glass jars filled with pickled eggs, pickled pig's feet, and Penrose sausages bursting with flavors of vinegar, brine, and hot spices. Today, she fries cheeseburgers on a one burner propane grill. It's a hard choice, but Finn and Bed Bug buy cheeseburgers with part of their dope bottle cash and sit outside on an old picnic table. They talk about going fishing as they chomp down on their burgers.

"Aw!" Bed Bug screams as he starts spitting out fragments of the cheeseburger.

"What is it?" Finn wants to know.

"It's a damn yellowjacket!" Bed Bug says as he pulls a wad of food from his mouth. "It must have landed on my burger when I looked away, and then I took a big bite. Damn thing sat on my tongue and just pumped his stinger into my tongue!" Finn tries not to laugh but can't help it.

Maude runs out of the store to see what's wrong. Finn explains, and Maude runs back into the store for ice cubes. Finn laughs so hard, tears run down his face. After Maude sees that Bed Bug is okay, she reaches into her apron and hands each boy a Black Cow, a chocolate flavored taffy on a stick.

"Come on, Bed Bug, let's go fishing!" They swing by Finn's house and pick up fishing poles with Zebco spinning reels. Finn strikes the fertile ground out by the barn with a hoe, and the boys drop worms into an empty Campbell's tomato soup can.

Few fish survived the pollution inflicted upon the South Toe River by up-river mining operations. After dump trucks bring the raw mica or feldspar ore to the processing plants, conveniently built on the banks of the river, the plant washes the ore, allowing all the water and sediment to go into the river. The mining companies have no restrictions since EPA did not exist at the time. Once the South Toe River was sparkling clear, full of native trout, but now is so muddy it is impossible for those kinds of fish to survive. Bottom-dwelling hogsuckers, with a mouth that looks like the bottom of a vacuum cleaner, and red-bellied, horny-head suckers are about the only fish ever caught from the opaque waters. Occasionally, a red "mudpuppy", a salamander, is reeled in.

"I get mad at those damn mining companies every time I come down here," Finn says as they arrive where a small creek flows into the river. "They've ruined this river." The only fishing spots in the polluted rivers are where creeks dump fresh water into the river.

"I'm puttin' on a fresh worm," Bed Bug says after nothing takes his bait.

"Not much biting today," Finn says. "But it gives you time to think, you know. I worry I'm just gonna end up like my daddy, no good, no count. That's what he says to me, 'Finn, you can try to be Mr. Goody-Two-Shoes, but you gonna end up like me.'"

ELEVEN

"I say you can be whatever you wanna be, Finn. Don't believe your daddy. He's just like that cause he screwed his life up. Just got one hand now, and just about everybody hates him," Bed Bug says.

"Cast upriver, above that big rock," a male voice says.

Finn turns around to see Grace and, surprisingly, her brother Grover looking through his thick lensed glasses, pointing to a large gray rock out in the river.

Finn casts above the rock. Bam! His rod at once jerks and bends almost double. Finn reels in a rare black rock-bass with striking white markings around the fins.

"How did you know where to cast?" Finn asks.

"Simple trigonometry," Grover points to the rapids out in the river. "Fresh water running in here, and river currents flowing at obtuse one-hundred and thirty-five-degree angles form a hydraulic vortex in front of that big rock. Fish can hover there effortlessly and wait for food to come by."

"Damn!" Bed Bug says.

"These mining companies gonna pay someday for what they've done to our rivers!" Grover says in a loud voice.

"I told you he was a brain," Grace says to Finn. Finn thinks he sees a thin smile on Grover's face.

"Grace and Grover, take this rock-bass with you. Will be good eatin' for your supper," Finn says.

"I'll make a deal with you," Grace says to Finn. "We'll take the fish, and you'll go to Burnsville with me. Grover wants to go home and read, but I'll come back for you."

"Okay," Finn says, "See you in about an hour."

Sixteen-year-old Grace Goins recently secured her driver's license. Her aunt gave Grace a set of keys to her 1959 white Chevrolet Impala. Rust spots speckle the lower side panels of the car, but most of the cars in the area have rust spots due to the heavy salting of roads from frequent snows in the winter.

Finn hops off the front-porch as Grace pulls up in front of the Boone house.

As he gets in the passenger side, Finn says, "Nice car."

"I thought we would go by the drive-in for footlong hot dogs on our way to water-tank hill," Grace says. Water-tank hill above the town of Burnsville offers some of the best views in the area and a favorite parking spot for young romantic couples. The extremely hairpin-turn dirt road is a see-yourself-coming kind of road.

"Grace, this car won't make it up the road to water-tank hill. You need a jeep or truck. The road is rough with big gullies," Finn says and then realizes he might have said too much. Grace is not the first girl that wanted to take Finn to water-tank hill.

Quickly offering an alternative, Finn says, "Let's go up South Toe River to the Carolina Hemlocks." The Carolina Hemlocks is a recreational area in the Pisgah National Forest. The South Toe River, with one of the best swimming holes in the area, runs through the campground.

Grace and Finn sit on top of a massive rock overlooking the giant pool of water below formed by rushing water squeezed between two giant boulders. They share a large order of french-fries smothered in ketchup.

"Hold still," Grace says as she takes her napkin and wipes ketchup out of the corner of Finn's mouth. They both take big bites from their footlongs, loaded with their favorite toppings, chili, slaw, ketchup, and mustard.

"I love this place," Finn says. "The rushing water so soothing. Life's been so crazy lately. Mama going down the country. Mickey taking his life. It's a lot, but you went through it with your mother and father."

"Life's so hard sometimes," Grace offers. "These Burnsville kids have everything. Both parents. Nice clothes. Money to go to college."

"You wanna go to college, Grace?"

"I do. We don't have any money, but I'm gonna find a way. How bout you?"

"Hoping for a football scholarship."

"Finn, you need to know something about me. It's why I wear these gloves all the time." Grace has always worn gloves at school and in public places. She told the kids at school she had a skin disorder.

Grace takes off her gloves and shows her hands to Finn.

"You have six fingers," Finn looks at each hand. "On both hands."

"I'm a Melungeon, Finn."

"Who cares?" Finn says as he shrugs his shoulders. "There's several Melungeon families around. Do you have the Melungeon bump?"

"Yeah, you want to feel?" Grace takes Finn's right hand in her left hand and pulls it to the back of her head. "Feel that? Grover's got one too. Not every Melungeon has six fingers and the bump, but most of us do. Grover says it is 'the Anatolian bump' that only people from Turkey and Asia Minor have. I guess some of my ancestors are from there."

ELEVEN

Finn's hand still rests on Grace's neck. He moves his left hand to Grace's shoulder as he moves his head forward. Grace moves her head forward. Eyes search each other. Lips touch. Grace pulls away.

"I've never kissed a boy before!"

"Glad I'm the first. Hope I'm the last!"

When school starts in August, Grace goes to school without gloves. Sitting in a math class, Grace reaches up and pushes her hair behind her ears. The classmate sitting across from her notices the six fingers. Students start to whisper, "Grace is not wearing gloves and has six fingers."

After lunchbreak, Cody Smith taunts Grace in the hall, "Melungeon! Melungeon!" Students start to laugh.

Finn emerges from the lunchroom and sees the spectacle in the hall. He pushes two students out of the way and goes to Grace.

"It's okay. They're just havin' some fun," Grace says, but Finn sees a tear in her eye.

"Cody, let's you and me step outside," Finn says. But the principal has emerged from his office to see what's going on.

"All right! Get to your classrooms! Clear out! Go on!"

Finn stares at Cody as he takes his hand and rubs it across his mouth in a signal to Cody to zip his mouth. Cody will never taunt Grace again. Not even the senior boys want to cross Finn due to his size and lightning-fast hands.

After school Grace says to Finn, "Maybe Grover did the best thing, just staying away from school and people."

"If anyone bothers you, just let me know," Finn promises.

"I hope they let Melungeons go to college?" Grace worries.

TWELVE

The sun goes down as Grace scrubs a pan with baked-on grease from macaroni and cheese at the kitchen sink. She furiously works the Brillo steel wool pad over the cast-iron skillet. A knock at the door, Grace quickly dries her hands and goes to the door. It's the nurse, Antionette Greene.

"Come in, Mrs. Greene," Grace says.

"Oh honey, I can't. I have to get home to check on the boys. Sometimes my husband fixes dinner for them, and sometimes he doesn't. You know how husbands are. Well, maybe you don't yet, but you will. I don't know what the world would do without women. Anyway, the reason I dropped by is you got approved as a candy-striper! Aren't you excited?"

"I am. When do I start?"

"This weekend! I work Saturday. I'll pick you up at six-thirty in the morning. Is that okay?"

"Sure!"

"Your uniform is in this poke. It's so cute and gonna look so good on you!"

After Antionette leaves, Grace goes back into her bedroom. She reaches into the paper grocery bag and pulls out the red and white pinafore jumper. She quickly slips off her sweatshirt and puts her legs through the jumper. Glancing in the mirror, she sees how lowcut the jumper is, revealing a significant amount of cleavage. She laughs at herself, realizing she needs to wear a blouse, probably a white one underneath.

Grover goes by her door and glances in. "You look like a candy cane!"

"I'm so excited. I start at the hospital on Saturday. I'm gonna be helping people."

Friday night as Grace prepares for bed, she winds her alarm clock sitting on her bedside table and sets the alarm for 5:30 A.M.

Grace is the first one up the next morning. The house is chilly because her aunt turns the thermostat on the Warm Morning oil heater down to its lowest setting the night before to save money. The cold floor stings Grace's feet as she makes her way to the heater in the living room. She learned to dress in front of the heater. The Warm Morning heater has a cast-iron burner, but a brown metal cabinet surrounds the burner. The cabinet gets warm but not warm enough to burn. She places her uniform and blouse on the heater. She slips her night gown off and pulls on her blouse and uniform. Down the hall in the bathroom, she admires her attire in the mirror. She brushes her hair for several minutes and braids her hair into several strands and then braids the strands into one large strand. A rubber band looped twice on the large strand will hold her hair in place.

In the kitchen, she quickly pours corn flakes into the bowl she left on the table the night before. A soft crackle rises to her ears as she pours fresh milk from Robinson's Dairy on the cereal. Robinson's Dairy delivers two quarts of milk twice a week. Delivery is made before sunrise. Grace realizes today is milk delivery day. She goes to the front door, and on the front porch sits the wire crate with the two quarts of milk, delivery as reliable as the sunrise.

Grace sees headlights coming up her driveway. Stashing the quarts of milk in the refrigerator and taking two more bites of cereal, she grabs a denim jacket, heads out the door, jumping into the passenger side of Antionette's green Ford pickup truck.

"Sorry for the truck. I ran off the road last week in my car and broke an axle. My brother has two vehicles and lets me borrow this old truck when I need it." As they speed down Highway 80, Grace notices flakes of hay from the bed of the truck being lifted by the wind and soaring into the air.

Thirty minutes later, Grace and Antionette arrive at the hospital. Grace's excitement causes her skin to tingle. Antionette works in Intensive Care but walks Grace down to the nurses' station where she introduces her to head nurse Wilma Gilbert.

"Honey, we are so happy to have you here. Most of the people your age are still in bed this morning."

Antionette tells Grace she will come by at three o'clock when her shift is over. Wilma begins Grace's orientation. She will fill water pitchers in patients' rooms. Other duties are to deliver mail and flowers to patients. She'll push wheelchairs when patients are discharged. In between those duties, she'll sit at the nurses' station and give directions to visitors.

"You look so cute in your uniform, and I love the way you braid your hair. I'm going to give you ten dollars before you leave today. Go buy some white tennis shoes. They'll look real good with your uniform," Wilma says, her voice full of kindness. Grace looks down at her feet and realizes her one pair of shoes, brown lace-ups, don't go well with her candy-striper jumper.

As her first duty, Grace goes down the hall pushing a cart with pitchers of ice water. In the first room, the female patient can barely hold her eyes open, apparently heavily medicated for her pain. Patients are appreciative of her efforts, and many comment on how cute she looks in her candy-striper jumper.

Grace knocks on the door of room 113.

"Come in," a gruff voice says. Mr. Burleson is recovering from a car accident that left him with a broken leg and wrist.

"I have you some fresh ice water, Mr. Burleson."

"You haven't been in here before. You're one of them candy-strippers."

"I just started today. I'm a candy-striper."

"Oh, I see. Are you one of them Melungeons?" Before Grace can respond, the man says, "I've always thought if you people just took a bar of good soap and some clean water, you could wash most of that brown off your skin."

Grace winces, like a knife has been stuck in her. She says nothing, exits the room with a tear running down her cheek, and continues her rounds.

The remainder of her rounds go smoothly, Grace thinks. Back at the nurses' station, Wilma asks Grace to sit down.

"Sweetie, we love you being here, but we have some patients who are backward. They think if you're not white like they are, you're not as good as they are. I'll take Mr. Burleson his water and mail from now on. Mrs. Jones in 145 doesn't want you to come into her room either. But don't pay them no mind, they're just ignorant. Too bad, there are still people like that."

THIRTEEN

An elite athlete, Finn rises in popularity in the eyes of the Burnsville "in" teens. The children of the Burnsville bankers, merchants, and factory executives tend to stick together, forming tight social groups. As teenagers, they shop in Asheville and wear all the latest fashions. They have parties and gatherings and don't tend to invite the teens who live out in the countryside. Finn is an exception since he is tall, handsome, and athletic.

Grace's friends live in Double Island, Boonford, and Micaville. Their parents work in the factories where the fathers of the Burnsville kids are the executives. It's like two different worlds, the haves and the have nots.

Several of Grace's friends have a unique way of acquiring spending money. Eighty-year-old Lester Roy Crowder's wife died nearly twenty years ago. Lester made his money on a small mine on his property he leased to Hightop Minerals Corporation.

"Grace, we have a little way of making money if you are interested," Sabra says.

"What's that?" Grace asks.

"Mr. Crowder asked my mother if she knew of anyone who could come cut his toenails. He can't bend over far enough. So, my mother sent me to his house after school. I cut his nails, and he gives me five dollars. He's so old and feeble he can't talk, but he writes notes on a pad. 'Take off sweater for five more dollars.' I figure he's so old he can't do anything, and he's hooked up to that oxygen tank with that hose in his nose. I need the money, so I took off my sweater. Then he writes, 'Take off bra for five dollars.'"

"I've done it, too," Ruth says. "He just sits there in that old ragged, upholstered rocker. He doesn't try to do anything. He paid me twenty dollars to take all my clothes off, and he started breathing really hard. I thought he was going to pass out or something, but he just sat there. Sweat was running down his face. It's easy money." They all laugh.

"If you go up there, just knock on the door and ask him if he needs his toenails cut, he'll know," Sabra says. Grace finds the whole idea repulsive but doesn't say anything to the other girls.

Finn encounters a moral dilemma of his own. As his sports fame increases, the Burnsville newspaper publishes stories about his athletic feats. His record setting performances on the football field, basketball court, and baseball field are the talk of the local barber shops and beauty salons. Men predict where he will play football in college. Women ask each other, "Did you see that picture of Finn Boone in the newspaper? He's a hunk!"

"I saw him cutting someone's grass down in Micaville. He had his shirt off. I got wet," Mildred tells her friends in the beauty salon. The other women laugh.

Lucille Barnes Fischer is married to Paul Samuel Fischer who is the CEO of a Burnsville manufacturing plant. He was transferred from a plant in New Hampshire to manage the plant. He's neurotic and constantly worries his plant will underperform.

Lucille has few friends in Burnsville. She wants more refined friends and looks down on the local borns. In her late forties, Lucille is very attractive. She exercises daily, and her figure is girlish. She gets her hair styled weekly and dyed monthly. With dark brown eyes, she has natural brunette curls that bounce on her shoulders when she walks. She drives into Asheville for all her shopping, even groceries. The local stores are just not up to her standards.

Lucille attends most of the high school athletic events, mostly out of boredom since Burnsville has few cultural events. She has taken note of the brown-haired Finn Boone and his perfectly sculpted body. Coming out of a Burnsville hardware store, she looks up to see Finn Boone about to enter the store.

"Hey, you're Finn Boone. I was at your basketball game a few nights ago. I like your game," Lucille says as she uses her right arm to imitate shooting a basketball.

"Yes, I'm Finn, just here to pick up some nails and helping a neighbor repair a barn."

"Hey, I've got some work to do at my house. You interested?"

"What kind of work?"

Lucille thinks quickly since they have a handyman already. "I've got some furniture that needs moving and some boxes that need to go to storage. My husband is the CEO at the mill and doesn't have time for things like that."

"Sure, but I have practice after school every day except Thursday when the JV team plays."

"Thursday would be great! You know where I live?"

"Well, everybody knows where you live, that's the biggest house in the county. I'll come by after school."

Finn drives the white pickup truck his father won in the infamous poker game to Lucille's after school on Thursday. He rings the doorbell.

"Come in, Finn," Lucille says. She wears tight workout pants that highlight her shapely legs and an athletic shirt that falls just below her bra-line revealing an almost flat stomach, quite an accomplishment for a woman in her forties. "Those boxes over there. Take those down to the basement and put them in the corner by the bicycles. I'm gonna take a quick shower. I just had a great workout."

Finn admires the lavishly furnished home. Fine hardwood floors glow in every room except the bedrooms that are adorned with expensive carpet. The basement has not only a home gym with exercise equipment but a game room with billiards, ping pong, and foosball tables. Every toy a couple could want.

"We have to entertain ourselves," Lucille says as she comes down the steps. "We didn't have children, so we have lots of time on our hands. Well, I should say I have lots of time on my hands. My husband works all the time, and when he is not working, he's thinking about work. Come on, let me show you the rest of the house."

After showering, Lucille wears a very short mini-bath robe that falls about halfway between her knees and her hips, revealing most of her tanned legs. As Finn follows her up the steps, it looks to him like she is not wearing underwear. Finn begins to sense he's not been invited just to move a few boxes.

In the den, Finn sees the largest television screen he has ever seen. It takes up half the wall.

"My husband gets home late every day. I always have a fine dinner ready, but after dinner, he comes down here and falls asleep in that rocker until bedtime. He says his work just exhausts him. Let me show you the second floor."

Between the kitchen and the dining room, a spiral staircase winds its way to the upstairs bedrooms.

"This is our bedroom," Lucille says as she grabs Finn's hand and leads him through the door. "We don't do anything but sleep though. Paul's so preoccupied with work he never gives me any attention. He's too tired or too worried about some damn production report or some visit by the top executives from New Hampshire. He always has an excuse. Never any time for me. I'm so lonely. I need a man to hold me and make me feel special. I want you to want me, Finn."

Lucille reaches down and pulls one end of the bow that holds the short robe around her body. The robe swings open. Finn looks at her perfectly shaped breasts, her large rosy nipples.

"May I take this off?" Lucille asks, her head turned slightly sideways and her left eye in a seductive stare. Before Finn can respond, the robe hits the floor. Lucille steps toward Finn with her hands going underneath his arms and around his back. He feels her hot breath on his skin.

The phone rings on the bedside table. "I'm not going to answer that," Lucille says. "It'll quit ringing in a minute."

Lucille pulls Finn down upon her on the bed. "Make me feel special," she says.

Finn dares not tell anyone about his Thursday encounter. Lucille tells him she will need him for some projects every Thursday after school.

The Thursday encounters go on for seven weeks until Lucille has some news for Finn.

"Baby, I've got some bad news for us. My husband is being transferred back to New Hampshire. The movers are coming on Monday."

Finn feels a wave of relief. Later that day after the relief wears off, he worries about what will happen if people find out about his "work" for Lucille. What would Grace think? Does this make him even more like his father?

In the fall of his junior year, the very popular Finn is elected class president, a position he did not seek. Before lunch, the junior class officers are invited to the principal's office for a swearing-in ceremony. To his relief, Finn finds out the class president is mostly a figure-head position. After the ceremony, Finn heads to the cafeteria. He spots Bed Bug and their mutual friend, Cornbread, about halfway up the line. Jerry Jones got the name Cornbread because that's all he eats. Three meals a day he has cornbread, usually cornbread and milk, the Micaville Milkshake. He brings cornbread to school in a paper bag and follows Bed Bug and Finn through the cafeteria line where he only picks up a carton of milk.

THIRTEEN

A common practice for kids when they come into the cafeteria is to move up the line to be with their friends, happens every day. But when Finn moves to the middle of the line to be with his friends, Mrs. Murphy, a math teacher who eats her lunch in the cafeteria, jumps to her feet and demands that Finn go with her to the principal's office. Mrs. Murphy explains to the principal that Finn has set a terrible example as class president and should be removed as junior class president. The principal agrees, and a new election is called.

At football practice after school, the coach says to Finn, "That's the shortest reign for a class president ever!" The players roar with laughter.

After practice, Finn heads to Grace's house for some comfort. He's embarrassed. "Geez, we do it all the time. Everybody breaks line now and then."

"I know, I know, they were just making an example out of you." Grace then explains to Grover what happened at school.

"Well," Grace says. "You can concentrate on football now."

"At least that is going well, I get a letter from a college about every week. Daddy wants me to go to Alabama or Notre Dame but no offers from them yet."

Grover standing nearby says, "No football for me. You players hit each other violently and in the head. I want to keep my cerebral fluid inside my head." They all laugh.

"Grover says there was a lot of excitement down Double Island last night," Grace says. "Grover, why don't you tell Finn about it."

"The Gordon family woke up this morning to find most of their cattle dead in the field, bellies already bloated, and legs sticking up in the air. Every electrical device in their house was fried. That mountain is a huge lightning rod. It's filled with iron, titaniferous magnetite. A typical lightning strike of three-hundred million volts and the entire mountain top is electrified. House current is only one-hundred and twenty volts. So they got quite a wallop," Grover explains. "They were lucky nobody got killed."

"How come a big mining company doesn't come in here and mine the iron?" Finn asks.

"Titaniferous magnetite does not smelt efficiently in modern blast furnaces. It would not be worth the expense," Grover explains.

"You are a walking encyclopedia," Finn laughs.

Finn receives invites to Burnsville parties almost every weekend. He invites Grace to go with him, but she always declines, saying she does not fit in. Grace is self-conscious of her fingers and her clothes from the secondhand store. Only the Burnsville elite teens attend the parties. Finn is so popular he is the exception. Finn takes Bed Bug and Cornbread when he attends the parties.

"Why do you take us with you? You could just hang out with the bankers' and doctors' kids?" Bed Bug asks.

"I know who my true friends are," Finn explains. "These people didn't want to have much to do with me until I made second team all-state."

When Finn goes through the door at the parties, girls start whispering and staring. "I wish he would ask me out. All he wants to do is hang out with that Grace Melungeon," Carrie says. Her friends laugh.

"She's got six fingers to wrap around that big penis," Mary says.

"That's sick," Donna says, holding back a laugh.

FOURTEEN

Finn invites Grace to go with him for a picnic at Hoot Owl Mine on Crabtree Creek. The mine was abandoned by the mining company years ago when the miners struck a large underground spring. As an open-faced mine rather than a tunnel mine, it quickly filled up with natural spring water to form a small, sparkling lake.

Finn picks up Grace in the poker-game-won pickup truck. Wearing cutoff faded jean shorts and a white-on-purple tie-dyed t-shirt, Grace sits by the passenger side window with her bare feet up on the dash. The pickup has a bench-seat. Finn turns down Santana blasting out "Soul Sacrifice" on the built-in 8-track tape player. "Why don't you slide across the seat and sit beside me, like the other guys' girlfriends do?"

"I'm not trying to be like the other guys' girlfriends, and I like sitting over here. It's not that I don't like you. It's just a personal choice where I sit, that's all. If you want to stop, I'll drive, and you can sit in the middle. How about that?" They laugh. "Grace, that's what I love about you. You have your own mind," Finn answers.

"I let a man have a piece of my mind yesterday," Grace says.

"What happened?"

"My aunt sent me to Pollards Drug Store in Burnsville to pick up a prescription. I had to get an orangeade. I can't go into that store and not get an orangeade."

"Yeah, they're the best, fresh squeezed. You see them do it right there. Cut the orange in half and put it on the machine and bring the handle down. I can taste one right now. We go there after practice if we can get there before they close."

"As I was going out the door, this man sitting at the counter said, 'Hey Melungeon, go back to your mountain. You ain't like the rest of us with your greasy hair and brown skin. You're a half-breed God never wanted born.' I looked him in the eye and said, 'I'm a human being just like you.' He didn't like that and mumbled something and turned the other way."

"Grace, I admire you."

The truck lugs up the mountain road. A chain is across the road about one-hundred yards from the mine. Finn parks the truck, grabs the sack with their lunch, and they walk the remaining distance. This part of the road is almost straight up. Finn and Grace breathe heavily. Rounding the last turn on the road, they eye the crystal-clear pool of water ahead. Splashes startle them. It's the swoosh of a large flock of white geese fleeing the pool. "So beautiful and graceful," Grace says. "Maybe, God's angels?"

The picnickers gained several hundred feet in elevation. The air is thin. The cooler air feels good to their skin. "Grover says the air is cooler at the higher elevations because the air molecules are farther apart, and they don't hold heat as long."

"Is there anything your brother doesn't know?"

"I'm beginning to wonder."

Finn packed bologna, swimming in mustard, and cheese sandwiches, potato chips, pickles, and two Cheerwines. He spreads out a blanket and invites Grace to join him. They sit with their legs crossed.

"Mr. Boone, do you dine often at the Grove Park Inn?"

Finn, puzzled for a moment, realizes Grace is transforming their picnic into a fine dining experience at Asheville's finest restaurant, The Grove Park Inn. Perhaps the Burnsville lawyers and physicians dine at the elegant and expensive Grove Park Inn, but for the average Yancey County resident, it's only a dream.

"I often have lunch here with business associates," Finn, catching on, answers while Grace giggles.

"These chips, so delicious. They must be prepared from potatoes grown in France," Grace adds more humorous sarcasm. "Likely, the Rhine Valley. The ham from one of the finest shops in Germany, I'm sure," Grace offers. "Normally, you only find this fine mustard on the Riviera. Mr. Boone, you know how to treat a lady."

Finn takes a football player size bite of his sandwich and starts laughing so hard he almost chokes.

"Mr. Boone, next Saturday is the Fire Circle. Would you join me?"

"Of course! I mean, I think so. I don't think I have anything else going on. I've heard about Fire Circles but don't know much about them."

"They're not secret but just a private kind of thing for those of us with the Anatolian Bump, but other families will attend and not all of them are Melungeon."

"My daddy says I am part Cherokee. We all got mixed blood in us," Finn offers.

FOURTEEN

"Things start on Friday night, but you don't have to come until Saturday afternoon. There'll be lots of dancing, mostly flatfoot-dancing, but some of the men buck-dance. Lots of scratchers to eat. Melungeons love those fried chicken feet. Men will bring their moonshine. The fortune tellers might be smoking Sweet Fern."

"Sweet Fern . . . is that marijuana?"

"Yes, but you don't have to do any of that. But you can get any curses put upon you banished. You might just have to hold some blood beads and chicken feathers and have smoke blown into your ears." Grace waits for Finn to respond.

"Are you for real?"

"Some of the old folks are still into those kinds of things, but it's mostly music and dancing. People getting together that usually don't see one another. Glass of all different colors will be hanging from trees and bushes, singing like wind chimes. Greens, ambers, blues, and cobalt blues are really striking. The different colors all mean something to the old folks. Cobalt blue chases away negative energy. Green brings healing. Oh, be sure to take home a jar of blackstrap molasses. My uncle makes the best!"

"Does Grover go?"

"He's the best dancer there!" Grace waits for Finn to register an expression on his face. When he looks puzzled, she says, "Are you kidding? He'll probably be home reading."

"Grace, I've been meaning to ask you. There's a story going round about a dead Melungeon preacher down at Lost Cove. The river got up and washed the dirt off his grave. People who saw him said he had not decayed . . . he was just like when they put him in the ground over eighty years ago. Is that true?"

"I didn't see it, but that's what some of our people are saying. He was found with his eyes wide open, staring up at nothing. And I heard some of the men put his body in a cave, but they won't say where."

"Grace, you are amazing, one foot in Melungeon culture and one in with the rest of us. Where's the Fire Circle held?"

"Up on the bald on Periwinkle Mountain."

"My mother used to go see the Periwinkle flowers in the spring. She would bring home purples and deep yellows," Finn chokes up, a tear runs down his face. "I'm gonna see her on Sunday. The last thing she says to me every time is 'You will be a better man than your father.' I keep hoping they'll release her."

FIFTEEN

On a hot July evening, Finn and Bed Bug stop at the Rainbow Roller Skating Rink in Burnsville. They haven't skated in several years, figuring they had outgrown the hobby, but some of their friends continue to whiz around the rink. A red-headed kid, who looks to be about their age, catches their eye. They've never seen him before and can he skate! "I Can't Go for That" by Hall and Oates plays on the jukebox.

"Did you see that!" Finn exclaims. Bed Bug's mouth is open in amazement. The red-headed kid skates backwards, jumps in the air, spins completely around, lands on one skate, jumps again. He weaves in and out of the other skaters. He does splits and quick circles. He jumps over a young kid.

Finn has an idea. The red-headed wonder makes his way to a chair and starts to take off his skates. Finn and Bed Bug make their way over.

"Man, that was some skating!" Finn congratulates. "I haven't seen you around before. I'm Finn, and this is Buster Blevins, but everybody just calls him Bed Bug. You move here or something?"

"Yeah, I'll be going to East Yancey High School in the fall. Where do you guys go to school?"

"East Yancey. You got some quick feet. You ever play football?"

"I wanted to, but my parents didn't want me to get hurt. I made a deal with them though. If we moved here, I could play football. You guys play?"

"I'm the quarterback, been since my freshman year," Finn says.

"I've always been too small to play. I find other things to do. Finn won't come out and say this, but he was second team all-state quarterback last year," Bed Bug says.

"How're your hands? Can you catch a football? I saw those quick feet on the rink. I bet you could turn defensive backs completely around, maybe break some ankles," Finn asks.

"I'll need to practice some."

"Coach gave me a key to the gate at the field. Meet me there sometime, and I'll throw to you. I'll ask Squirrel to join us?"

"Squirrel?"

"He's one of our receivers. He got his nickname because he's quick and shifty, like a squirrel. We want to win the state championship. You know, go out on top. We could do that with one more really good receiver. It'll be fun!"

"How come you moved to this end of the world place? We're all trying to get off these mountains, not much to do around here," Bed Bug moans.

"We're from New Hampshire. My father got transferred here. He's the new top dog at the big plant. He replaced a man named Fischer, who got moved back to New Hampshire. We even bought their house. You'll have to drop by soon."

Finn feels a chill sweeping to the marrow of his bones. Does this family know Mrs. Fischer? Has she told them about their Thursday afternoon romances? Will it all come out now? It could be a big scandal? Would he get kicked off the football team? Everybody gonna know I am a no good like my daddy. Finn shudders as thoughts race through his mind. He begins to calm himself down. She wouldn't go around telling people she fucked a highschooler, would she?

Bed Bug starts talking. "You haven't told us your name?"

"Jared Murphy. We're Irish, my parents tell me. I guess that's where the red hair comes from."

"I got a nickname for you already. Everybody gets a nickname around here," Bed Bug says.

"Yeah, what's that?"

"On Fire!"

"Really? Why?"

"Dude, on those skates with the spinning in the air and those red locks swirling around with you, it looked like you were on fire!"

"Jared, you're gonna be On Fire from now on," Finn adds. They all laugh.

Rumors circulate a new teenage gang has formed in west Burnsville. It's called the Cane Gang. They gather in an old, deserted barn in a field next to Cane River, drink beer, and masturbate as they look at Playbook magazines. A member of the gang, Jimmy, often entertains the gang. Like the famous French flatulist Le Petomane who performed at Moulin Rouge in Paris in the early 1900s, Jimmy uses his abdominal muscles to pull air into his rectum and fart at will. He blows out a candle from several yards away.

To become a member of the Cane Gang, a guy must go to Asheville and bring home a cane, a cane being used by a person walking on the street. The guy walks up and down the street until he sees a person, usually an elderly person, walking with a cane. Then, he grabs the cane and runs. He brings the cane back to the gang gathered in the barn, and they celebrate with rounds of Pabst-Blue Ribbon.

If the guy goes to Asheville but does not bring home a cane, the group gives him another assignment. One guy was sent to shoot a hole in the water tank above Burnsville. He drove up water-tank hill, aimed his father's rifle at the tank, but the weak .223 Remington bullet bounced off the tank. The last guy who did not bring home a cane was assigned to burn down the railroad trestle spanning the river near Kona, and he was successful. Helicopters were sent in to remove the damaged sections of the trestle.

Finn becomes enraged when he hears what the gang is doing. He recruits Bed Bug, Cornbread, On Fire, and several East Yancey football players. They approach the old barn on a Saturday night when the initiations usually take place. Finn easily kicks down the barn side door that only has one working hinge.

"What are you doing here?" One of the gang members screams.

"We know what you're doing to those old people in Asheville. Let me ask you this. What if that was your grandfather or grandmother? What would you do to a bunch of jerks who stole their cane? Huh? What would you do?" Finn elevates his voice.

The cane thieves hang their heads and don't say a word.

"All right, you jerks, get out of here! If we ever hear of you stealing canes again, we'll come back and stomp your asses. You understand?"

The humbled gang members file out of the barn one by one.

"Did you see the look on their faces?" Bed Bug laughs.

"I guess we should take their beer for our trouble," Cornbread states.

Such was the life of many teenage boys in Yancey County!

SIXTEEN

Finn's senior football season starts with a bang. In the first game against Avery County High School, Finn throws for a school record two-hundred and forty-nine yards. Against Yancey County rival Cane River High School, he smashes the conference record with three-hundred and ninety-five yards. With Finn flinging the ball to water bug-like receivers, Squirrel Renfro and On Fire, the East Yancey Panthers roll over the next four opponents.

Major colleges from the southeast have their assistants at every game. The flat-topped press box roof usually has two or three cameras on tripods filming the star quarterback. The assistants take the film back to review with the college head coaches. Scholarship offers have already arrived from small colleges in the Asheville and Boone areas. Big name college coaches have been more cautious, but by mid-season Finn holds offers from major colleges in three states. Finn has told all the coaches he will not decide until the season is over. The team has a goal to win the state championship in their classification, and Finn does not want his decision to detract from his team's accomplishments.

Reuben Boone embarrasses the other parents in the stands with his antics. When a ball carrier on the other team breaks into the open, Reuben might scream, "Kill him! Kill him!" When a penalty flag is thrown against the Panthers, he calls the referees vulgar names. When Finn breaks free on a quarterback keeper, Reuben shouts, "Eat! Finn! Eat!" He's so obnoxious hardly anyone sits within ten feet of him, but otherwise the bleachers are packed. The East Yancey Panthers are rolling toward an undefeated season. Spruce Pine's Harris High won the conference championship for the last three years and sits as the last opponent on East Yancey's schedule. Beat Harris High and East Yancey gets a berth in the regional playoffs, one step away from the state championship.

The Harris High and East Yancey rivalry cuts across families and communities. Harris High sits in Mitchell County while East Yancey is in Yancey County. The counties are rivals in many ways, including commerce and manufacturing sites. Chambers of Commerce lobby manufacturers from up north to locate their plants in their respective counties. Some say the county rivalries go back to the Civil War when Yancey County was sympathetic with the South and Mitchell with the North.

Bets are made between the mayors of Spruce Pine and Burnsville. Fist fights break out in pool halls and even restaurants when opposing fans get too uppity. Students from respective schools "roll" each other's schools overnight with hundreds of rolls of toilet paper.

The Panthers have the home field advantage this year. By conference rules, the opposing team fans get the bleachers on one side of the field. Panther fans plot against Mitchell fans though. Panther fans are encouraged to come early to the game and take up as many parking spots as possible with the hope that Mitchell fans cannot find a parking spot.

It's also homecoming for the Panthers. The lovely Patty Young, daughter of Dr. and Mrs. Theodore Francis Young, MD, of Burnsville, is elected the homecoming queen. The homecoming king is star quarterback, Finn Boone, son of notorious bootlegger Reuben Boone and Fiona Boone who was "sent down the country." It is quite a contrast.

Homecoming festivities will have to wait until halftime. The players have gone through pre-game stretching and warmups. College coaches fill the press box to see one player, the star quarterback. When the players appear from the locker room for the coinflip and kickoff, On Fire trots alongside Finn. "Damn, look at all these fans. This is insane."

"It's bragging rights for these fans for a whole year," Finn says.

The Panthers win the toss. Finn calls heads, and heads it is. The Panthers choose to kick-off since that will allow them to receive the second half kick-off. Harris is stopped on their first series and punt to the Panthers. Squirrel Renfro calls for a fair-catch at the Panthers' forty-yard line. The Panthers have great field position. Finn hands the ball off on the first play to tailback Scooter McMahan. Harris expects Finn to come out throwing, but the Panther coaches decide to surprise Harris with some running plays to begin the game. Scooter breaks into the open for consecutive runs of fifteen and twenty-five yards. Harris coaches call a timeout as the Panthers are quickly in scoring position. Harris coaches move their safeties closer to the line of scrimmage figuring that the Panther coaches will keep calling running plays until they are stopped. Indeed, Scooter only gains three yards on first down and one yard on second down.

SIXTEEN

In an obvious passing situation, Panther Head Coach Price sends in the play. Finn will drop back to pass, Squirrel will go long taking the cornerback and safety with him, and On Fire should be open on a down and out of fifteen yards which would give the Panthers a first down.

Something strange happens when the ball is snapped to Finn. All eleven Harris players rush the quarterback. The Panther blockers are overwhelmed. Finn sees the wave of players coming at him. He flicks the ball to a wide open On Fire who trots into the endzone. Harris players continue their momentum toward Finn. Just after Finn releases the ball, the first lineman reaches him, grabbing him around the chest. The second lineman wraps himself around the other side of Finn. Harris' largest lineman, weighing over two-hundred and sixty pounds, throws his body into Finn's left leg. The leg bends unnaturally. Finn collapses to the ground with the three linemen falling on him. All eleven Harris players leap on the pile.

Finn feels something pop in his left knee. Pain shoots up and down his leg.

The Harris lineman who fell on Finn's leg and now on top of Finn snorts, "How's that leg feel, pretty boy?"

East Yancey players clear the bench and head for the pileup. They drag Harris players off the pile. Finn writhing in pain doesn't even try to get up. East Yancey players go after Harris players. Obscenities are yelled. Players pushed. Helmets swung. Coaches separate the players.

The Harris head coach approaches a furious Coach Price. "I didn't know about this. I didn't tell them to do that. The players did this on their own. What happened was terrible! We'll forfeit this game and get on the buses and go home. I am so sorry."

"You can't control your players any better than that!" Coach Price roars.

"I'm sorry is all I can say."

"Get your players and get your asses out of here."

College scouts in the press box have already started folding up their tripods. The quarterback they wanted is now seriously injured and his football career in jeopardy.

In the stands, Reuben Boone feels so much anger he looks like he might turn himself inside out. He screams at the Harris players, "I'll kill you sons-a-bitches! I'll kill every damn one of you!"

Two of East Yancey lineman grab Finn under the arms and start to lift him up.

"Don't do that!" Coach Price screams. "Get the stretcher from the locker room. Let's don't take any chances with that leg."

The Burnsville rescue squad ambulance takes Finn to Asheville Memorial Hospital. The emergency room doctor wants Finn to stay the night. X-rays will be taken in the morning. An orthopedic specialist, after viewing the x-rays and examining Finn, says to Reuben and Seth. "I'm sorry, but this is one of the most serious knee injuries I've seen. He has a torn ACL and MCL of the left knee, but the worst part is a patellar fracture of the kneecap in the same knee. I hate to say it, but his football career is most likely over. I wish I had better news."

Reuben turns over Finn's food tray cart. Finn's breakfast flies across the room. A water pitcher hits the floor, and water explodes across the room. Seth grabs his father, "You've got to settle down."

"They'll pay for this!" Reuben promises as he threatens Harris High.

Back to business, the doctor says, "We'll schedule surgery for Monday morning and hopefully your boy can go home in three or four days."

Later in the day, a knock on the door. Bed Bug's head peers around the door. "Can we come in?" A small delegation of Bed Bug, On Fire, Grace, and, surprisingly, Grover enter the room.

"Yes, of course, come in. They've got me on some high-powered pain medicine. So, no telling what I might say."

"That was a terrible thing those Harris players did. Their coach said he didn't know anything about it, but nobody in Yancey County believes it," Bed Bug says.

"We're gonna get even," On Fire says. "Coach don't know about it, but there's a meeting of the players later today. We're gonna fix those losers."

"Don't you do anything foolish and get yourselves in trouble. They're doing surgery Monday, and I'm gonna be good as new."

"Finn is right," Grace says, "you can't undo what's done. Finn doesn't want you to mess yourselves up over this. Besides, Grover's gonna join the team as the new quarterback. Right Grover?" They all laugh as Grace tries to get Grover involved in the conversation with a little humor.

"I'll bet Grover could design some great plays using his math skills," On Fire says.

"I could predict play success based on probability theory. You know mass, speed, resistance," Grover smiles.

SIXTEEN

After the surgery on Monday, the doctor tells Reuben, "Surgery went well. We got everything back in place. He'll just have to heal and that will take several months. He'll be on crutches for a couple of weeks."

"Will he ever play football again?"

"I don't know. He's a senior. Does he have a scholarship?"

"He wanted to wait until the season was over before signing."

The next Friday evening East Yancey faces Sylva High School in the first round of the Mountain District playoffs. On crutches, Finn cheers for his teammates. The new quarterback's weak throwing arm means East Yancey must run the ball. Sylva realizes this and crowds the line of scrimmage. East Yancey plays hard but loses by two touchdowns. The dream of a state championship was ruined by the crutches on the sidelines.

SEVENTEEN

"Grace Goins, please report to the guidance counselor's office," the school secretary announces over the PA system.

"Grace, you in trouble?" one of Grace's Algebra II male classmates teases. "Let's be nice," Mr. Burns, the algebra teacher suggests.

Grace makes her way to the guidance office in the rear of the library. Larry Howell, who would eventually be the principal of Mountain Heritage High School when East Yancey and Cane River High Schools merge, invites Grace to sit.

"Grace, I've got some good news for you!"

"Really, what's that?"

"You've been accepted at a very prestigious university in Durham."

"Is this a joke? I didn't even apply."

"I know you didn't, but I thought you had an excellent chance of getting in. So, I applied for you."

"Who paid the application fee?"

"I did. I won some money playing golf against this racist guy. Figured I'd put his money to good use."

"My family doesn't have money for me to go to college," Grace protests.

"You don't need any. You get a full scholarship. Grace, your grades are outstanding, and your test scores are very good. Maybe not as good as your brother's scores, but they really want you in Durham. They have a divinity school as well. I know you're interested in those kinds of things."

"How do you know about Grover's test scores?"

"Came across my desk the other day. Even though he didn't go to school here, his scores were on the printout since he lives in the county. Grace, your brother had a perfect score on his SAT. He's going to hear from elite universities and colleges. He can go wherever he wants. He'll get full scholarship offers from places like Harvard, Yale, MIT."

"I don't know what to say?"

"You don't have to say anything. You're smart, and you've worked hard. We're proud of you here at East Yancey."

SEVENTEEN

Grace tells Finn her incredible news after school. He's incredibly happy for her. "Let's celebrate with cheeseburgers and fries at the Circle Drive-In!"

Still learning to navigate on his crutches, Finn slips into the front seat of Grace's car, and they speed toward Spruce Pine. A carhop takes their order of cheeseburgers, fries, and vanilla milkshakes. The Circle Drive-In is the first restaurant in the mountains to have a milkshake machine. The stainless-steel beast does all the work at the touch of a button. Milkshake fans flock to the Circle.

Two Harris football players walk back to their car after dining inside. They see the crutches sticking up above the back seat of Grace's car. They walk by the car. "How do you like those crutches, Mr. All-State Quarterback?" Finn holds up his middle finger as they walk away.

"Grace, I am so excited about your scholarship. What will you major in?"

"I'll have to take the basic courses first, but maybe theology. I have all these questions about God and the universe. Maybe I'll find some answers."

"My college prospects are lookin' pretty dim. I didn't sign a scholarship. I wanted to wait until the season was over and maybe have a state championship. I thought I might get a scholarship offer from Alabama or Notre Dame. My daddy put that idea in my head. I guess I got greedy. Now, it looks like I'll turn out like him. Who wants a quarterback with a bad knee?"

"You're not gonna to be like your father! You're better than him! Your mother is right! You have a heart, you have a soul! I don't know if your daddy does!"

"When I was in the hospital, I started thinking about joining the Marines when I graduate. Bed Bug's talking about joining the Navy."

"What? They'll just send you to Vietnam! That's crazy! They'll get you killed!"

"No one else in our family, not my grandfather, not my father, not my brother, has served their country. They wouldn't want Seth, anyway, missing a finger. If I serve my country, I'd prove I'm a better man than my daddy."

"You need to talk to Grover. He watches the news every night, keeps up with the war, and reads about it all the time."

Two days later, Grace and Grover pick up Finn, drive across the one-lane bridge over the North Toe River, and head down river to Loafers Glory in Mitchell County on another cheeseburger adventure. Rumored to have the best cheeseburger in the mountains, the restaurant tops their burgers with both Swiss and American cheese, chili, slaw, mustard, and onions, instead of the traditional lettuce, tomato, and mayonnaise.

The seventeen-mile drive takes almost an hour. Highway 80 twists and turns along the steep riverbanks. Along the way, they observe the odd mixture of old farmhouses, abandoned home trailers, and artist studios where New Yorkers and other "Yankees" have summer homes to enjoy the cool air and produce pottery, paintings, and sculptures that will be sold in expensive shops in Asheville and Blowing Rock. In front of the Sinclair gas station in Loafers Glory during daylight hours sit without fail a few idle, elderly men in overalls and long-sleeve wool shirts, loafing the day away.

A sparkling, sunny, fall day with a slight breeze, Grace, Grover, and Finn sit outside at a picnic table. A big white cat jumps on the table and just as quickly jumps off. The burgers are sloppy and impossible to eat without chili and slaw falling on the table. They giggle and laugh at the droppings on the table and take turns accusing each other as to who is making the biggest mess.

Grover takes a bite of cheeseburger and then sticks his finger in his mouth to push cheese off his front teeth. He raves about the onion rings, "Fried to perfection, I tell you. I love their hot sauce too, better than any ketchup." Grace and Finn shake their heads, their mouths full of burger.

"Grace says you're thinking about joining the Marines and going to Vietnam?" Grover asks.

Finn swallows and wipes his mouth with the oversized white napkin. "I'm thinking about it. My football days are probably over. Several guys on the team are thinking about signing up. Might be good for me to serve my country."

"Well, it would be if it was a winnable war," Grover explains. "We've already dropped more bombs on them, called Operation Thunder, than we dropped during the entire World War II. The Vietnamese are fiercely independent people. They defeated the French. Ho Chi Min who rules North Vietnam sided with the United States against Japan. He thought he could take over Vietnam when Japan was defeated, but the United Nations divided the country into North and South. President Diem rules the South, and he's very corrupt. The peasants and the Viet Cong hate him and side with the North. They hide in the jungles and use hit-and-run tactics. We'll never win, just make a lot of mothers cry."

"My daddy talks about the domino effect that if we let communist North Vietnam have South Vietnam then communism will spread and take over the world," Finn injects.

"Yeah, that's what the President and Robert McNamara, the Secretary of Defense, preach, but I seriously doubt it. Communism has some good intentions, like equality for all the people, but is based on flawed economics. They don't use supply and demand principles, and communism's means of distribution is decided by a few government officials. They just send goods where they want to without knowledge of demand or need."

"Damn!" Finn says. "That's way over my head!"

"Do yourself and my sister a favor. She'll worry her head off. Join the Peace Corps," Grover adds.

"You'll have to tell me about this Peace Corps sometime," Finn says.

EIGHTEEN

Finn will miss basketball and maybe the baseball season in the spring as well. He often stays after school and watches his former teammates practice basketball in the gym. He is off crutches now, the large stiff brace removed, but he limps noticeably when he walks.

Football coach Price also coaches the basketball and baseball teams. East Yancey is a small high school in a poverty level county with resources spread thin. Coach Price jokes that he won't be surprised if the principal asks him to teach home economics in addition to his health and physical education classes.

When basketball practice concludes, Coach Price walks over to Finn and asks him to wait for him in his office. "I need to talk to you about something. But first, I have a parent to talk to. She doesn't think her son gets to play enough, but it won't take long."

"Finn, I've got some great news for you," Coach Price says as he walks in and drops into his desk chair and breathes a huge sigh. "Teaching classes all day and coaching after school makes for a long day. I don't know if I can keep this up until I retire. Maybe I'll start selling insurance or something."

Finn chuckles. "That is a long day."

"Finn, I got a call this afternoon just before practice from Coach Sweazy. He says he wants to honor your football scholarship."

"But the doctor said I shouldn't play football again. Says another injury to this knee might put me in a wheelchair for life."

"He knows that. But here's his angle. He needs to get the best players from these mountain high schools. He doesn't want all of them going to other schools to play. If he honors your scholarship, word will get around to these high school coaches. They'll think highly of his program and steer their players there. I'll get the paperwork in a few days. You're going to college!"

Finn stands, starts to jump in the air, but remembers the knee. "Coach, I don't know how to thank you. You've been great and so good to me even after this injury."

EIGHTEEN

Finn's world becomes a brighter place. Electrified with new energy, Finn rushes to Grace's house. Grace hangs clothes on the clothesline beside the house. A clothespin between her front teeth, she uses another clothespin to attach a blouse to the clothesline. Finn shares his wonderful news. She invites him to stay for dinner. "Just pintos, sauerkraut, and cornbread," she adds.

After Grace and Grover's mother died, Aunt Linda sold her house and moved in with them. She wanted her niece and nephew to have as much stability as possible. The house is as plain inside as it is outside. A well-worn sofa and two upholstered rockers sit in the small living room. A black and white tube television sits on a chipped wooden table. Rabbit ears reach toward the ceiling. Finn wonders what kind of reception they get back in this holler. A large, well-worn, braided rug covers most of the floor. Finn imagines Grace's parents sitting in the rockers, watching television, while Grace and Grover play on the floor. Little did the children know their parents would be taken away from them at a very young age.

A large bowl of pintos, a jar of homemade sauerkraut, and a plate stacked with cornbread squares sit on a white vinyl tablecloth-covered kitchen table. Grover comes out of his bedroom, says hello to Finn, and then places scoops of beans and sauerkraut topped with cornbread on a plate. Finn notes the plates are unmatched. Some are white, and some are light brown. He thinks broken plates were probably replaced by plates from the Burnsville thrift store. Grover explains he will have dinner in his room since he is in the middle of a very interesting book.

Finn notes that Grace's aunt, Linda, eyes him suspiciously. She offers him beans and kraut, but otherwise doesn't say much. Grace and Finn talk about classmates. Finn laughs in disbelief as Grace talks about Claire Wiseman who wrote Mike Phillips a love letter. Before the teacher got to the room, Mike read the letter to the history class, embarrassing Claire. "That was mean," Finn says.

"What are you gonna major in at college?" Grace asks.

"I don't know, haven't thought about it much. I didn't think I was going to college."

"Why don't you major in criminal justice? You say you don't want to be like your father. That's about as different as you can get," Linda says with a stern, serious look.

"I'll think about that," Finn responds, surprised by the directness of the aunt's statement. Finn thinks the aunt doesn't want him there. It is the first time Grace has invited him into the house. Finn wonders if the aunt holds his father's abundance of sins against him, and perhaps Grace was hoping that Finn's college plans might warm her aunt's feelings toward Finn. But it doesn't seem to be working.

After dinner, Grace and Finn sit on the front porch. The stiff winter air cools their faces and hands.

"I'm gonna leave these mountains soon," Grace says. "Probably going to summer school. Get a head start on college. It's gonna be a big change for me. Hanging out with those big city people from well-off families. All my clothes are from the thrift store."

"You'll be fine. I doubt those kids got a full scholarship. Their tuition is paid by their rich parents. Still thinking about majoring in theology?"

"Religious studies, but yeah, that's theology. Courses too like church history, world religions, and several philosophy courses, along with the basic math, English, art and music history. You'll be taking those kinds of courses, too, until you get into criminal justice," Grace laughs when she says the last part.

"The future is happening fast," Finn declares.

NINETEEN

An unexpected happiness sweeps over Finn. His football career, likely over, but he's going to college while falling more and more in love with Grace. He seizes every opportunity, after school and weekends, to be with Grace. They hit the movie theaters in Spruce Pine and Burnsville, and, of course, share many cheeseburgers. In the fall, Finn figures he'll be traveling from his campus to see Grace in Durham.

One afternoon after school, Finn receives a stunning jolt. Grace says she needs to spend her time working on herself and can't go out with him anymore. Finn begs for an explanation, but Grace sticks to her story. Finn wonders if Grace is seeing someone else, but there's no evidence of that. Still, Finn's insides feel like a plate glass window that a large rock has just shattered.

Bed Bug and On Fire try to comfort Finn, but his hurt is deep. "I'll never trust happiness again," Finn tells them. "I guess it's my family," he tells them. "Grace probably started thinking I would turn out like my father after all."

When the young women in the area hear that Finn is back on the market, they start showing interest. Flirtations shower upon Finn. At first he shows no interest.

"You wanna go for a ride in my new car?" Alicia asks Finn as they walk toward the school parking lot after school. Brown hair goes perfectly with Alicia's brown eyes, and her hair falls just above her shoulders. With a cute figure, Alicia is a very popular cheerleader and part of the Burnsville elite crowd.

"You got a new car?"

"Yep, a Mustang. My father said that if I got into State he would buy me a new car. It's sort of an early graduation present, too." Alicia's father is president of the Burnsville Bank and Trust. Money is not a problem.

"You wanna drive?" Alicia asks as she dangles the keys in front of him.

Finn eyes the brown Mustang with a tan interior. It's a two door with a five speed.

"Take me up South Toe River," Alicia says.

"This thing has a lot of power," Finn says, going through the gears as the sleek Mustang speeds up Highway 80.

"Turn up there on Swinging Bridge Road," Alicia says. "Pull over right up there. It's a great place. You can hear the roar of the river."

"I love the sound of the rapids," Finn adds. Alicia and Finn sit in silence for several minutes and listen.

Alicia leans across the center console and puts her left arm around Finn. He turns his head to her, and she looks into his eyes. "Your eyes look lonely," she says. Stretching across the console, she moves her head toward Finn. She looks at his lips and turns her head slightly to the right. She looks up into his eyes, and she sees hesitation.

"You don't like me?" Alicia asks.

"I do. It's just happening fast."

Alicia rubs her hand across Finn's chest. "You like that, don't you?" Finn nods.

"You wanna get in the backseat?" Alicia asks. Finn hesitates and looks out over the steering wheel. He releases a big breath of air. Alicia kisses Finn on his ear, and then moves her tongue into his ear. Finn feels something happening in him as the tongue is moist and warm.

"Come on. Get in the backseat with me. You're not gonna hurt my feelings, are you?"

"Okay." They open their car doors. Each one has to fold their seats forward to get into the back seat. Finn motions Alicia to go first. Their eyes meet.

"Watch me get undressed," Alicia says. She slips her blouse over her head. She unzips her skirt, slides it down her legs, and kicks it off with her feet. She reaches around her back and with both hands unsnaps her bra that falls on the seat. Finn feels his breathing race. She pushes her panties down to her knees and uses her feet again to push them down her legs and onto the floor. She grabs Finn's hands and places them on her breasts.

"You like that?" Alicia asks.

"How couldn't I?" Finn says as he enjoys her soft warm skin.

"It's your turn now," Alicia says.

When they have finished, Finn feels a relaxing relief. He holds Alicia and says, "Thanks, I needed that."

"Anytime you want to do this, you know, just let me know," Alicia says with a twinkle in her eye.

NINETEEN

Finn and Alicia speeding away from school in the brown Mustang becomes a regular event. Several times per week they make the trip up Highway 80.

For a summer job before college, Finn works for Hightop Minerals Corporation in Kona. A tiny community, Kona has a scattering of houses, maybe ten total, and a small white clapboard church, giving Kona an end-of-the-world feel. The plant sits on the banks of the North Toe River with the railroad track between the plant and the river.

Finn loads railroad boxcars with hundred-pound bags of fine-ground feldspar. He wears a respirator while in the boxcar to protect his lungs from silica and silicosis that killed his grandfather. Even though mountain air is cool in the summer, the temperatures get quite warm inside the boxcar. When the boxcar is loaded, the loading crew gets a break while the boxcar is pulled away and another brought in. The men of the crew are local and uneducated. One man finished the eighth grade, and he is considered a scholar among the less educated crew. Tobacco juice drools from the corners of their mouths. Every employee makes minimum wage. Jobs are scarce, and the wealth making companies need only pay the minimum. Finn notes how happy these men seem to be. They entertain themselves with humor and wit during the long hard workdays. They talk of wives and children and dream of getting a raise so they can take their families to Myrtle Beach. Most have never seen the ocean before. They are flattered that a former football star now walks among them.

On Saturdays, Finn works at a furniture store on Upper Street in Spruce Pine as part of a two-person crew. In his mid-forties, Chuck has a chauffeurs driver's license which means he can drive large trucks. During the week, he drives a dump truck for a mica mine operation and delivers furniture on Saturdays to make extra money. His wife has multiple sclerosis, and money is tight.

Across the street from the furniture store a hair salon welcomes men as well as women. During his lunch break, Finn walks in for a haircut.

Desari doesn't have a client now and invites Finn to her chair. "I'm Desari. You're that football star from Burnsville working at the furniture store. We see you going in and out of the store on Saturdays but never during the week."

"I only work here on Saturdays. I work at the feldspar plant in Kona during the week, that is until I start college in August."

"How do you want your hair cut, sweetie?"

Finn explains. He wants his hair to grow out some and only wants Desari to even up his dark brown locks.

"Gonna let your hair get long and be one of 'em hippies at college?"

"Don't know about that."

"Hippies believe in free love. Maybe that's not a bad idea, but I don't know about that LSD and stuff they take," Desari remarks as she pulls a comb through Finn's hair and holds it steady while she uses scissors to cut away the layer of hair sticking out of the comb. She repeats the procedure several times.

"Want me to shave your neck? We keep some hot cream here for our male customers."

"Sure," Finn feels the pleasure of the hot shaving cream on his neck.

"I'm all done, sweetie. How does it look?"

Finn says it's fine and asks how much she owes her.

"Not a thing, for you."

"What do you mean?"

"I just want you to come to my party tonight at my house in Penland. My parents went to Asheville to stay with my brother and his wife this weekend. We're just gonna listen to some music and hang out, that's all."

"Sounds like fun. I don't have any plans."

Finn works until six o'clock, drives home, showers, and dresses in Wrangler jeans and a white college sweatshirt. He arrives at Desari's house in the Penland community at eight o'clock. Penland sits between Burnsville and Spruce Pine and hosts an interesting blend of people. Factory and mine workers have small homes scattered along the road. Just off the main road sits the world famous Penland School of Craft and Gallery. Artists from all over the world come here for intensive training for their artistic talents.

Desari is petite, maybe five feet tall, with short strawberry-blonde curls and bright blue eyes. She is seductively dressed in a black miniskirt that falls just below the hips. Her breasts push out against her yellow blouse. Finn only sees one other person at the party.

"Where's the party?" Finn asks.

"Oh, it's just me and Louella. Everybody else went to Sarah Gibson's party. Her parents are out of town too, and she has a heated swimming pool and a band. We didn't get invited. So, we thought we would have our own party."

Desari introduces Finn to Louella. Much taller than Desari, Louella has a curvy figure that is squeezed into her tight white jeans and a green tank top. With a narrow face, long nose, and dusty brown hair, Louella has an almost blank stare, slumps her shoulders, and says very little until she has her first beer of the evening.

Desari hands Finn a tall Budweiser. He pops the top and sips the foam.

"That's my daddy's beer. He won't notice it gone. He goes to that bootlegger on South Toe River just about every week for his beer."

Finn realizes Desari is talking about his father, but they haven't connected Finn to Reuben Boone yet. Finn decides in his mind he doesn't care if they do figure it out.

"What do you do, Louella?" Finn asks.

"I dropped out of high school after my junior year to work at the hosiery mill. Figured I'd just start making some money. If I finished my senior year, I'd probably go to work there anyway and do the same boring job. I pack for shipment, one box after another."

The three continue to chat, sip on beer, and listen to a series of 45-rpm records including John Fred & The Playboy Band's "Judy in Disguise," Mary Hopkins' "Those Were the Days," and Marvin Gaye's "I Heard It Through the Grapevine."

"I can't play Marvin Gaye when daddy's here. He says he doesn't want any soul music in his house cause they're sung by black people. Mama don't care. So, we play what we want when he ain't here."

"Finn, you like to play poker?" Desari asks with a twinkle in her eye.

"I've played a little. I always lose money, so I quit."

"Wanna play strip poker?" Desari flirts. "You know, all three of us. Lose a hand and you must take a piece of clothing off. Socks don't count."

They all feel a buzz from the alcohol. Finn laughs, and the women giggle.

Finn loses the first hand and takes off his sweatshirt. "Look at those pecs!" Desari says. Louella whistles.

Desari loses the second hand and takes her blouse off. Her breasts have her bra stretched to its limit.

"Hey, this is not fair. You women have on more clothes than I do. You know, counting the bras."

"Okay, I'll take the bra off!" Desari quickly says as she winks at Finn.

Louella takes off her blouse when she loses. Finn loses the next hand and takes his pants off. "I told you I'm not any good at poker."

"We're glad you're not a good player," Louella giggles.

Finn's hand is the loser again, and his shorts come off. He's completely naked.

Louella reaches for her blouse and puts it back on. "I'm gonna go. Desari likes you, Finn. I'll leave the two of you to figure things out. Besides, I told mama I wouldn't be out late."

The spring on the screen door causes the door to slam shut as Louella leaves. It's a warm summer evening. The main door and all the windows are open.

"Well, this party just got even smaller, Mr. Finn Boone," Desari quips. "Why don't we take this party up to my bedroom."

Finn now has a sex partner in both Burnsville and Spruce Pine, and before the summer is over, a new love interest in Linville.

TWENTY

Cornbread waits for Finn on Friday afternoon at the road that leads up by Tinnie Wilson's house, the dilapidated barn, and to Finn's house. Finn has finished a hard day loading boxcars in Kona.

"If you don't have anything planned, go to Linville with me tonight," Cornbread invites.

"Why Linville?"

"My daddy worked there a couple of days this week. You know, he's an electrician. I went with him yesterday to that fancy lodge. He needed an extra hand. The electricity was out in a dormitory building where the college students stay. The students are from all over the place, and they work at the lodge during the summer. You know, waiters and dishwashers and stuff. I figure we would go up there and meet some girls. I saw some pretty ones."

"Sounds like fun. I gotta get cleaned up," Finn says.

Cornbread holds up each arm and smells his armpits. "I got some deodorant in the glove compartment. I'll wait here for you. I'd rather not be around your daddy."

"I don't blame you."

After showering, Finn puts on khakis and a white button up shirt. Cornbread drives his daddy's black Pontiac Bonneville, a massive car with a huge engine. "This thing drinks the gas," Cornbread says as they roar up 19-E toward Linville.

They pull into the dorm parking lot. "What'll we do now?" Finn asks.

"Let's go in. You know, just see what's going on." Finn notes to himself that Cornbread says 'you know' a lot.

Stepping inside the dorm, they don't see a soul. They hear television. They walk down a short hall and enter a television room with almost a dozen different sized chairs spread around the walls.

"How you guys doing?" a male voice asks.

In a corner, they see a guy slumped into a well-worn recliner. Cornbread introduces himself and Finn. He explains how his father did some electrical work during the week, and how he and Finn thought they might stop in and see what's happening. The young man explains the other young people will get off work soon, some at nine and some at ten, depending on if they are servers or kitchen staff. He has the day off since he worked seven days in a row.

A few minutes after nine, summer staff trickle in and head to their rooms. Bill introduces himself. He is from Charlotte and goes to Clemson University. He's worked here three summers in a row, says the tips are fantastic, and will graduate next May with a degree in engineering. Three more staff come through the door and introduce themselves with stories like Bill's.

The next student through the door quickly catches Finn's eye. Monica is at least five feet and eight inches tall, he figures. Her eyes are brown, her hair jet black, and skin chestnut brown. In black pants and a white blouse, she is more formally dressed than the others. Bill introduces her to Cornbread and Finn.

"Monica, I know this is kind of abrupt but just wondering what you're doing tonight?" Finn asks quickly, not wanting to let her get out of his sight.

"Just hanging around here. Not much to do unless you go into Boone."

"You're welcome to hang out here with the rest of us and watch a movie. *The Graduate* comes on at ten o'clock. We've all seen it but that's the only station we get here in the mountains," Bill suggests. Finn and Cornbread look at each other and indicate they're in.

"I got to go to my room first," Monica says. "It's been a long day."

With Monica upstairs, Bill explains that Monica is the host at the restaurant. "With those looks it's not hard to understand why they put her at the front," Bill adds.

Monica enters the tv room in bell-bottoms covering her long shapely legs. A white cotton shirt with UNC on the front fits tightly around her upper body. To Finn's eyes, her body looks perfectly contoured.

Three more student workers now sit around the room as *The Graduate* begins. The first time Dustin Hoffman appears on the screen, Bill quips, "Watch out, Benjamin! Mrs. Robinson wants to lay you." The viewers all laugh.

When the movie ends, Bill says, "Good night, everybody. Gotta work tomorrow."

Before Monica can get away, Finn asks, "What about tomorrow night? You got any plans?"

"No, but the restaurant stays open until ten o'clock. I'll just crash in my room after work. I'm off Sunday."

Finn seizes the opportunity. "How about I come up? We'll do something."

"I'd like that," Monica says. Finn is smitten.

Sunday afternoon, Finn arrives at three o'clock in the poker game won truck. Monica comes down the steps dressed in light blue, tight-fitting slacks and a red, long-sleeved, button-up blouse. The colors make her dark hair and brown skin pop.

"Not many pickup trucks where I'm from," Monica says as she slides into the front passenger seat. Finn explains how his father won it in a poker game. Finn has decided to be honest with Monica about his background and situation. If she is going to like him, she'll like him for who he is and not who he pretends to be.

"Where are you from?" Finn asks.

"Chapel Hill. I'm a junior at the university," Monica explains.

Finn realizes she's probably three years older. Finn learns Monica's parents fled from Barcelona in 1958. Her father, a leader in the Catalonia separatist movement, became an enemy of General Franco, the Spanish dictator. Her father became a political science professor at the University of North Carolina in Chapel Hill.

"Life was good until my father died of a heart attack when I was six years old. My mother didn't have a lot of education. She took a job in the cafeteria at UNC. We had to sell our house and move into a cheap apartment in Durham. I got good grades and an employee family scholarship. That's the only way I could go to college."

Finn tells Monica his history and realizes they have more in common than he first thought. "Hold on. We're gonna go up a rough road. This old truck gonna come in handy. Most cars can't go where we're going."

"Where are you taking me? Should I be concerned?"

"It's going to be a surprise, but if you're in the mountains, you need to see this place."

The truck bounces and tires spin up the steep and rutted road. They meet a Jeep Wrangler coming down. Finn gets as close as he can to the bank on the right, and the Jeep does the same on the other side of the road. The Jeep's top is down, and four college age boys are aboard.

"Probably summer school students at Appalachian State in Boone," Finn says.

After nearly thirty more minutes of bouncing, the truck arrives at the small parking lot at the top of the mountain. Two other trucks are in the parking lot. A white truck has a camper on the back. The red truck is a four door with a mini bed.

"It's a short walk up that trail," Finn points.

The air is even cooler on the mountain top than at the lodge. Monica wonders if she should have brought a sweater.

"You promise me it's not far?"

"I promise."

The couple make their way up the trail. Beech and white pine trees line the trail.

"Why don't you go first?" Finn asks as they approach the end of the trail.

Monica takes a few steps past the end of the trail. "Oh my God! I've never seen anything like this!"

The couple enjoy the vistas from Wiseman's View. Table Rock Mountain and Hawksbill Mountain reach to the sky on the other side of Linville Gorge. Linville River looks like a white thread at the bottom of the gorge. A small plane, looking like a mosquito, flies just above the river below.

"They're tiny, but I see people on top of the mountain on the other side of the gorge," Monica says.

"They hiked up Table Rock, a much longer hike than we took."

"It's so peaceful up here," Monica says. "I feel like I'm at the beginning of creation. It's so primitive and rugged."

Finn explains the mystery of the Brown Mountain Lights. "After dark, people come up here. It must be a clear night. People see mysterious lights moving around in the gorge. Scientists studied the area but have never come up with an explanation. The local legend is people, carrying lanterns, got lost in the gorge while looking for a man lost on a hunting trip. Their ghosts, carrying the lanterns, are still wandering around down there."

"You're sending chills up this girl's back! Have you seen them?"

"I've been up here several times over the years. A couple of times I thought I saw something, but I can't say for sure. Hey, let's go. We've got lots more to see."

The truck bounces down the mountain road, and Finn turns into another parking lot at the base of the mountain. They walk out on another trail. In a few minutes, they hear a roar.

"What's that roar?" Monica asks with concern in her voice.

TWENTY

"Linville Falls." Finn explains how the falls cut the gorge out of the mountain over millions of years. "The falls used to be down river, but the force of the water cut out the gorge. I can show you some great views of the falls, but we'll have to be careful. A lot of people have fallen to their deaths off the narrow trails."

"I can't think of anything I could be enjoying more," Monica adds.

On the way back to the lodge, Finn stops at an Italian restaurant in Pineola. "You like Italian?"

"My favorite!"

The server places a plate of rolls splashed with olive oil and garlic on the table. "Good thing we're both eating this bread. We're gonna have strong garlic breath," Monica says.

Finn orders meat lasagna while Monica has eggplant parmesan. "I don't eat meat," Monica says. "Since my father died, we haven't had the money. Now, I hear it's much healthier." With a mouth full of lasagna, Finn just shakes his head.

Back at the lodge, Monica and Finn sit on the porch and watch fireflies flicker against the background of the dark forest. Crickets chirp their songs.

Monica explains this is the first time she has been away from home. "My mother never had money for us to go on vacation. When I got old enough, I had to work in the summer. I thought it would be a good idea to come up here and work this summer. My mother agreed."

"I'm glad you did. Can I come back next weekend? There's lots more to see. Grandfather Mountain, the oldest mountain in the world. Blowing Rock, where you can throw a handkerchief over the cliff and it blows back in your face. And there's lots of great hikes off the Blue Ridge Parkway."

For the rest of the summer, Finn visits Monica every weekend. They take in all the natural sights and eat at the college pizza joints in Boone.

In early August, Monica tells Finn the following week will be her last week. Classes start in Chapel Hill the third week of August. "They're having a going away banquet for the students on Wednesday. I checked, and you can come. Would you like to come?"

"Sure! I'll be there."

Instead of his usual jeans, Finn arrives on Wednesday in gray pants and a white shirt. A tan leather miniskirt reveals most of Monica's long brown legs. A yellow ruffled blouse ignites her brown eyes and jet-black hair.

Finn has never heard of a seven-course meal. Wealthy tourists are the only ones who can afford the meals at the lodge. Monica assures Finn she doesn't eat like this back at the apartment. Waves of food sit before them: shrimp cocktail, oysters on the half shell, salads, pasta, duck, and dessert.

"Bed Bug and Cornbread won't believe this," Finn says, and they laugh.

On the lodge porch after dinner, they enjoy the crisp mountain air. Finn feels love pangs sweeping over him. The words start forming in his mouth to say, "I love you."

Monica speaks first. "Finn, there's something I haven't told you. I find myself wishing I had met you first, but I am already committed." Finn feels a coldness moving over him. "I have a boyfriend back in Chapel Hill. He's older and in medical school. He's doing his final residency this summer. He wants to get married next spring."

"Have you told him," Finn pauses, ". . . . yes?"

"I have. He's so busy this summer he thought it would be good for me to work here this summer. Next year he'll practice at the hospital in Chapel Hill while I start working on my law degree."

"I guess this is goodbye forever," Finn says.

Emotionally crushed, Finn drives back home. She was perfect, too perfect, he thinks. Women throw themselves at him, but the two women he loves don't want anything to do with him.

Finn tells Bed Bug and Cornbread he wants to go on a weekend camping trip before he leaves for college. Finn liberates a case of beer from his father's bootlegger storage shed. There's so many cases of beer in the shed he doesn't think his father will miss it. The forecast calls for a clear weekend. With no rain, they decide they don't need tents and will simply sleep on the ground in sleeping bags.

Budweiser tops pop off almost as rapidly as machine gun fire. The guys sit on logs as a campfire roars. They tell stories and laugh.

Bed Bug tells how the basketball coach at a high school in a neighboring county volunteered to take girls home after practice. One of the girls is now pregnant. She has quit school, and apparently the coach will not lose his job. The father is threatening to kill the coach.

Cornbread shares a story. A mother from the head of Shoal Creek is teaching her young son about parts of the body. She tells the little boy his wee-wee is really called a penis. The husband works at the plant in Burnsville but preaches on Sunday at the little church on Shoal Creek. The mother and the children sit at the back of the church. She doesn't want to have the preacher's children disrupting the service.

Before the service starts, the father-preacher goes up and sits in the big chair behind the pulpit. The piano player softly plays the gathering music. Standing in the back pew, the little boy points to the front and shouts, "That's my daddy, and he has a big penis!"

Bed Bug and Cornbread roar with laughter. They look over and see Finn passed out, a pile of crushed beer cans beside him.

"Finn has a barrel of hurt inside him," Cornbread says. "And his hurt has no place to go."

"Maybe college will be a new start for him," Bed Bug hopes out loud.

TWENTY-ONE

Even though first-year students for the first time in school history can bring a car to campus, Finn doesn't have a car of his own. Tommy Dunnegan, a distant relative of his mother and a recent graduate of Bakersville High, will give Finn a ride. Finn slings an Army duffle bag, bought at the Burnsville Army-Navy Surplus Store, over his shoulder. Finn wonders what soldier carried the bag in its first life.

"You're off to college," Reuben says. "You'll be back here in a few weeks. Like the rest of us, you're not cut out for college. You'll be back here with me and Seth."

Stunned, Finn doesn't know what to say. Finally, he says to Seth, "Help me carry this footlocker down to the road." Tommy arrives a few minutes later in a baby blue Chevelle decorated with dual chrome exhausts and chrome running boards.

The Chevelle roars west on Highway 19, passing Burnsville and Asheville. Tommy's car has a built-in 8-track tape player. They listen to James Taylor, The Hollies, and Sly and the Family Stone. Despite his father's dismal prophecy, Finn feels a sense of pride. He's the first member of his family, both sides, to go to college.

Finn's room is on the third and top floor of Hudson Dorm. The high-ceiling room has two sets of bunk beds. His three roommates and all the boys on the hall share one bathroom with five toilets and three showers. The other three boys have already arrived. Finn will have a top bunk. Two of the boys, Todd and Alan, went to high school together in High Point. A country boy, Fred lives on a farm near Franklin. They'll go to orientation and sign up for classes tomorrow. Tonight, they'll go down to the lounge on the first floor, drink beer, and brag about the girls they've made-out with. Finn realizes not many of these boys have the sexual experiences he has in his background, let alone a seduction by a much older woman.

The first semester, Finn takes World History, Math 1, Art Appreciation, English Literature, and Physical Education. On the weekends, he goes to campus concerts with friends in the dorm. Chicago Transit Authority (later to become Chicago) plays to a rocking group of students sitting on blankets in the basketball gym. Finn notices the long-haired lead guitarist on stage wearing a green t-shirt with Filmore East on the front when he notices a cigarette being passed around the group around him. He takes a big draw and coughs. People around him laugh. "Take it easy. Just little puffs and hold it in a few seconds," a young woman says. This is the seventies, and marijuana is challenging alcohol for students' favorite drug.

Fall break rolls around, and Finn heads home, stopping in Burnsville for an orangeade. Bed Bug is in the Navy, but Cornbread is at home. Finn stops for a visit. Cornbread says he is working at the new yarn plant in Marion. It's a long drive every morning down the mountain and back up after work, but the pay is good.

"Did you hear about Grace Goins?" Cornbread asks.

Finn says he has not. Cornbread explains that Grace was arrested the past weekend in DC.

"What?!"

"Yeah, she went with some students from Durham to protest the war, and they got arrested. They were released the next day, but it was a big story in the Yancey newspaper."

"Wow! She's a free thinker for sure," Finn says.

"How about Grover? Have you heard how he is doing?"

"No one has heard a word since the van picked him up."

"A van picked him up?"

"Yeah, a white one. It had Massachusetts Institute of something on the side of it."

"Grover's going to be famous someday. What a brain!"

"Their aunt died, too."

"Really, what happened?"

"A stroke, they think. They don't have any family left. Poor kids."

TWENTY-TWO

Immediately impressed by Grace's keen intellect, faculty members are also touched by her amazing life story. She arrives in Durham on a Greyhound bus and walks several miles to campus in her baggy clothes, carrying a battered suitcase her aunt gave her. Her bargain store clothes often misfit, but her smile is contagious. She has the only set of unpierced female ears on campus. She wears peasant blouses and authentically faded jeans to class. In the classroom, she is quick to answer questions posed by the professors. Several times per week, Grace receives invitations into faculty homes for dinner. For the first time in her life, she dines on seafood and international dishes from Asia and Europe. She develops a love for Italian cuisine.

A faculty family invites Grace to attend church with them. The progressive church is deeply involved in inner city ministries for the homeless. On Saturdays, Grace often helps with the soup kitchen and food pantry. Church clergy and student organizations on campus work together on social justice issues. Church vans transport interested students to peaceful protests in Washington, D.C. and across the south. The Vietnam War is winding down, but race relations remain tense.

The pastor invites Grace to go on a summer mission trip to Guatemala. The church will take care of all her expenses, including airfare. Grace has never flown before but is excited about the opportunity. She attends orientation sessions at the church in the spring. College classes are over in mid-May. In early June, a church van transports Grace and eight other church members to Charlotte International Airport. They leave Durham at 2:00 A.M. to catch an early flight to San Salvador Airport. From there, they board a flight to Guatemala City. An old bus, spot-painted with bright yellows and greens, takes them into the Guatemala Highlands. The bus stops when two passengers develop elevation sickness. The driver seems used to the predicament and patiently waits for the passengers to stabilize.

Grace eyes the unspoiled green mountain tops as they make their ascent. Their destination lies between Sierra Madre de Chiapas in the south and Peten in the north. The remote village is nestled on the side of a mountain at ten thousand feet above sea level. Active and dormant volcanoes are in the area. Excited villagers greet the bus. A converted warehouse will be their hotel. Bunk beds line the walls with a curtain separating the women's side and men's side. Like the villagers, their bathroom will be an outhouse where gagging odors hang in the air.

Warnings are given about drinking the local water. Dinner consists of greens, rice, boiled peanuts, and tortillas. Although temperatures can be quite warm during the day, nighttime temperatures drop dramatically. An old, noisy generator helps small heaters produce some heat.

A breakfast of scrambled eggs, sprinkled with local red pepper, oatmeal, and watermelon prepare them for their day of work. The group is divided into teams that will build concrete block stoves in one-room shanties where most people live. The small huts have dirt floors with no windows or ventilation. When temperatures drop, families build small fires inside the huts. Smoke fills the space, resulting in respiratory and eye illnesses. Families also cook inside over the fires. The outside ventilated concrete block stoves will be lifesavers.

Up early the next day, local men are off to work in the coffee fields on the side of the mountain. Pastor Diego and his assistant Lupe arrive and greet the mission workers. Families are at first suspicious of the mission workers but quickly become very appreciative. The group is divided into teams and assigned to the huts. Most stoves are completed in three days when the team moves to another hut.

The mission workers hear the stories of life in the Highlands. Villagers have been promised new highways and clean water systems for decades, but corrupt governments never come through on their promises. Elections are in a few months, and, once again, they are promised the improvements.

At the end of the twelve-day mission, a mariachi band and thankful families bid the workers farewell. Happy families shower the mission workers with gifts of colorful beads and fresh avocados. Children say, "Tank you Jesus!"

The mission workers board a bus bound for El Pedoregal over the mountain. A chalet with a hot shower is a most welcome sight. A breakfast of pancakes and fresh fruit restores the workers' energy. Back on the bus, the group spends the night at the San Sebastin Hotel before boarding a flight to Charlotte.

Less than twenty-four hours into the experience, Grace begins to sense she is having a deeply transformative life experience. She has an urge to stay and help the villagers, forsaking her education. Life for her family in Yancey County was not easy, but nothing like the extreme poverty she is witnessing. Although lacking in luxuries, she felt very fortunate to have running water, inside bathrooms, and adequate nutrition back home. She would devote the rest of her life to educating people about the dramatic poverty she has witnessed and the need for economic justice for all people.

TWENTY-THREE

Back on campus, Finn thinks about reaching out to Grace but realizes he doesn't have an address, let alone a phone number.

College days and weeks fly by. Finn studies hard. He won't allow his father's curse to come true. He'll prove him wrong. He makes the Dean's List fall and spring semesters. In his sophomore year, he must declare a major, at least a preliminary one. He can change it later, but he must be careful not to add an extra semester due to required courses in a new major. Grace's aunt said he should major in Criminal Justice if he wanted to be different from his father. Most of his friends declare a business major. One chooses biology and another history.

The evening before the deadline to declare a major Finn takes a break from studying and goes to the dorm lounge. Some guys have just finished watching a rerun of *The Smothers Brothers* when the detective series *Columbo* begins. Finn finds the character interesting. Criminal Justice, it will be!

Finn spends his summers working two jobs, one at the Kona silicosis mine and a weekend job delivering furniture. He must work hard and save as much money as possible. His college tuition, dorm, and a cafeteria meal ticket for three meals a day are provided by the football scholarship, but he has to earn and save spending money.

Finn hangs out with Cornbread in the summer. They hop a moving freight-train in Boonford and jump off in Erwin, Tennessee. They must wait three hours to hop a train back to Boonford. Cornbread slips when he grabs the edge of the boxcar at the open door. Finn, already in the box car, grabs Cornbread and pulls him aboard. Cornbread breathes a sigh of relief, and they laugh about the near serious accident.

The guys at college talk about the fun they have at Ocean Drive Beach, just north of Myrtle Beach in South Carolina. Finn asks off from his weekend furniture delivery job. Finn and Cornbread hitchhike to Ocean Drive. It takes several different rides to get them to the beach. They have interesting conversations with drivers as they travel down the east coast. A life insurance salesperson gives them a ride and offers them his business card should they ever want one of his policies that he assures them they will need.

Two summer school students on the way to the beach and from Grace's college in Durham take them on the last leg of their journey. They know who Grace is but not much about her. She's really smart, they say. The Durham boys give them pointers on how to best enjoy Ocean Drive since they've been many times.

Upon arrival and finding a cheap motel room, Finn and Cornbread follow the Durham boys' instructions that simply involve rotating from one beachside club to another. The Tams are playing at The Pad. Finn and Cornbread catch a few songs by the Embers at The Barrell and run into the Durham boys who invite them to a party that starts at midnight.

The party features "PJ." Gallons of grape juice, orange juice, ice, and a case of vodka poured into a large, galvanized tub give birth to Purple Jesus. For good measure, orange slices and grapes swim in the tub. The partygoers have already consumed bottle after bottle of beer in the bars. Normally they would stumble into bed at this point, but at the beach, the party just begins.

Julia is a sophomore at UNC-Greensboro. Her head rests on Finn's chest when they open their eyes later the next morning. Their mouths are dry from the dehydration and their heads pound. They re-introduce themselves to each other since their encounter earlier in the morning was quick and swift. They danced together for three songs when the guys who had rented the house declared the party over.

On the way back to the mountains, Finn and Cornbread talk about their weekend. Finn slept with Julia both nights while Cornbread made love to his hand.

"All you have to do is snap your fingers and a woman jumps in bed with you," Cornbread whines. "Must be nice."

"It's overrated," Finn says, trying to help Cornbread with his disappointment. "I've loved two women. We didn't have sex, and I was happiest with them. I think I have sex trying to be happy. Football made me happy. Grace and Monica made me happy. I feel like I'm just going through the motions of life and having sex trying to feel alive again."

Julia and Finn stay in touch for a few weeks until their relationship fizzles out due to Finn's lack of interest.

TWENTY-FOUR

On campus Finn is good friends with several of the brothers of Kappa Alpha fraternity. They invite him to join the fraternity, but Finn explains he cannot afford the monthly dues. They understand but tell him he is always welcome to come to their weekend parties at the fraternity house. Finn often takes them up on the invitation and takes random dates to the parties. He is taller than most of the fraternity brothers except for a couple of football players. They are offensive linemen. They tell Finn they've heard about an All-State quarterback on a scholarship but not playing football.

Finn works four evenings per week at the University Center. He manages the billiards hall. Back in Burnsville, it's called a pool hall. Male students who are just trying to pass their courses but not impress anyone with their grades spend their evenings here playing billiards. Finn sits behind a counter and checks the student ID cards as they enter. Otherwise, he does his required class readings and makes a little money while doing his homework.

During his senior year on a Monday evening in mid-October, Finn recognizes a man when he walks into the billiards hall.

"Finn Boone, I'm Coach Sweazy."

In September, the KA brothers invited Finn to play on their intramural football team, a flag football league among the fraternities where tackling is prohibited. A player is down when the opposing player pulls a flag from a special belt on the other player. With Finn flinging the ball all over the field, team KA rolls along to an undefeated season. Finn stands in the shotgun formation and throws bullets to the KA brother wide receivers. They're not used to catching balls at Finn's velocity. Finn takes a little off his throws. Finn doesn't even try to run with the ball, fearing what could happen to his bad knee.

"I hear you can still really spin a football. Some of my players have watched your intramural games. My top two quarterbacks are hurt and out for the season. My freshman quarterback has really been struggling. I worked him too hard in practice trying to get him ready, and now his arm is sore. I want you to come to practice and throw to my receivers. I can rest my only quarterback's arm."

"Sure, I'd like to help you out, but I have to be here at five."

"Not a problem. Jim Jones, your boss, and I go back a long way. I've talked to him, and he'll punch your timecard. You'll still get paid the same, but you won't have to be here until football season is over. Practice starts at three o'clock. What size shoe you wear? The equipment manager will have you a set of cleats ready."

"Size thirteen."

"He'll have you a pair of football pants and a red practice jersey. The players know not to hit a player with the red jersey on."

The coach doesn't give Finn any time to argue or even ask questions. He spins out the door, and Finn is on the football team.

Finn calls his father later in the evening from the dorm phone and tells him about the coach's invitation that felt more like a command than an invitation.

"Finn, you just be careful. Football won't last long anyway. You have to walk the rest of your life." Finn thinks to himself that was the most caring thing his father has ever said to him.

"I hear you're majoring in criminal justice. You gonna come back here and arrest me?"

"No, it won't be like that."

Finn clicks with his new teammates and wide receivers. "You have the best arm of any of our quarterbacks," Tommy Lane, a wide receiver, tells him. "I wish you could play in a game."

In the next to last game of the season against Catawba College, freshman quarterback Billy High leaves the game in the fourth quarter due to a vicious hit on the shoulder of his throwing arm. The Cats have a two-touchdown lead and simply run the ball as the clock winds down.

The hall telephone rings on Sunday evening in Hudson dorm. Joe Simpson answers as he often does since his room is next to the phone. "Somebody get Finn. Coach Sweazy wants to talk to him."

Hearing the phone ring and his name, Finn walks down the hall and grabs the black phone hanging by the cord from the box on the wall. "Hello."

"Finn, this is Coach Sweazy. You're gonna be my quarterback on Saturday. All my quarterbacks are hurt. We go to the regionals if we beat Appalachian. I'll put you in the shotgun formation. You'll hand the ball off most of the time. If I send in a play where you have to throw the ball, you can just throw it away if you're about to get sacked. We need you to do this."

"Okay coach, I'll be ready to go at practice tomorrow," Finn says, knowing Coach Sweazy won't take no for an answer and feeling some obligation since he has been on scholarship for four years.

With his red jersey on, Finn practices as the starting quarterback all week. On Saturday when Appy State comes to town, he won't be allowed to wear a red jersey. He'll be tackled if he has the football.

The Cats win the coin toss and choose to kick off. Finn watches from the sideline as Appy marches down the field for a touchdown on the opening drive. Appy kicks off. Brent Slaughter returns the kick to the Appy fifteen-yard line. Coach Sweazy calls three straight running plays, and the Cats tie the game at seven.

At the half-time break, Finn has attempted three passes. One dropped, another for a first down, and a touchdown pass to tie the game at fourteen to fourteen.

Coach Sweazy screams at the players in the half-time locker room. "You have to want to win! You have to give it your all! This is for all the marbles! For a trip to the regionals!"

Both teams come out of their locker rooms inspired and hit each other viciously. During the second half two Appy defenders, a linebacker and a cornerback, must be helped off the field. The Cats lose their right guard to a knee injury.

The game is tied twenty-one to twenty-one to start the fourth quarter. Appy scores a touchdown on a punt return. Scooter Wilson, the Cats' tailback, takes a handoff from Finn and goes sixty-five yards to tie the game with eight minutes remaining in the game. Appy drives the ball inside the Cats twenty yard-line and kicks a field goal to go up by three points. Three minutes and forty seconds remain in the game as Appy prepares to kick off.

"Finn, on this last drive we'll need to throw the ball when they think we're gonna run it, and we'll run it when they think we're gonna throw. Their starting right cornerback is out of the game. That's a freshman in his place. That's where you'll throw it. You got it?"

"Yeah, coach, I got it!"

The Cats return the kickoff to their thirty-nine-yard line. Finn hits wide receiver Jimbo Tyner up against the freshman cornerback on the first down for fifteen yards. Scooter Wilson gains nine yards on two carries. Finn passes to Tyner for another first down on a twelve-yard gain. Scooter runs for eight yards. The obvious call is another running play to gain at least two yards for a first down, but only two minutes and twelve seconds remain in the game.

Coach sends in the play. Tyner will fake a ten yard down and out. Hopefully, the freshman cornerback will expect another down and out. The ball is hiked to Finn. Tyner makes his move. Finn fakes a pass to Tyner. The freshman cornerback bites on the fake. Tyner streaks down the sideline. Finn launches a perfect spiral. Tyner hauls in the pass in the endzone.

From Finn's blindside, an Appy defensive end slams into Finn just as he releases the ball and smashes Finn into the turf. After the jubilation at the apparent winning touchdown, everyone on the sideline and in the stands turns their attention to the quarterback on the ground. Finn is motionless. The crowd grows quiet. Finn puts both hands on the ground, pushes up, going to one knee, the good knee. Slowly, he brings the injured knee forward, rises to his feet, and waves to the bleachers. Cat fans roar their approval. Finn takes a few steps, feels dizzy, and goes back down on one knee.

Examined after the game, there's no knee injury this time, but Finn does have a mild concussion. He won't be able to play in the regional game the following week. Coach Sweazy gets back one of the injured quarterbacks, but the Cats fall to the perennial powerhouse Lenoir-Rhyne.

Just as Grace's arrest in DC made the Yancey County newspaper earlier in the fall, Finn's football heroics are on the front page of the paper, making East Yancey alums proud. The newspaper reports another Grace arrest. She spends a night in jail in Alabama along with other students who are there in a civil rights march.

TWENTY-FIVE

Finn's spring and final semester winds down. Seniors sign up for employment interviews starting in mid-March. Finn wonders if he made a good decision majoring in criminal justice. His grades are fine, but only banks, textile factories, and Sears Corporation come to campus. Finn signs up for a bank and a Sears interview.

The bank interview is first, on a Wednesday afternoon. Finn goes to the assigned room, 143 in Anderson Business building. He knocks on the door.

"Come in," a strong male voice barks. As Finn enters the room, he sees three serious looking men all in dark suits sitting behind a rectangle table that has metal legs and a fake wood grain top. The man in the middle's coat hangs on the back of his chair. The man on his left stands up as Finn enters the room and takes his coat off, hanging it on the back of his chair. He sits back down. Three cups of coffee on the table let off steam. An open bag of mini donuts sits on the right side of the table. Three little white paper plates hold leftover crumbs.

"Finn Boone?" the man in the middle asks.

"Yes, sir."

"Have a seat," the man in the middle motions. Finn sits down in the metal folding chair in front of the table.

Getting straight to business, the man in the middle says, "I'm Special Agent Willoughby, director of the mid-Atlantic branch of the FBI." Pointing to his right, Willoughby says, "This is Special Agent Crowder," and pointing to his left, says, "Special Agent Banks."

"There must be some mistake," Finn explains. "I'm supposed to interview with Central Carolina Bank and Trust."

"We've asked them to step aside. We want to interview you," Willoughby states firmly.

"How did this happen?" Finn asks.

"You don't need to know. We get recommendations. If you take a job with us and get killed in the line of duty, you can probably blame one of your professors in the Criminal Justice Department."

All three agents chuckle as Finn tries to adjust his thinking.

"If the FBI hires you, will you be able to kill a man if you have to?" Willoughby bluntly questions.

Stunned by the directness of the first question, Finn hesitates, "Well . . . if it's necessary."

Willoughby stares into Finn's eyes. "If you're tough enough, you're the kind of man we're looking for. You've done well in school. You're an athlete. You got a serious girlfriend?"

"No."

"Good, you won't have time for one. We checked, and you're not in debt for college. That's good. We don't want people who are desperate for money. Might accept a bribe. Tell us about your family."

"It's not pretty. My father is a hillbilly bootlegger. My mother cut off his hand, and they sent her to a mental hospital. That probably rules me out."

"We know about your family. We just wanted to make sure you would tell us the truth."

The other two agents ask a few questions, and Willoughby wraps things up. "If we want you, you'll get a letter in a few days. If we don't, you won't hear from us. It'll be like this never happened. But if you want to be an FBI agent, you'll tell us now. If you need to think about it, we don't want you."

"If you want me, I'm in."

"One thing to be thinking about. You'll want to decide if you prefer to be on support staff or a field agent. Support staff training starts in Greenville, South Carolina, on June 15. If you prefer to be a field agent, training starts at Quantico on June 1. Can you be ready?"

"Yes, sir. Classes are over in early May."

"Just remember if you choose field agent, you might have to kill somebody one day."

Finn shakes the hands of all three and thanks them for their time. As he turns to go out the door, Finn spins around, "I want to be a field agent."

Always hoping for a letter from Grace or Monica that never comes, Finn checks his campus mailbox every day. Three days later, a note in his mailbox says to come inside to the postal clerk to sign for a certified letter.

TWENTY-FIVE

It's from Regional Director Joe Willoughby. Finn quickly rips the envelope open and scans the letter. "Yes! I'm in the FBI!" Finn shouts. Both postal employees look up from their counters. "Congratulations!" They both say. The letter informs Finn another package with forms to sign and further instructions will arrive soon.

In mid-May, Finn finishes his exams. Three professors in the Criminal Justice department allow him to skip his final exam. "I know you'll study and do fine. You're already in the Bureau," they say.

After graduation, Finn waits around two days to catch a ride to Burnsville with Hal Wagner, another graduate. His footlocker packed for days, Finn stuffs his remaining clothes in his duffle. Hal says he cannot take Finn all the way home because he and some friends are headed to Nashville in a couple of hours to celebrate graduation, and he just doesn't have the time.

Hal drops Finn off in front of Pollards Drug Store on Main Street. Finn buys a large orangeade and sits outside on his footlocker as he thinks about how to get home. Call his dad? He'd rather not do that. If he gets in touch, he knows Cornbread will pick him up when he gets home from work in Marion but that would be hours.

Finn eyes a car parking down the street. The car backs into the space and then pulls forward into a straight position. Grace Goins steps out and walks toward Pollards. They exchange greetings. Grace seems more friendly than before. Finn explains his predicament. Grace offers to give him a ride home after she buys toothpaste and, of course, a fresh squeezed orangeade.

Driving down 19-E, Finn tells Grace about his new job with the FBI. He hopes it's a career, he explains. Grace seems genuinely happy for him.

"FBI! That's exciting!"

"Your aunt suggested criminal justice. She said it would make me quite different from my father. The idea stuck with me."

Grace explains she finished her undergraduate degree in three years by going to summer schools and taking a heavy load each semester. Already in the PhD program, she plans to start on her thesis soon. She will receive a divinity degree at the same time.

"What's your PhD going to be in?"

"Process Theology"

"What's that?"

"It's theology that uses the process philosophy of Alfred North Whitehead and the quantum physics of Einstein. It's quite fascinating."

"Way over my head!" Finn motions with his right hand over his head.

"I'm also interested in cults, religious cults. Why do people join extremist cults? What's the attraction to these bizarre cults that aren't based on traditional religious experience? Maybe it's the Melungeon in me," Grace laughs. "But we're not a cult."

While Grace talks, Finn sees just how beautiful she has become. While she still has skin the color of cinnamon, she is no longer the skinny, girlish kid from South Toe River. She's plenty tall and filled out. Her brown hair now in long ringlets almost touches her shoulders. Her blue eyes still dart about as she seems to take in everything going on around her. She no longer dresses in thrift shop clothes. Her bell-bottom jeans fit perfectly around her round buttocks and long legs while her tie-dyed tee shirt has a huge peace sign on the front. Large gold loop earrings blend perfectly with her natural tan coloring, making her a stunning natural beauty.

"I thought about a master's degree in criminal justice, but my advisor told me the training at the FBI would be just as good. By the way, how about your brother? How's Grover doing?"

"Beats me!" Grace throws her hands into the air for an instant and then grabs the steering wheel again. "He left for college a few days after I did. Before my aunt died, she said she hadn't heard from him. I've not heard from him in almost three years. I sent birthday and Christmas cards for a while, but then I started getting 'return to sender.' So, who knows? Maybe he'll show up some day. He still had so much anger in him over how our mother died, and how the medical community treated her. I never want to be in that much pain for so long."

"I'm going to see my mother soon. I wonder if any of these dealers around here would sell me a car. I've got a job, just no money yet."

"Usually, you must pay some money down. I don't know what I would have done if my aunt hadn't helped me. She was so good to us. I miss her."

Finn asks Grace to drop him off where Highway 80 and his road intersect and not take him all the way up the road to his house. "I just never know what could be going on up there. I'll get Seth to help me with this footlocker later."

Grace makes a U-turn at the intersection. They look at each other, eyes searching for a few seconds.

"Grace, thanks so much for the ride."

"Glad I could help. Sorry, I gotta run. I'm going to Asheville to meet up with some friends from school. We're going to a James Taylor concert tonight. I'm going back to Durham tomorrow. Not much for me around here anymore," Grace says before she speeds away in her yellow VW Beetle. Finn listens as Grace shifts through the five-speed transmission. She disappears around the curve.

Finn tells his father and Seth about his job and upcoming training with the FBI.

"You're not gonna turn us in? Are you?" Reuben inquires, his eyebrows raised. What his father just said confirms what Finn has suspected. Seth quit his job and is now helping his father with the illegal sales. Finn notices that the operation has expanded. Seth handles the marijuana and narcotics side of things. Seth's hair falls over his ears, and he hasn't shaved in weeks, maybe months. He dresses in bell bottom jeans and an orange tank top with the Zig-Zag man on the front. Finn thinks Grace and Seth dress in hippie attire for entirely different reasons. Grace is a war protestor while Seth has much lower motives.

"I don't think you're breaking any federal laws. That will be my jurisdiction. Anyway, I need to finish training before I can arrest anyone."

Over the next few days, Finn notices a distinction in the customers arriving at his house. Older people, men mostly, purchase beer and liquor. Seth handles the transaction with the younger customers. Most want dime bags of pot, amphetamine pills called Black Beauties, or they ask for painkillers. Finn's not sure what Seth gives them, but it's pills, probably barbiturates, he thinks. Finn thinks it's funny because most of these young people, unless they have a terrible disease not visible to the naked eye, don't seem to be old enough to be in much pain.

The next day Seth gives Finn a ride to Burnsville.

"I'm going to see if Mr. Whitson at the Chevrolet dealership will let me have a car without a down payment."

"If not, I can help ya, little bro. Business booming right now. I've probably got enough for a down payment in my pocket."

Finn thanks his brother but thinks to himself, "I don't want to accept drug money." Finn hopes to get out of the house as soon as he can but has almost three weeks until Quantico.

"Finn, you've meant a lot to this county. We all read about that game for the Cats. Brave of you to risk your knee for them," Mr. Whitson says after Finn explains his predicament with the FBI job on the horizon but no car to drive. "There's a Triumph Spitfire at the back of the lot. Jeb Johnson's boy got a big promotion at the hosiery mill and traded it in on a new Chevelle a few weeks ago. It looks good. British Racing Green with a black rag top. I'll let it go for eight hundred. Just mail me a hundred a month after you get your first government check."

"Deal!" Finn says, excited to finally have a car. He signs some paperwork, heads out the door, and feels like he's walking on clouds. Mr. Whitson is elated to have the problematic Spitfire off his car lot.

"That's pretty cool looking," Seth says as they arrive at the back of the lot. The Spitfire fires up the first time Finn turns the key. "That car is a chick magnet, but you don't need that."

Finn heads down 19-E. He takes a right turn onto Highway 80 at Micaville and speeds toward South Toe River. The Spitfire starts sputtering and dies. Seth turns around and comes back to see what's wrong.

With natural mechanical ability, Seth conceptualizes quickly. Under the hood, Seth says, "Looks like the coil wire burned in half. Let's go to Burnsville and see if the auto parts place has one."

Jerry behind the counter at Mac's Auto Parts turns the wire from side to side. "She's ruined all right. We don't stock foreign car parts, except Volkswagen. I'll have to order a new one. I hope I can find one in the U.S. If it has to come from England, it might take weeks or more. I'll call your house as soon as it comes in."

Finn feels his spirit sink. Weeks? But the next day, the phone rings. It's Jerry. "I found one in upstate New York. Be here in a few days. We got lucky. I'd get rid of that car as soon as you can. Those things ain't nothing but trouble."

Three days later, Seth takes Finn to pick up the coil wire. Finn's not very mechanical, but this is easy. He just snaps the wire into the coil and to the spark plug cover.

"I gotta say, bro, this car's wiring bout burned up. Somebody probably crossed poles when jumping the battery. Cheap wiring to begin with, didn't take much."

Finn jumps behind the wheel. The engine roars. "At least it's running now," a happy Finn says.

The next morning, Finn tells Seth, "I'm going to see mama."

"I ain't been down there in a while but tell her I'm comin' soon."

Finn enjoys downshifting as he goes down the hairpin mountain road to Marion. He eyes the Harvest Drive-in on the right side of the road as he enters the town of Marion. He thinks about the night he met Mustang Sally at the drive-in. That's what the Marion boys called her. She drove a bright green mustang. She was single and in her mid-twenties, much older than the high school boys who hung out at the drive-in. Evenings, when lonely, Sally would pull into the drive-in, order a Coke, and hope a high school boy would pay her some attention. Finn remembers the night when she rewarded him for some attention in the backseat of the Mustang down a dirt road about a mile away. Finn felt a wave of embarrassment as he thought about some of his earlier behaviors, which were unbecoming of an FBI man.

At the prison, locals called a hospital, Finn tells the receptionist he is here to see his mother. "She's such a sweet lady and so kind. We all love her. I don't know why they keep her here. One thing, she never wants any of us to mention her husband. She loves to talk about her boys. So sad about the younger one though."

Finn knocks on the door. His mother reads from a Ladies Home Journal when he enters. Later Finn notices the magazine is about two years old. She stands, and Finn moves to embrace her.

"You're such a handsome boy!"

"Mama, I'm going into the FBI!"

"Oh!" Fiona puts her hand over her mouth. A smile erupts across her face. "I'm not surprised. You're a good man. I told you!"

They chat for over two hours. Fiona asks about Seth, Grace, Grover, Tinnie, and several others. When it's time to leave, Finn says, "Mama, I'm going to get you out of here if it's the last thing I ever do." He cries. She cries. They hug. Finn heads to the parking lot cursing his father as he goes. 'Son-of-a-bitch. He and his local buddies keeping her here. Their time's a coming.'

Tires squeal as the Spitfire churns up Marion mountain. Finn stops and visits Cornbread. They plan a camping trip to Mount Mitchell State Park. They're hoping Bed Bug will be home on leave from the Navy soon.

Before leaving for Quantico, Finn blasts Seth with strong words. "You're part of this now, keeping mama in that mental hospital. Daddy won't forgive her and pads the local official's income to keep her in there." Seth stomps off, not wanting to talk about it. Finn thinks Seth stays stoned and numb to the guilt he should be feeling.

TWENTY-SIX

"Quantico's kicking my butt," Finn tells Cornbread over the phone. "We're up at five-thirty for physical training and in classes all day long. Then firearms training for a couple of hours before dinner. Most evenings, they make us watch training films. I'm seeing J. Edgar Hoover in my sleep."

"I guess packing boxes at the plant ain't all that bad," Cornbread chuckles.

"I get a long weekend off soon. Maybe, we'll do something?"

"Ocean Drive might be fun again."

Quantico FBI training runs twenty weeks. Finn's classes include basic law, forensic science, behavioral science, interviewing techniques, counterintelligence, counterterrorism, cyberterrorism, and weapons of mass destruction. At times, Finn feels like his head will explode with all the new information being crammed into it.

FBI trainees can't wait for the December 15 graduation ceremonies. Finn is the only person who doesn't have a family member to attend. Good friend Alex Moore's family notices Finn's predicament and invites him to a celebration dinner with them in Alexandria. The Moore family buys Finn the Captain's Platter at a harbor restaurant. Finn falls in love with Maryland style crab cakes and oysters on the half shell from the Rappahannock River in Virginia.

The graduates get two weeks off and report to duty on January 2. Finn doesn't want to go home. As a law enforcement officer now, he has a serious conflict of values with his father and brother. He does, however, have money in the bank since he's been paid full salary during his training.

Finn calls Cornbread and invites him to go to Gatlinburg with him for the holidays. To his surprise, Finn hears Cornbread married his pregnant girlfriend the previous Saturday. The couple went to the justice of the peace and spent a quiet honeymoon in Asheville. Cornbread will spend the rest of his working life doing shift work at the thread mill in Marion.

Cornbread tells Finn that Navy Seaman First Class Buster "Bed Bug" Blevins is coming home for a two-week vacation. Finn and Bed Bug hit the ski slopes in Gatlinburg. Neither have skied before but catch on quickly with lessons. They drink cold lager and eat steaks each evening. Bed Bug says he's enjoying life on the aircraft carrier, seeing the world, and plans to make a career in the Navy.

Finn goes to an after-Christmas sale and buys two dark suits, three white and two blue button-down shirts along with three ties. On January 2, Finn reports to the FBI field office in Richmond, Virginia, 1970 East Parham Road. Special Agent in Charge Eric James LeComte greets Finn and introduces him to his partner, Field Agent Jonas L. Brown. Brown is in his mid-fifties and has worked in the Atlanta and Charlotte field offices. He looks strong and muscular, his barrel chest about to pop his sport coat.

"The orientation is going to be quick, Agent Boone. We try to keep things informal and simple around here. There's been a bank robbery in east Richmond this morning. Robbers hit the bank just as it opened. We'll take two cars. Agent Richard Sparks will ride with me," LeComte says.

Sparks drives the lead car as they head to the bank on Laburnum Avenue. In the second car, Finn makes small talk with Brown. Finn picks up on Brown's frustration. He feels stuck as a field agent, not having had a promotion in his career.

"I give them two reasons not to like me. I'm black, and I'm gay," Brown laments. Finn doesn't know what to say. "Don't worry about it. It's not contagious, and I'm in a committed relationship," Brown adds.

"I'm just glad they put me with such an experienced agent," Finn says.

A bloody teller lies dead in the bank. Another teller lies on the floor behind the counter seriously wounded by gunshots while treated by emergency medical personnel. A security guard spawls dead in the parking lot. Apparently, the guard got to work a few minutes late. He confronted the robbers as they fled from the bank, and they shot him in the chest.

"Finn, this is your baptism by fire. I want you and Brown to start knocking on doors and see if there are any witnesses. City police have surrounded the area. Our lab unit will be here soon to look for DNA evidence. Richard just interviewed a customer who was in the bank. The customer said it was two men. One had on a white hoodie and the other a black hoodie," LeComte says.

"If you've just robbed a bank, which street do you use to run away?" Brown asks Finn as they plan their search outside the bank.

"Depends on where the get-a-away car is parked?" Finn answers.

"Some of these guys aren't very smart but wouldn't you park the car on the less conspicuous street?" Brown offers. "Let's go up this one."

There are no cars in the driveways of the first two houses, and no one answers the doors. The elderly woman at the next house says she saw two men running up the street at about nine-thirty.

A woman in her late twenties answers the door at a house down the street. Brown notices she seems nervous. "Do you mind if we come in?"

"There's nobody here," she says.

"We just want to ask you a few questions."

The woman says she has not seen anyone, explaining she just got back from dropping her daughter off at preschool. She tells the officers her husband left almost a year ago and she lives alone.

"Do you have an attic?" Finn asks.

"No. No attic."

"Do you mind if we look around?"

"Go ahead. Ain't nobody here."

As they walk down a short hall, Finn motions with his eyes for Brown to look up. A pull-down attic door looms in the ceiling.

"I need to check this out," Finn whispers as he pulls his service revolver out. "Wait here."

Finn pulls down the folding steps. The steps creak, as if they can barely hold Finn's weight. Finn peaks his head into the attic and shines his flashlight around.

"I think we got something here. I see a white and a black hoodie as well as some other clothes."

"How did you know to look up here?" Jonas asks.

"I noticed a bit of sheetrock bulging in the ceiling in the hall. I think one of the robbers stepped on the sheetrock up here when he was changing clothes."

"I'll call Lecomte and get the lab people over here as well."

As Finn descends the rickety steps, Brown says to the woman, "You need to start talking. Let's sit down at the kitchen table."

After she spends several minutes denying she knows anything, the woman admits her boyfriend and another man came into her house while she was taking her daughter to nursery school.

"We're going to need some names. You could be in some big trouble, but if you cooperate, you can help yourself," Finn says.

TWENTY-SIX

After much encouragement, the woman gives the agents her boyfriend's name but says she does not know the other man's name. Brown talks to LeComte and gets permission for them to track down the man. LeComte says the evidence technician, after examining spent shells, has determined that two guns, a Lorcin 380 semiautomatic handgun and a TEC-9 semi-automatic handgun, were used in the robbery.

Finn calls the field office with the name, and in a few minutes, they have an address and a search warrant. There's no answer when they knock on the door. Brown's legs are thick and strong. His right foot hits the door three times. The door swings open, the lock yielding to his violent thrusts. No one is in the apartment, but the kitchen floor and walls are spattered with red dye. Twenty-dollar bills and one-hundred dollars bills covered with red dye remain on the kitchen table.

"I bet that dye bag was quite a surprise," Brown chuckles.

By the next afternoon and after contacting relatives of the fugitives, the officers track down the two men in a rundown southside Richmond apartment. After hearing the FBI stands outside their door with warrants, the men put up no resistance. Under the sofa, Finn finds a Lorcin 380 semiautomatic and a TEC-9 semi-automatic. Special Agent Finn Boone makes his first arrest. Five months later, the two men are convicted in federal court and sentenced to life.

After the arrests, the two agents head to Brown's favorite diner, Mama Sara's on Church Hill, to celebrate.

"I live not too far from here," Brown says as he sops sausage gravy with a large cathead biscuit. "Church Hill used to be a rough part of town, but that has changed. Lots of young couples have moved in. Patrick Henry gave his famous speech just up the street at St John's Church. You know 'give me liberty or give me death.' By the way, where do you live?"

"I got a tiny apartment in the Fan District," Finn says. "It's not very big, but I can walk to a lot of restaurants. The Virginia Museum of Fine Arts is just a few blocks away."

"Sounds like a good location. Let me tell you some things about LeComte. He says his mother lost him in a poker game when he was three years old, and he was raised in multiple foster homes. Apparently the older he gets, the more bizarre he becomes. The Bureau moved him out of DC. He drinks a lot, keeps a bottle of Jack Daniels in his desk drawer. He eats constantly, too. He downs Bavarian pretzels covered with bright yellow mustard with part of the mustard in the corners of his mouth the rest of the day. Pieces of potato chips lie all around his desk. He's putting on lots of weight. He can be rude. When I'm in his office, he farts every thirty seconds or so, acting like he enjoys it. Maybe you noticed already, but I don't think he bathes more than once a week. In the summer, he reeks. I bet they push him into early retirement soon."

Over the coming months, the general expectation grows into the belief that Finn will eventually become the Special Agent in Charge of the Richmond office. He has natural leadership skills and is well-liked by the other agents. However, Finn's career takes another path. The main office in DC sends Finn on special assignments, "going-under." Going-under is the Bureau's way of saying going "under cover" or taking on a fake identity to penetrate a crime network or conspiracy.

In July of 1973 former FBI agent and Kansas City, Missouri, Chief of Police, Clarence Kelley becomes the new FBI Director. Reorganizing the FBI's intelligence gathering, Kelley puts the General Investigations Division in charge of investigating domestic terrorists and subversives. The Intelligence Division, renamed the National Security Division, continues foreign counterintelligence operations. Finn is often called upon by the General Investigations Division when a "Red Notice" is issued. A "Red Notice" means a person is placed on the "most wanted list." Finn works closely with the FBI's Special Unit for Behavioral Analysis. Finn remains stationed in the Richmond office but is often on assignment across the country.

Finn goes-under for the Charlotte office investigating insurance fraud in western North Carolina. Contractors and insurance representatives overbill the government for flood damage. Finn poses as a fictitious contractor from a small town in North Carolina, eager to overbill the government he thinks overtaxes him. Arrests and convictions are made for five men.

In coastal South Carolina, Finn, after letting his hair grow longer and not shaving for over a month, pretends to be a drug dealer from Norfolk, Virginia, who has lots of drug money to launder. A gold and silver dealer keeps ten percent, but the laundered money comes out as unreported tax-free money. More arrests and convictions take place.

After the FBI receives a tip, Finn gets as close as he can to members of the Symbionese Liberation Army. Their hideout is an apartment in Los Angeles. The Brigade hangs out in a nearby coffee shop. Finn becomes a regular customer and vocally condemns the government as he sips on fresh brewed. He convinces their leaders he is murderously angry at the government. They are planning to kidnap the Dean of the National Cathedral in

Washington D.C. and hold him captive while demanding several of their colleagues be released from prison. According to the terrorists' plan, the government will supply an airplane that will fly them to Cuba. Finn finds out the date for the planned kidnapping, and his team intercepts the would-be-kidnappers with convictions following.

Agents are impressed with the coolness with which Finn operates. Even in high stakes settings, he is never rattled or anxious. "I grew up with so much violence in my family these tense situations seem normal."

Deep inside his psyche, Finn worries people will see how flawed he really is. His deeply dysfunctional and abusive family haunts him. What if his colleagues find out about his father's lawlessness? He thinks the worry probably contributes to the dusty gray streaks forming in his otherwise full head of dark hair. He wonders how many bad guys he must arrest before he fulfills his mother's wish that he be a good man?

Special Agent Brown supports Finn on most of his assignments. He stays in a hotel room since they cannot be seen together in public while on assignment. A tracking chip planted in Finn's shoe enables Brown and the main office to track Finn's movements and send emergency backup if necessary.

TWENTY-SEVEN

Back in Richmond on a blustery, cold, Saturday evening in January, Finn, Brown, and Brown's lover, Pernell, put their topcoats and scarves on hooks at their favorite booth at a casual restaurant on Grove Avenue. Finn has not been in a relationship in years. Most of his life is spent on assignments. Finn often goes with Brown and Pernell for dinner.

"The cold out there is growing teeth," Brown says to the server. "Wind chill approaching zero."

The server knows the three well since they are regular customers. "Your regular? A pitcher of Stella and three frosted mugs?"

"You got it," Brown says.

Finn orders his favorite, a grilled salmon reuben sandwich with sauerkraut and thousand island dressing with a side of blackened brussels sprouts. Roma spaghetti and green beans with almond flakes sit on Brown's plate. Pernell enjoys fish and chips.

With his plate empty, Finn wipes the corners of his mouth with a blue napkin and tells Brown he will be right back. As he steps away from the booth, headed to the men's room in the back, he sees the back of the head of a woman several booths away. The woman's hair, jet black and smooth, instantly reminds him of Monica.

Finn flushes the urinal, washes his hands, and opens the door. Looking down toward his booth, he sees the face of the woman. Her head is slightly turned so she does not see him. Finn's eyebrows lift as he walks forward. The woman has chestnut brown skin like Monica. Her head turns and her dark eyes meet his eyes. 'It can't be Monica,' Finn says to himself.

The woman moves her head slightly forward and focuses directly on Finn's face.

"Monica?"

"Finn, is that you?"

"Yes," Finn, stunned, barely mumbles.

"I don't believe this!" Monica says. "What are you doing here?"

"I live here. What are you doing here?"

TWENTY-SEVEN

"I live here."

"I thought you lived in Chapel Hill, married to that doctor."

"I'm divorced now, but that's a long story. This is my friend and colleague, Lexi. We're both attorneys at Baxter and Short. You've probably seen our commercials on television. Personal injury attorneys, but we do more than that. I work with corporate accounts. Lexi is a personal injury attorney. You should see her in the courtroom. Something to behold."

"Well, Lexi, I hope I never see you in a courtroom, but it is good to meet you," Finn says.

Pernell's phone buzzes, and he steps back towards the men's room. When he comes back to the booth, he whispers something to Brown.

"I want you to meet my friends," Finn says to the women. "Jim, Pernell, come meet an old friend and a new one."

Introductions are made, and greetings exchanged when Pernell says, "I just got a call. My ex is sick, and I must pick up the kids. I'll have to go."

"Sorry to pull you away from your old friend," Pernell says to Finn.

"We can give them a ride," Monica says.

Pernell grabs his topcoat and scarf and heads out into the cold.

"I get the impression you're a couple. You and Pernell?" Lexi asks Brown pointedly.

"We are. I always knew I was gay, but Pernell tried to make a go as a heterosexual, got married, had kids, but just couldn't live a lie. He feels bad about hurting his wife, but we are in love."

"What do you do, Finn?" Lexi asks. Lexi is petite and looks to be fit, probably hits the gym every morning before work. Her short skirt hugs every curve of her buttocks. Brown hair falls just below her ears while intense hazel eyes communicate a seriousness that probably helps her personal injury attorney career.

"I work for the federal government."

"Doing what?" Lexi asks. Finn feels like he is being cross-examined.

"I'm a special agent for the FBI. Brown is my partner," Finn says, not revealing too much as his FBI training had taught him.

"You're a field agent?" Lexi pushes Finn.

Brown answers before Finn can. "Finn won't say much. He's modest and trained to keep things quiet, but he's one of the FBI's best. He was there when they arrested the Unabomber, John Wayne Gacy, and a bunch of others you've seen in the newspapers. He's brought down some plots against the government that never made the news, too."

"Impressive! A real secret agent man!" Lexi jabs at Finn as Monica grows uncomfortable with her friend's aggressive nature.

The server comes to the booth. "You guys need anything else?"

"Anybody?" Finn asks. When the others shake their heads, Finn says, "Bring me the checks for both tables."

"You don't have to do that," Monica protests.

"Just spending your tax dollars," Finn teases.

Monica's silver Mercedes drops off Brown at his Church Hill home first. The others discover they all live in the Fan District. Lexi exits the Mercedes at her house on Park Avenue.

"Wow, that's a big house," Finn says as he moves to the front passenger seat.

"She's a force. Makes a lot of money. Sorry she pushed you so hard on your professional life. Lexi thinks she's always in the courtroom," Monica says. "What's your address?"

"Belmont. I'll show you, not far. Just ahead on the right."

"You've got parking here. That's great. I must drive around and around sometimes on my street to find a parking spot."

"How about dinner tomorrow evening? Pick you up at 6:30?"

"Sounds wonderful!"

On Sunday evening Monica and Finn park on Franklin Street and walk down North Harrison. Finn made a reservation at a very popular restaurant. Wooden tables sit just a few feet apart. The small kitchen means a limited menu, but the food is incredible. The emphasis is northern Italian with heavy garlic. The server brings tall, slender glasses filled with ice and water. Finn orders a whole branzino. The head and tail hang off the ends of the plate. Heat rises from the gray scaled fish. Finn takes his fork and pulls back the skin, revealing hot white flaky meat. A very generous dusting of cracked black pepper raises the deliciousness to yet another level. Monica orders seafood pasta swimming in a rich marinara sauce. On first bites, they both roll their eyes and moan with the flavors exploding in their mouths.

"I've seen the last two governors here," Finn says.

"As good as this food is, I believe it. How did you end up in the FBI?"

"Surprising, I guess, with what I told you about my family. I wanted to be as different as I could be from my father. So, I chose criminal justice, and then the FBI recruited me." Finn went on and told Monica how the Bureau asked the bank to step aside during his interview time.

"You carry?"

"Not now, but yeah, while on duty. I've never had to shoot anybody, but I've pulled my gun many times when making arrests. We plan things very carefully, so we don't get in situations where the suspects could get the drop on us. So far, so good. I do have to travel a lot. You know, special assignments."

"How about you? How did you end up in Richmond?"

"I had a good job at a firm in Raleigh, a little bit of a commute, but I was making it work. My husband worked a lot at the hospital, but I knew that's what doctors do. He was caught with a nurse in the doctor's lounge. They were screwing. The hospital put him on probation, and I forgave him. Then, it happened again. At least it was a different nurse. That was it for me. I think my husband lived such a sheltered life growing up. His father was a doctor and pushed him hard to make the best grades. John never had a normal adolescence and just started acting out. I needed to get away from Chapel Hill. Interviewed and got this job here. Love it."

Monica and Finn spend every moment they can together when their busy careers permit. Monica attends First Presbyterian Church on Cary Street. After six months of intense romance, they talk to the pastor and set a wedding date. Neither have families in the area. So, the wedding gathering is small with cadres of lawyers and FBI agents, a potentially explosive mixture, Finn jokes. They use the small chapel rather than the much larger sanctuary.

Both Monica and Finn like the Fan District but grow weary of the parking problems. The couple buy a house in the Glenburnie section of the near-west end of the city. Mr. Brown becomes the third member of the family. Mr. Brown is an English Cream Golden Retriever. Pleasure sweeps over Special Agent Jonas Brown's face when Monica and Finn tell him their puppy is named after him.

The couple can walk from their home to the Continental, Pegasus, and several other fine restaurants. For home cooking, an outdoor wood oven sits on the opposite side of the swimming pool, located behind the house. Finn cooks wood-smoked pizzas with varying degrees of success. Guests chuckle as Finn struggles with an overheated oven resulting in burnt crusts or insufficient heat resulting in undercooked, gooey crusts.

Soon rumors circulate that the new resident, the tall, shapely, brown skinned, voluptuous, woman of pure Spanish descent sunbathes in the nude by the pool. Wives accuse husbands of staring out second floor windows at their new neighbor's poolside activities. But when word circulates that the nude sunbather's husband is a six-foot-three FBI agent, men think twice about their aristocratic voyeurism.

While on assignment in Virginia Beach (to investigate another money laundering scheme involving a state government official), Finn's phone buzzes. The call is from a member of the North Carolina State Bureau of Investigation. Finn worked with SBI Agent Scott Norman on an investigation the previous year. Norman tells Finn, while reviewing a list of arrests from the previous day, he noticed Seth Daniel Boone of Yancey County had been arrested in Charlotte on a drug charge. Finn acknowledges it's his brother. Fortunately the arresting charge is for possession of a controlled substance and not for trafficking or distribution. Norman tells Finn that Seth will probably get a two-year sentence and will most likely be released after a few months.

Finn asks for some family leave time and visits his brother in jail in Charlotte before his trial begins. Finn explains to Seth there's nothing he can do since this is not a federal trial, and there would be nothing he could do even if it was a federal charge. Finn encourages his brother to rethink what he's doing with his life. "Our father doesn't have a conscience, but I think you do. When you get out, you need to move away from there and start your life over."

TWENTY-EIGHT

Two months after his sentencing, Seth is released and heads back to South Toe resuming his illegal business ventures with his father. Four months later, Finn gets another phone call from Norman at three o'clock in the morning.

"Finn, something terrible has happened. Your brother and your father have been shot. I'm afraid they're both dead."

Norman explains that while Seth was in prison he met some very bad guys. The men were members of a drug cartel based in Atlanta. They convince Seth to work for them instead of a Charlotte based gang. Seth used the Charlotte gang as his wholesale drug supplier for many years. The Atlanta cartel promised Seth cheaper prices and purer products. Insulted and angered, two Charlotte gang goons made the two-hour drive to South Toe. Arriving at 3:00 A.M., when Seth and his dad were sure to be asleep, the hooded men kicked the door down and shot Seth and Reuben dead in their beds.

Finn makes arrangements at the funeral home in Burnsville. Monica postpones meetings with clients, and they attend the service. Seth has a few high school friends who attend. Reuben, so feared and hated, has only two people paying their last respects, Finn and Monica.

Monica and Finn spend two nights at the Terrell House, a classy bed and breakfast, in Burnsville. Finn takes Monica sightseeing. They go to South Toe where Finn shows Monica the house where he grew up. She gets to hear the roar of the South Toe River. Finn explains that the North and South Toe Rivers come together and form the raging waters of the Nolichucky Gorge, a favorite place for whitewater rafting. Monica wants to come back for the adventure. They spend one night in Asheville with a quick tour of the Biltmore House.

On the drive back to Richmond, Finn asks Monica to get behind the wheel of her black BMW. She sold her Mercedes after several expensive repairs. Finn had long since sold his Spitfire and drives his government issued, plain and simple, dark-blue, Ford Fairlane.

Finn has a long phone conversation with SBI agent Norman. Finn explains the illegal enterprise of his father and brother and how his father and a local official, who received monthly bribes, conspired to keep his mother in the mental hospital. Norman promises he will undo this great injustice since Reuben is probably burning in hell and the local official will not be receiving any more bribes.

Six weeks later, Finn checks his mother out of the hospital. Since her name is on the deed of the family home, she goes home.

During the drive up the Marion mountain, Finn asks his mother, "A lot of terrible things happened in that house. You must have some awful memories. Are you going to be okay there?"

"Finn, in the end, good wins. Your father was an awful man. I hate what he got Seth into. But justice has been done as far as your father is concerned. No. I'll be fine. I'll miss my boys, but I'm strong. I'll appreciate the good memories. I'll concentrate on how well you've turned out. I love Monica. Who knows, maybe the two of you will give me grandchildren?"

That was not to be the case, however. The following year, Monica tells Finn her annual mammogram showed an abnormality. A later biopsy reveals a malignant tumor that has spread to her lymph glands under her arms. Chemotherapy and radiation try to turn the tide, but the malignancy's tentacles quickly spread to her liver and pancreas.

Finn takes a leave from the FBI. He sits by her bed in a straight-back chair during the day. If she coughs or moans, he springs to his feet to see if there is anything he can do to comfort her. At night, he sleeps in a lounge chair nudged between the hospital bed and the wall.

Morphine eases Monica's pain but not Finn's. Her last words, "I love you," cause Finn's knees to buckle. He weeps for almost an hour.

Brown and Pernell visit Finn that evening in his near-west-end home.

"You two were the perfect couple. I can't believe she's gone," Brown shares.

"I told myself never to trust happiness again. I let my guard down. Monica was too good to be true. She came back into my life when I thought I would never see her again. But now, she's gone. Gone forever," Finn says as he weeps.

Fiona takes a Greyhound bus winding its way through Marion, Greensboro, and Durham to Richmond. After the memorial service, Finn invites his mother to spend a few weeks with him. He'll drive her home when he can take a long weekend.

TWENTY-EIGHT

After spending two nights with his mother in his boyhood home and returning home to Richmond, Finn sells his house and buys a condo overlooking the James River. A brewery sits around the corner. Finn knows he spends too much time at the bar and drinks way too much beer. He knows he's burying his sorrow in the foamy mugs.

TWENTY-NINE

Grace Goins, PhD, joined the faculty of a seminary in Atlanta after finishing her academic work in Durham. She taught theology classes and was soon churning out book after book. Her writings were popular and controversial with titles like "Feminism and Theology," "Rethinking God: Deconstructive Theology," "How Racism Shaped Evangelical Theology," and "Religious Cults Plot Dominance." Her "Theological Basis for Equality and Human Dignity" is required reading for most seminary students in the United States.

Due to the popularity of her book on cults, the Department of Homeland Security invites Grace to present a series of workshops to their staff on the dangers and methods of cults in the United States. The workshops are offered in Washington, DC. A theology teaching position opens in Richmond, Virginia. Grace interviews and accepts the position. The Homeland Security work looked like it might go on for several years, and the Richmond seminary is only two hours away from DC, much closer than Atlanta.

Over the years, Grace's research and teaching is all consuming. Although quite attractive, she is single and rarely dates. She is tall and slender, and her curly hair cascades across her shoulders. Her brown complexion stays smooth and almost wrinkle free. Only half-jokingly, she attributes her smooth skin to her Melungeon genetics.

At the conclusion of a Homeland Security workshop in DC, FBI associate director Carla Frances Johnson approaches Grace as she packs up her laptop. After having a total laryngectomy, Johnson uses a voice prosthesis held to her throat to restore some ability to speak.

Her voice garbled and raspy, Johnson says as the prosthesis rattles, "Dr. Goines, I'm Carla Johnson, associate director of the FBI, and this is Special Agent Ben Carson. We want to talk to you about a special consultation position. Could you talk a few minutes back in the conference room? The staff gave us permission to use the room." Grace agrees, although feeling quite surprised.

TWENTY-NINE

"Coffee?" Carson offers. "They put on a pot for us," Carson says as he points to a table on the other side of the room.

"Sure. I would love a cup."

"Cream or sugar?"

"I'll fix my own, thank you," the fiercely independent Grace says. "You never know what the FBI might slip into your drink." They laugh. Grace pours a cup, leaving room for just a splash of cream, and returns to her seat.

"The consultative work can all be done in Richmond. There'll be no travel, and it'll be part-time. Might you be available?" Carson asks, not wanting to reveal too much in the event Grace is not interested or does not have the time. "And you can name your hourly rate. We're spending government money." They all laugh. "Seriously, you can set your rate to a point. Just let me know."

"I'm interested," Grace says as she begins to realize Carson will do most of the talking since Johnson struggles with the voice prosthesis.

"Okay. Good. Really good! Your country needs you. We're facing a threat from a very sophisticated cult led by a real mastermind. We don't know the name of the cult or the leader. We do know they have an operation underway in Irvington, Virginia, and at some other location. But we don't know where the other location is found. We don't know exactly what they're up to, but we know enough to know they are a serious national security threat. Maybe a threat greater than any we've ever faced."

Grace feels engaged. "So, it's a greater threat because of AI?"

"Exactly! It's scary what an evil-minded person could do with AI technology that's being improved every day. We have a special agent who is willing to infiltrate the group. We're going to set him up as a right-wing preacher in Irvington, Virginia, where part of the cult operation is set up. What we need you to do is this: Get the agent up to speed on religious cults, how they talk, what they believe, and you'll need to give him some pointers on preaching. He's never done it before. You'll help him with sermons that talk about the coming end of the world and how to prepare. We want his preaching to attract the attention of the cult, and hopefully, they'll let him get his foot in their door."

Grace agrees to the undertaking.

Having done their homework, Johnson's team knows Grace and Finn grew up in the same area and went to high school together. They also know they have not kept in touch over the years. Wanting to take one step at a time, they don't want to tell them just yet that they'll be working together.

THIRTY

Finn and Brown know they will spend two hours beginning at three o'clock on Tuesday afternoon with an expert on religious cults at the FBI office at 1970 East Parham Road in Richmond. Special agent Carson notified Finn and Brown he wants to meet with them at two o'clock. Carson wants Finn and Brown to know the identity of the expert before the training starts.

"Wow! Small world!" Finn says when he hears it is Dr. Grace Goins. "I knew she was very bright and would go a long way in this world, but this is really a huge surprise." Carson uses the remaining time to get the two agents up to date on what the Bureau knows about the cult in Irvington. Only one person has been seen going into the bunker. He explains all communications are coded.

"They're either using burner phones or destroying SIM cards after each call," Carson says. "We'll get Finn on the ground there real soon. Brown, we've rented a small house for you in Urbanna. That's straight across the Rappahannock River. Special Agents Lisa Jones-Turner and James F. Dooley will join us soon. They'll be your backup team here in Richmond."

There's a knock on the door and agents Turner and Dooley enter the room. Greetings are exchanged. Another knock on the door and Carson welcomes Dr. Grace Goins.

"Dr. Goins, welcome, and let me quickly tell you that you know someone in this room. You and Special Agent Finn Boone went to high school together."

Stunned, yet quick on her feet, Grace says, "Finn, it's been a long time."

Finn rehearsed in his head what he might say at this moment but still has trouble forming the words. "Yes . . . yes, it has. But it's good to see you."

"Dr. Goins will take a couple hours today and go over the nuts and bolts of religious cults and their activities in this country. She'll be spending added time with Finn and Brown since they'll be on the ground in Irvington. Any questions?" Carson asks. Hearing no questions, Carson adds, "Dr. Goins, it's all yours."

THIRTY

"I'm Dr. Grace Goins and, like Special Agent Boone, a native of Yancey County, North Carolina. I've taught theology and religious cults at two seminaries. The first was in Atlanta, and now I'm in Richmond, Virginia. I've done several of these workshops for the Department of Homeland Security as they have looked to better understand religious cults.

"Cults are all over the world and have sprung off every religion. Today, I'll talk about religious cults that have developed from the Christian faith. If we look at the First Testament in the Bible, we can read about cults there, Baal cults and Canaanite cults. Keep in mind that the Baal and Canaanite followers probably thought the Hebrews were a cult.

"We'll focus on the cults that developed after the formation of the Christian Bible and what I call the Second Testament. Of course, most people say Old Testament and New Testament, but aren't they both old? But that's not the reason I use First and Second Testaments. In the third century, a few church theologians began to say that the Old Testament should be discarded because the New Testament replaced the Old. This was called Supersessionism, Replacement Theology, or Fulfillment Theology. Take your pick. The Early Church Fathers, they didn't let women have any input then, called this a heresy and held that both testaments were of equal value. So, in the Christian Church, the first cult might well have been the Supersessionists who wanted to do away with the First or Old Testament.

"But they were certainly not the last. This was just the beginning. Around the same time, the cult of Gnosticism arose. These people believed they had received special knowledge from God, called gnosis. Gnosis is Greek for knowledge. They believed they were the true Christians. This cult was condemned as well.

"In these two movements in the first century, we see two traits that distinguish most cults today. First, they believe they are the special people of God, and second, they believe they have received special knowledge from God.

"By strict definition, every Christian denomination today is a cult. A cult, by definition, requires that a person believe, and often declare in a gathering of followers, that they believe certain things. For membership in any church in America, a person must declare they believe certain doctrines or statements of faith. There are a few exceptions, one being the Unitarian Universalist Church that does not require adherence to any doctrines.

"And most of us have professed faith and belief in specific doctrines if we have joined a faith group. We've said in a church or synagogue that we believe in certain theology. And that's harmless, probably beneficial in many ways. So, we might even categorize some religious groups as beneficial cults.

"In harmful cults, the leaders of the cults demand control of individuals' behaviors. Members of these harmful cults are expected to turn over their earthly possessions, live in communes, and perhaps even submit to the sexual demands of the leaders. They might even have to give up their children for special training. In extreme situations, they might have to give up their lives for the cult. We saw that in Jonesboro with the Jim Jones cult."

James Dooley's hand goes up. "Yes, James, you have a question?" Grace asks.

"Not a question, but Finn and Brown went to Jonesboro," James says.

"Not as cult members, I hope," Grace jokes.

"Finn saw the Kool-Aid, but he didn't drink it," Brown jokes as well. "Seriously, it was a terrible situation, decaying bodies all over the place. The Bureau just sent us in to make sure there were no outside influences upon this group of people and to collect any evidence that anyone still alive there or anywhere in the world might be responsible for this tragedy."

"Yes, that must have been awful to see that carnage. And how senseless! The Jonesboro cult is an example, as well, of another feature of most religious cults. The leaders preach a kind of paranoia. Perhaps, they teach the world is evil and the cult is the only escape from this evil. The leaders teach a fear of government. They want their followers to think the government is trying to brainwash them and control their minds. The cult promises to be a haven from these evil forces of government.

"In personality cults, the charismatic cult leader has tremendous control over the followers. Not too long ago, a charismatic cult leader in California told his followers God had told him the end of the world would be in a few days. He told his followers God had told him they should come together on top of a mountain to escape the horrors of the coming end times. So, the followers obeyed, gathered on the mountain top, but the end of the world did not happen. The cult leader quickly pivoted and told his followers God had just told him that this was a test. God wanted to see if these followers would obey. The cult leader congratulated the followers on their obedience and told them the true end of the world date would come soon. Clever, don't you think?

"And you know much of this already, but one other important characteristic of a cult is disinformation. Misinformation is when people just have their facts wrong. Disinformation is when people deliberately spread information the person or group knows is false.

“In Christian cults, we see a fear of One World Governments. Passages from the Revelation to St. John, of course the final book of the Christian Bible, are used to prove the danger of this One World Government. The Devil will lead this One World Government.

“In most of these cult belief systems, there is a bending of reality and, sometimes, a spreading of complete falsehoods. The cult leaders point out how current events and current political figures are profiled in the Bible. I’m sure you are familiar with this story. High ranking members of the Democratic Party were said to be sexually abusing children in the basement of a pizza shop in DC. A fanatical and armed follower of one of these cults entered the pizza shop to liberate the children. Alas, the pizza shop did not have a basement.

“Conspiracy theories are the lifeblood of any cult. The development of social media has enabled almost anyone to develop and spread conspiracy theories. So many people live in an epistemic bubble. They get their information from one source. You know about “Q,” a still unidentified individual, who using his or her computer and social media, developed a far-reaching group of followers. A lot, and I mean a lot, of churches are now having to deal with the followers of Q. Pastors are being pushed out of their churches because they won’t spread these conspiracy theories. Of course, some pastors go along with the conspiracies.

“Conspiracy theories and misinformation can now spread much, much quicker because more and more people are getting their news and information from online platforms like Tik-Tok and other social media outlets.

“We are seeing a fascinating new development in the cult-world, and it’s coming from the wellness community. A wellness community website blamed the wildfires on Maui on the government. Another blamed the fires on Oprah. She was attempting a land grab. And yet another accused the military of setting the fires to cover up a military blunder.

“What’s sad is the more extreme the conspiracy theory becomes the more internet clicks the person or organization gets. Their thinking has changed now, but at one-point, right-wing conspiracy theorists were pushing the idea that Taylor Swift was an Aryan goddess who was rising to lead the righteous at the end of the world.”

Grace continues the workshop until the adjourning time is reached. Finn and Brown hang around as the others thank Grace for her presentation.

"Finn, I'll be in the car and give the two of you a few minutes to catch up on things," Brown offers.

"Sure," Finn says. "We won't be long."

"Grace, I'm still shocked. The Bureau prepared me for lots of unexpected consequences, but this is off the scale. You did a great job with the presentation. I see why Homeland Security gets you to do these workshops."

"Pretty surprised as well," Grace adds. "You live in Richmond?"

"Yeah, down by the James River. I live by myself."

"I'm in the Fan District. So, we're not far from each other."

"Are you married or living with someone?"

"I'm single. Kind of a life choice."

"How about we get together for dinner? Catch up on things."

"I'd like that. Here's my card. Call me."

"I'll do it. Here's my card."

THIRTY-ONE

The following Saturday evening Grace and Finn meet at the Rappahannock Restaurant at 320 East Grace Street in Richmond. Grace orders oysters while Finn chooses rockfish.

"Your oysters are out of the Rappahannock River, as well as my rockfish. That's where I'm going soon. The cult is operating out of an old military bunker near Irvington on the Rappahannock. The creeks of Irvington flow into the river. I'll be living in an old Airstream trailer in a campground."

"That should be good cover."

"Brown will be in a house in Urbanna. I can't be seen with him in public while I am under. It might blow my cover. You could visit though, but you'll have to call me Jonah or Reverend Crow. That's my cover."

"I'd like that, Reverend Crow! Lots of oysters in that area."

"I got a lot out of your workshop. Brown was impressed, as well, with your knowledge of cults and conspiracy theories."

"I didn't tell the group about the greatest conspiracy theory of all time. I didn't know how the members would take it."

"What conspiracy theory is that?"

"That men are superior to women."

Finn smiles but stops short of chuckling when he sees how serious Grace is.

"You think I'm kidding? Listen, men have used that to control and dominate women for thousands of years. It has worked very well for men."

"I've never thought about it like that."

"Yeah. Most men would rather not. And here is another top conspiracy theory that has worked well for whites. Europeans are superior and ordained by God to rule the world. That has allowed them to murder the indigenous people of America and take their land."

"And enslave millions of another race," Finn adds.

Smiling, Grace says, "You're catching on."

Genuinely interested but also knowing that he is no match for Grace's intellect, Finn changes the subject. "I heard your Aunt Linda died."

Grace's face turns sad. "Thanks. I've been on the sad side of things. I don't have anyone now."

"You still have Grover."

"Sounds like you didn't hear. Grover died. I had not heard from him in years. I stopped sending letters, but I did hear he went to work for an organization in Europe. But about a year ago, I got a letter from the State Department, saying Grover was killed. His motorcycle went off a cliff in Turkey where he was on vacation. Turkish authorities found the motorcycle in the sea near Kusadasi, but not his body."

"That's terrible."

"He lived in a shell most of his life after our mother died. So angry. And he was almost too smart. He was always in a league by himself. I might have heard from him once every five years. I hadn't seen his face since we left for college. He said he was working on big, secret projects and didn't have time to meet with me."

"That's sad. I bet he made some good contributions to whatever he was working on before he died. I'm going to make a quick trip to North Carolina to see my mother before I go-under. I might not be able to visit her for months or longer. I don't know how long this operation is going to take. I'll let you know when I get back. Do you need anything taken care of in Yancey County while I'm there?"

Grace says she does not, but Finn realizes this is the friendliest Grace has been since high school. Maybe it's just because two former residents of Yancey County met up in Richmond, Virginia, and are working on the same FBI case? Maybe a life situation has caused Grace to warm up toward him?

THIRTY-TWO

The next day, Finn travels down I-85 and then heads west on I-40. Four hours later, he charges up Marion Mountain, crosses over the Blue Ridge Parkway, takes a left on Highway 19, and then a left on Highway 80. Rural Yancey County is a place where few things change, Finn thinks. Fifty years ago, a person driving on Highway 80 would see the same pastures, fencing, barns, and houses. Except for a few cows grazing, most of the farms are now non-operating. A new house or mobile home sits here or there. Evidence of continued depression-era type poverty can be seen on side roads. Families scrape enough money together to buy the least expensive car they can find. When the car no longer runs, it is pushed to the side of the house into a graveyard of abandoned cars. Most commerce is now centered in the strip malls of Spruce Pine and Burnsville. However, the towering mountains with the protected national parks give the area a perpetual beauty.

Tinnie Wilson's house sits empty now for over twenty years. Missing roof shingles and broken windows reveal the years of neglect. Finn smiles when he sees his mother sitting in her rocker on the front porch of her house where he spent his first eighteen years. When she stands as he pulls into the driveway, he notes how elegant she is with her gray hair pulled behind her head. Her face still shows the scars from the grease thrown on her by her husband nearly fifty years ago. She probably weighs about what she did then, and Finn thinks he has forgotten just how tall she is. He thinks she is as much responsible for his height as his father. Tears trickle down her face when she eyes her only surviving son.

They hug, sit in the porch rocking chairs, and share the recent events of their lives. A neighbor takes Fiona to church every Sunday. Fiona goes grocery shopping every Wednesday with another neighbor. Her neighbors take good care of her.

Fiona's jaw drops when Finn tells her about meeting Grace Goins. She read the story of Grover's accidental death in the county newspaper, so that did not come as a surprise. Finn does not share anything about the nature of the FBI operation because, as in all cases, he is sworn to secrecy and because he does not want to worry his mother.

When they enter the house, Finn feels another wave of warmth sweep over him as he eyes a traditional South Toe dinner. On the kitchen table sits a bowl of pinto beans with a jar of homemade chow-chow, chopped white onions, corn bread and butter, ears of fresh yellow corn, and fried golden-brown pork chops. A sad feeling crosses over Finn when he thinks about how a burned pork chop resulted in the scarring of his mother's face.

They eat and talk. Fiona wants to know how his work is going. Finn shares what he can. He tells her he might be undercover for a few months, and she might not hear from him. Fiona updates Finn on recent deaths and marriages in the community. She likes the new pastor at the church. On special occasions like Christmas and Easter, she gives in to the choir's demands and joins them for special music. At her age, her voice is still clear. They talk about memories of Seth and Mickey. They laugh about the time Seth fell in the river and the time Mickey brought a baby squirrel into the house.

Finn points to a stack of books on a table beside the sofa. "You still read a lot? Most of those books are by David Joy and Ron Rash. I haven't heard of them."

"Read, that's all I could do in the hospital. I read everything I could get my hands on. Ron Rash writes novels about this part of Appalachia. *The Cove* is about Madison County. David Joy, I don't know if I hate him or love him. But I've read every one of his books. He describes a scene, a sunset, a mountain, anything, in such vividness. He's a gifted writer. He writes about the area around Sylva, the opioid addictions, crime, gruesome murders, and abusive, dysfunctional families. It reminds me a lot of what it was like around here when Reuben was bootlegging, drinking, fist-fighting, and good lord, the preacher gets hanged in his own church."

"I still think daddy had something to do with that hanging."

"I think he did too."

"I can't believe that old clock still works," Finn says as he looks at the ancient wood framed clock on the mantle. He's thinking he needs to go to bed soon due to the long drive the next day back to Richmond.

"I just change the batteries about every six months, and it just keeps on going. Finn, there's something I need to tell you I should have told you a long time ago, but there just wasn't a good time with me in the hospital all those years. And since you're going undercover for a few months, now might be a good time. I would hate for something to happen to me, and you never know."

"Okay," Finn nods, not knowing what to expect but bracing himself emotionally.

"I'll just be blunt. It's the easiest way to get it out. But your father . . . ," she hesitates and takes a deep breath. "I know about the DNA testing out there, and before you do that, I need you to know something. Reuben Boone is not your father."

Stunned, Finn takes his hands and rubs them down his legs to his knees again and again. Where he rubs starts to feel warm, and he feels a little more energy, "I'm . . . I'm . . . I don't know what to say. I know how he treated you."

"I was so lonely. Reuben Boone was an awful man. Young and in a family where sometimes we went hungry, I was desperate to get married. He was violent, and he made me feel like I was just a hunk of meat. I know you know that. Oliver was such a kind and caring man."

"Oliver, the insurance salesman?"

Fiona nods. "That was your father."

"I remember him. He was tall." Finn starts to ask about Seth and Mickey but decides against it.

"That's him. Oliver would come by when Reuben went to Asheville to get beer and stuff. Oliver died a long time ago. Finn, I hope you'll forgive me."

"Of course, Mama. We hated him. I'm glad to know he was not my father. I always worried I was stained because he was my father. And something just now hits me. That's why when I was growing up you said, 'You don't have to be like Reuben Boone.'" Finn moves to the sofa and puts his arms around his mother. "After you cut his hand off, he never hit us again. He wanted to several times, but we would just get clear of him. He couldn't grab us and hit us at the same time." They both cry tears of relief.

The next morning, Finn and his mother hug. He promises to be in touch as soon as the undercover operation is over. To see different scenery, Finn decides to take a different way home. He goes past Burnsville, gets on I-26, and jumps on I-81 near Bristol, Tennessee. Near Charlottesville, Finn exits onto I-64 and arrives at his condo at a few minutes past five o'clock.

During the drive, Finn answers a call from Special Agent Carson. The Bureau's Cyber Security team assigned to this operation has picked up on some new chatter from the bunker to another location. The communications bounced off several servers and locations making it impossible for the team to find out where the messages were coming from, and the messages were coded. One message was intentionally not coded: "Minotaur is almost ready." Carson tells Finn they want him to move into his position near Irvington in two days. The Bureau senses something is about to happen.

Finn calls Grace during the drive and asks if she can meet for dinner. She has a faculty meeting but should be finished in time. Finn makes a reservation at the Athens Tavern on North Robinson Street. The restaurant is near Grace's apartment and makes it convenient for her. Finn and Brown both love Greek food and have dined at Athens Tavern many times. The restaurant has been owned by a Greek family since 1981.

When Finn arrives, after circling the block several times to find a parking place, Grace stands outside the entrance. She greets Finn, and Finn opens the door. Pictures of Greek ports, villages, and many houses with the classic blue roofs adorn the walls of the small restaurant. When making the reservation, Finn asked for a table in the rear and in the raised section. Their table is close to the kitchen. Finn likes to talk to the owner and the servers. He orders a bottle of Greek white wine.

"I've never found a Greek wine I really like," Finn says as the bottle of wine arrives. "Dionysus should have tried another profession. I haven't tried this one before. The bottle says it is Agiorgitiko from Nemea, Greece."

Grace swirls, sniffs, and sips. "That ole wine god did a nice job with this wine." Finn agrees as he takes a sip.

The server delivers a dish of saganaki. She pours ouzo over the cheese, flicks a lighter, and in seconds the cheese is flaming. The server tells the two guests this is their prized kefalotyri cheese. Finn asks for honey as a saganaki topping. The next wave of food soon arrives, dolmades and small spanakopita slices. Traditional Greek salads, without lettuce, come with kalamata olives, thick tomato and cucumber slices, feta cheese, and chunks of sweet white onion and red bell pepper. The eye-popping bowl is splashed with olive oil, red wine vinegar, and oregano.

Grace informs Finn she is a pescatarian, and she orders pan-seared jumbo scallops with oregano-lemon butter and topped with feta. Finn orders Arnaki, thick chunks of lamb braised in red wine and tomato sauce.

While they wait for the entrees, Grace quizzes Finn. "Your doctor hasn't told you about the health value of not eating red meat?"

"Yes, but it's a habit hard to break."

"I abstain from meat because of the terrible cruelty meat companies inflict upon these sentient beings," Grace adds.

"I'll have to work on that."

The entrees arrive, and the conversation wanes. "Greek food is so filling I can never eat dessert," Finn says.

"I never eat dessert. Avoid the sugar," Grace says.

"How about a cup of Greek coffee? It's thick and sweet. I think I just answered my own question. You probably don't want the sugar."

"How about I fix coffee for us at my apartment?"

Finn agrees and starts to pay the bill. Grace insists on paying for her meal. Reluctantly, Finn agrees.

In a few minutes, they are inside Grace's apartment on Grove Avenue in the Museum District.

"You're really close to the Virginia Museum of Fine Arts?" Finn says.

"I go to their restaurant a lot. Good food and very convenient."

Grace's apartment has a vaulted ceiling with large crown molding. Finn sees stainless steel appliances in the kitchen and a granite countertop. He eyes a bathroom with tile flooring and a claw foot tub.

"Nice place you have here."

Grace pours beans into the stainless Cuisinart Coffee Center. "I get my beans from Carytown Coffee. Their beans come from small sustainable farms in South America." She pushes a button. The machine groans and grinds. The sound of hot coffee hitting the bottom of the cups fills the room.

"Let's take our coffee out on the balcony," Grace says. Her balcony overlooks North Boulevard where people walk briskly to their apartments after dining or maybe to a show or movie.

"I don't have classes to teach tomorrow afternoon. Why don't you come back around two o'clock? We've got to get you ready to preach down there at the Rivah. You know that's what they call it, 'the Rivah'?"

"Yeah, I know. I hear people saying they are going to the Rivah for the weekend, but in all these years, I've never been there."

"The theology department had a retreat in Deltaville a couple of years ago. There's a lot to do at the Rivah, little coastal towns with antique shops and fresh seafood right out of the Bay. In that respect, that's a nice assignment but sounds like a dangerous threat is brewing."

"Yes, this could be quite a challenge, but I've got great backups. Brown is going to be just minutes away in Urbanna."

"Oh, I did go with some friends to the Urbanna Oyster Festival a few years ago. It's the largest continuous oyster festival in the United States. But tell me how things were in Yancey County. You must have left early this morning."

"I had a good visit with my mother. You remind me of her. You're both fiercely independent. She's doing quite well. She carpools to the grocery store. She reads a lot. I envy her. She can sit on the porch and listen to the South Toe River. It's very relaxing. I might move back there someday.

"I got quite a surprise though before I left. I'm not sure I've come to terms with it yet. But my mother told me that Reuben Boone is not my father. My father was Oliver, the insurance salesman. Everybody knew him, and my mother knew him really well. I don't blame her. My father, I mean Reuben Boone, was a terrible husband. She deserved someone who really loved her."

Finn notices Grace has stopped listening. Her hands are placed on the side of her head with her head between her legs. When he stops talking, she lifts her head. Finn sees anguish in her face that is turning red with anger. Why is she angry?

Grace bites her bottom lip. Tears stream down her cheeks. "Grace, what is it?" She puts her head back down. In a few minutes, she raises her head and blows out a deep breath.

"I'm in shock."

"Why? What happened? What's wrong?"

"It's nothing you have done. It's not your fault. Where do I start? I've lived with a lie since I was a teenager. I can't believe this. You're saying Reuben Boone is not your father?"

Finn nods.

"I started liking you in elementary school and sent you that note with check a box instructions if you liked me. You used to walk up the river trail, and we would look at the stars. I think we were sixteen, maybe seventeen, and we started spending a lot of time together. We went on picnics to the Carolina Hemlocks. Aunt Linda took me aside one day. Remember how the bulldozer turned over on my father and how he was in the hospital for a month or more before he died? My aunt said Reuben Boone came to visit my mother, saying he wanted to comfort her. Turns out he raped my mother. Nine months later I was born."

Now Finn has a look of horror on his face.

THIRTY-TWO

Grace continues. "My aunt said I could not get serious about you because you were my half-brother. That's why I started being so cold toward you. I had loved you since elementary school, but I had to stop. Now, I find out Reuben Boone is not your father, just mine. It's not fair. My whole life I've loved you but avoided you!" Grace wails.

Finn moves to hold her. "I'm floored," Finn says as he cries.

Grace sobs. "This is going to take some getting used to."

"Wow, this feels like a major life adjustment," Finn adds.

"I'm angry. So angry I can't think straight!" Grace blurts as she puts her elbow on the table and rests her head in her hand like her head is so heavy with this stunning information that she can't hold her head up. "Finn, why don't you go? I don't want you to see me like this."

"Okay. I'll go."

"I don't want you to go! I've denied myself for over forty years. Stay with me."

The next morning while Grace showers, Finn fries eggs and butters toast. He sits two glasses of fresh orange juice on the table. "I can't get the coffee to brew," Finn says as Grace enters the room. She wears bell-bottom jeans with a large belt and buckle and a long-sleeved white blouse. Her brown, wavy hair wet from the shower dances just above her shoulders.

"You have to push the heat button first," she says. Finn pushes the button, and the machine hums into action. Seated now at the table, Grace says, "I love the sound of eggshells cracking and eggs sizzling in the pan. You fry some good eggs, just like I like them, and to think you could have been frying my eggs for the last forty years or so." They both chuckle with a hint of sadness.

"It's really been a broken road for us," Finn says.

"Maybe now, it is a blessed broken road. Are you still okay meeting here at two o'clock?" Grace asks.

"I better. I've got to preach soon. But I think it's going to take several weeks, if not months, to get the church open. I'll have to find out about county permits, get signs made, do advertising. But it will give me good cover to find out what's going on in Irvington. What are you teaching this morning?"

"Eschatology."

"Okay, that sounds interesting, I guess."

"Eschatology comes from the Greek word eschatos, the end of the world. In my course on eschatology, we study apocalyptic literature about the end of days. At least, that's how I teach it. We're looking at the Revelation to St. John, the Book of Daniel, and various contemporary writings on the subject."

"So, you know when the world is going to end?"

"No, and no one does. Most of these ancient writings were in reaction to the persecution the early Christians faced from the Romans. It's one of the most difficult things to get out of the conservative students' heads, that anyone can predict how or when the world is going to end. I should get paid extra for that," Grace laughs.

"Grace, about last night . . . . I don't know what to say. Things happened so quickly. I'm glad they did, and I hope we have a future together."

"I do, too! And we must get you ready to preach. See you at two o'clock," Grace says as she puts her napkin on the table.

"I'll go back to my condo and check on a few things. I'll also swing by the RV store and check on the trailer the Bureau has rented for me. They've also leased a pickup truck for me. I'll be towing tomorrow. I haven't backed a trailer since I was a teenager helping Mr. McKinney get up hay. No one knows the rentals are for the Bureau. They use a third party. And starting tomorrow I'm going to be the Reverend Jonah Crow from Elkhart, Indiana."

Grace gives Finn the code for the door in case he returns before she does.

At the door, they kiss.

"Grace, I'm so excited about the rest of life."

"Me, too. Gotta go."

Finn returns to the kitchen, scrubs the cast iron frying pan, and puts the other dishes and utensils into the dishwasher. He enters the code into the door lock and turns the handle to make sure it is locked. He's off to prepare for a new life as The Reverend Jonah Crow.

THIRTY-THREE

A few minutes before two o'clock, Finn returns and knocks on the apartment door. Grace does not answer, apparently not back home. She arrives a few minutes later and explains a student was upset with her for something she said in class that offended his conservative theology. After class she took a few minutes to explain and calm the young man down.

"It's a big adjustment for some of my students," Grace says. "They come from conservative families and churches with it all figured out. Then they hear from me about the different interpretations of the Bible and theology. It's a shock sometimes."

"Finn, before we get started and before I start billable hours, I need to tell you something else."

"Okay."

"When Aunt Linda told me about my real father, she also told me that Grover was not my brother."

"What!?"

"About the same time Reuben Boone raped my mother, Aunt Linda thought she was in love with a man of strong Melungeon descent who lived near Lost Cove. When the man found out she was pregnant, he left, never to be heard from again. Feeling terrible shame, Aunt Linda went into hiding. Grover was born about the same time I was, and my mother agreed to take him in and say we were twins. And that's why Aunt Linda was so involved in our lives, that plus our father and mother both died when we were so young."

"Did Grover know that?"

"I never told him, but I bet he figured it out. In one of our last conversations before he was killed, he told me his new hobby was genetic research. His brain and the new DNA testing would have been quite a combination."

"Are there any more surprises? I don't think I can process more," Finn quips.

"I hope that's the end of them. I want to do all the things we missed out on because I thought you were my half-brother. I want to share sunsets, thunderstorms, go dancing, to movies and shows, to dinner, fall asleep in your arms. Maybe we'll return to Yancey County, hike the trails, and see a play at the Parkway Playhouse in Burnsville. And go to Asheville and really eat at the Grove Park Inn. Remember how we used to pretend to eat there?"

"Sounds good to me. Count me in!"

"All right, Reverend Jonah Crow, let's talk about preaching. Do you need a pen and paper? It's in that top drawer," Grace points to a desk in the hall.

"First, you need to know your audience. The best sermon or lecture in the world will fall flat on its face if the talk is not tailored for the specific audience. From what I understand, your advertising will be directed toward conservative and fundamentalist Christians. You will need to be concrete and practical. Most of these people have a fear of an angry God baked into them. The world was literally created in six days. They believe in a three-story universe. God sits on a throne in heaven. He's probably old with a long beard. A blue-eyed, fair skinned, smiling Jesus sits to God's right. A vaguely formed Holy Spirit hovers at God's left. Angels occasionally fly by the divine throne. This God sits in judgment. Unsaved sinners are cast into hell where they will suffer eternally.

"Your audience is looking for deliverance from this angry God. You will need to give them special knowledge, a way to escape God's judgment and the coming end of the world. So, you need to claim you have a 'special anointing' from God.

"A very popular strategy used by fundamentalist preachers who pastor fast-growing churches is Seven Mountain Dominionism. This approach is based on Revelation 17:1-18 that talks about seven heads and seven mountains. These preachers take this as instructions from God to influence religion, family, education, entertainment, media, business, and of course, government. They also believe the church is to be God's governing body on earth, which of course puts these pastors as rulers of the world. One of these pastors became a spiritual advisor to a recent president. So, this is no small thing.

"And you will need to preach some Christian nationalism. God ordained the United States as a Christian nation to rule the world. You could preach a coming Great Storm when the ungodly will perish.

"You'll want to preach against Critical Race Theory and the intellectual elites who want to destroy the Christian values this country was founded upon.

"But most importantly you will need to offer a plan for individual salvation from the coming Armageddon and end of the world. You can promise to share steps in a plan of salvation only given to you. In the coming weeks or months, you will reveal those steps to your congregation.

"And you could invent some outrageous claims like some of the fundamentalist preachers do. Maybe Satan is engineering a pregnancy for Taylor Swift and her child will be the awful Anti-Christ. We chuckle, but some of these preachers come out with stuff like this.

"Finn, the Bureau has given you a tough assignment. I've got a few books you can have, and you can go on-line and read about most of this stuff. It's scary what some of these pastors claim and what the followers seem ready to do. I'll be happy to review your sermons, but I couldn't preach them with a straight face."

For the next hour, Grace goes over more sermonic material and strategies. Little does Finn know, but he will never preach a sermon in his new church. The conspiracy moves ahead more rapidly than the Bureau realizes.

At the end of the billable two-hour session, Grace and Finn sip on glasses of Argentinian merlot and then make love.

Dinner awaits at Lemaire at The Jefferson Hotel, one of Richmond's fine restaurants. Grace sips on a red pepper bisque with arancini. Finn enjoys a Caesar salad with white anchovies and Parmigiano-Reggiano. For entrees, Grace feasts on Wester Ross salmon with trout roe butter. Herb Roasted Halibut sitting on spring vegetable fricassee provides Finn with his nourishment.

The next morning, Grace sets off to teach a morning class on Celtic Theology. Finn speeds down I-64, pulling an Airstream International. The twenty-three feet of aluminum glistens in the June sun. He exits I-64 and slows down as he goes through West Point, Virginia, a town with a massive paper plant. Finn crosses the Pamunkey and Mattaponi Rivers, their vast waters flowing quietly toward the Chesapeake Bay. Past West Point, he obeys the posted speed limit of fifty-five while he sees field after field of young corn and soybeans. He enters the county of Middlesex and passes through Saluda.

The campground sits on the banks of the Rappahannock River. Finn feels relieved when the office clerk finds his registration. He is delighted to find out he has a river-front site and feels a sense of accomplishment when he successfully backs the Airstream into the designated spot. He did research on-line and knows how to hook up a water line and an electricity cable. The website recommended that he bring rubber gloves for the attachment of the sewer line. Stepping inside, he flips on a switch to test the electricity and makes sure he has water at the kitchen sink. Realizing he does not have bed linens, pillows, or kitchen supplies, he heads to the WalMart in Kilmarnock, Virginia.

As he crosses the Robert O. Norris, Jr. Bridge spanning the two-mile-wide Rappahannock River, Finn eyes the blue water of the river and of the Chesapeake Bay, visible to his right. The bridge has one lane each way and is so narrow some people drive miles to the north to cross a wider bridge. Finn white knuckles his way and is glad to be safely on the other side.

With his bed made and pantry stocked with instant oatmeal, multi-grain bread, and cans of soup, Finn decides to drive into Urbanna. At the popular Something Different restaurant, Finn orders crab cakes with slaw and french-fries. He says to himself he will bring Grace here when she visits. It's open mic night, and he admires the locals who do their best at versions of musical hits from the 60's and 70's.

Later in the evening back at the trailer, Finn calls Grace and tells her about the crab cakes and the views of the Rappahannock. He invites her down on Friday evening to spend the weekend.

The next morning, Finn calls Brown who has checked into his rental in Urbanna. Brown says he will have all his electronics set up by mid-morning. Before he left Richmond, Brown gave Finn a microchip to place in his shoe that enables him to track Finn.

Finn heads back across the Norris Bridge wishing the Bureau had located him on the other side and saved him from the scary passage high above the deep water of the Rappahannock. Passing through White Stone, Finn admires the markets, shops, restaurants, and even a bakery. He makes a left turn toward Irvington. Finn noticed in a magazine a few days earlier that Irvington was the second most popular place to retire in Virginia with Williamsburg coming in at number one. The Bureau technicians pre-programmed Finn's phone with the address of the bunker where the quantum computer is housed. It will be up to Finn to find a spot where he can observe what goes on at the location without being spotted.

Finn passes over small bridges and deep looking creeks. His GPS takes him down a partly graveled side road with green grass growing in the middle hump of the road. Ahead of him is a new metal storage building and another that looks like it hasn't been used since World War II. He spots what appears to be a huge generator between the buildings. The generator is not running. The buildings probably have electricity, and the generator is only for emergencies, he thinks. He realizes his arrival is going to be too obvious. He turns his truck around and heads back out toward the main road where he finds a parking place along the creek. Observers will think he is fishing on the creekbank. He walks back towards the metal buildings, and when he gets close, he steps into the woods and inches closer. There is not one vehicle to be seen. Finn begins to wonder if he has the correct location when a car comes up the road where he was just walking.

The late-model gray Mercedes sedan pulls in front of the first metal building. An older man, probably in his late sixties, steps out of the car and straightens his back. His hair is mostly gray, while his eyebrows are white and bushy. He wears khakis and a blue button-down shirt. He hardly looks like a terrorist, Finn thinks. Finn checks his watch. It's a few minutes after nine. Finn watches and waits. His plan today is to observe. Boredom is his enemy now, sitting in the woods on a stump and watching. At exactly noon, the man walks out to his car and drives away. Finn noticed a security camera on each metal building, and each pointed at the other building. He doesn't want to risk being caught on camera. About an hour later, the vehicle returns. The man exits the car with what looks like a cup of coffee in his hand and enters the metal building again.

Finn leaves his observation spot long enough to drive back into Irvington and pick up a pre-prepared cheese and ham sandwich and a sixteen-ounce Lipton tea. He's glad Grace is not there to witness him eating part of a sentient being.

With no activity around the metal buildings, Finn finds himself daydreaming and looking forward to a weekend with Grace. At five o'clock, the man leaves the metal building, locks the door, and drives away. When the man's car is out of sight, Finn hustles to his car and follows.

The man pulls into the parking lot of the Kilmarnock Inn. Pressing the remote as he walks away, the car security system beeps. Finn doubts the inside of the car will tell him much, but he does walk by the car glancing inside. The inside of the car is as clean as a pin.

Finn thinks about returning to the metal buildings but decides he might learn more if he waits around for the man to emerge from the Inn. In the meantime, he calls Brown.

"This is the most boring assignment I've ever been on," Finn says after Brown answers his phone. "It's as still as concrete."

"I almost fell asleep tracking you. You hardly moved all day. By the way, the thermal camera on the drone just picked up one person in the buildings."

"This man is about as ordinary as they come. His khakis and shirt were perfect, laundry starched stiff. He looks like a guy who gets his hair cut every week, just to look neat. If he's up to something, I'll be surprised. I'm going to hang out here in the parking lot and see if he goes to dinner. The Inn has its own dining room. I don't know if he'll go out. But I'll wait."

"Okay, are you observing the site again tomorrow?"

"Yep, that's the best I can do at this point. The place has security cameras. I don't want to tip them off if there is anything going on. I know the Bureau tech guys have traced some disturbing chatter to this location, but our guy doesn't seem to be in a hurry to do anything. He's been very punctual, arrived at nine o'clock, took an hour for lunch, and left at five, right on the dot."

"Interesting. Well, it's not, but it's interesting that it's not interesting."

Finn chuckles. "I can give you an excellent restaurant suggestion. Something Different in Urbanna is very good. Can't be too far from where you are. I had crab cakes last night. When I go back, I'll try the oysters. All the seafood is right out of the water."

Finn's eye catches a glimpse of a man going out the front of the Inn. The white bushy eyebrows make him hard to miss. The parking lot is in the rear, but Finn is quite sure his man is on the move.

"Gotta go. I got movement."

Finn sets a quick pace but slows up before getting too close to the briskly walking man. 'Mr. Starch, it is,' Finn chuckles to himself. The man takes a right on North Main Street, waits at a crosswalk for traffic to clear, and turns down West Church Street. He enters Nacho Average Brewpub.

"Well, our terrorist likes to drink craft beer," Finn tells Brown, after thinking he would give Brown an update. "I'll go in, have a beer, get something to eat, and get a closer look at our guy."

Mr. Starch sits on the left end of the bar, and, except for some large tables, the only other seat is at the bar beside Mr. Starch.

"Are you saving this stool for anyone?" Finn inquires.

"No, have a seat."

"Thanks," Finn says as he decides not to say another word as he doesn't want to appear too eager.

"Are you gentlemen together?" the bartender asks.

"No. We're not," Finn says.

"Okay, just making sure," he says.

"Go ahead," Finn says, deferring to Mr. Starch.

"I'll have your Trotline Amber Lager," Mr. Starch says.

"I'm a lager man, myself," Finn says, hoping to establish some immediate rapport.

"I like their Devil's Backbone IPA as well," Mr. Starch says.

"Yeah, I like lagers, and Belgian Ales. I'll have to try the Devil's Backbone. I'm Jonah," Finn says, holding out his hand.

"Ken, nice to meet you," the man says as they shake.

The bartender comes back. Ken orders the Nacho Mama's Burrito. Finn orders tacos stuffed with beer battered cod, pico de gallo, sliced red onion, and cheese.

"I love places that have small batch craft beers," Finn says. "You can get a small variation week to week. I'll be coming back here. I just moved here from Indiana."

"I'm here just on a temporary job. Are you retiring here?" Ken asks.

"Oh no, I'm just getting started. I'm going to start a church here. I had a falling out with my church in Elkhart. They weren't ready for the kind of gospel that needs to be preached."

"I haven't been to church since my wife died. I guess I'm disappointed with God. We went to church every Sunday. She even helped prepare Wednesday night dinners. She got cancer, and nobody came to see her. The preacher was so busy traveling for denominational meetings he hardly ever visited us."

"That's terrible. The church must do better than that!" Finn snaps.

"When I got this job, it was good to get away. I only have a few more weeks, though. Then, I'll be completely retired."

"What do you do?"

"I used to manage the data processing division for a large corporation in northern Virginia. We did a lot of work for the federal government. I've always been fascinated with computers. My first computer was a Radio Shack TRS-80 back in the day. The data was stored on a cassette tape. Things have really changed.

"I retired last year. Then I got a text message about this job. I did not respond, figuring it was a scam. Another text told me to open my bank app. The message said to look for a $10,000 deposit, and sure enough, there it was. Another text message told me to go to the bank the next day and verify the deposit. And then to call a phone number. Everything checked out at the bank. So, I called. The man said to just call him 'G' and offered me this job. This job here is the easiest and best paying job I've ever had. I've never met my boss. I've talked to him a few times on the phone and get an occasional text message. I get a very generous direct deposit every week. Since my wife is gone, it's good to be away for a while."

"So, what do you do?"

"Not much. I babysit this powerful computer. I occasionally get text messages or an email. The emails are all encrypted. I get asked to compile databases, that's all. Otherwise, quiet as a library."

"Sounds like a great job! What kind of databases?" Finn asks and then realizes he might appear too interested.

"Oh, just different things. The first was a database of all the phone numbers of hospital corporation executives. Another was a list of all the governors and their contact information and then Senators and House of Representatives. I figure it's some political organization. I still don't understand why the computer is here and underground."

"Is there a humidity problem?"

"Nope, dry as the desert down there. Huge dehumidifiers run all the time. The computer is unusually powerful. I think somebody made it. It's nothing like what an ordinary person can get their hands on."

Finn realizes he has gotten about all the information he will get out of this man. He seems completely in the dark about what else might be going on.

"Is this the first time you've been in the area?"

"Oh no, we used to come down here from Fairfax. It's just a few hours. I still have a boat in Deltaville. I'm thinking about taking it out Saturday. Would you like to go?"

Finn realizes the lonely man has taken a liking to him. "My friend, Grace, is coming down Friday. Could she join us on Saturday?" Finn realizes he used a fake name but gave the man Grace's real name.

"Oh, sure. My boat is a big Grady White. It's way too much for me. I'll probably sell it soon and get something smaller. I'm thinking about cruising through the Hole In The Wall. It's not far from Gwynn's Island and near Stutts Creek. It's important to stay inside the markers, but I've done it a couple of times already."

"I'm sure Grace will want to go. What time do you want to meet?"

THIRTY-THREE

"Meet me at ten o'clock. There's a marina at Stove Point Neck in Deltaville."

The bartender scoops up their dirty dishes and returns with their bills. Finn glances as Ken signs because he wants to find out Ken's last name.

THIRTY-FOUR

Finn observes the metal buildings on Friday. Once again, Ken arrives at nine o'clock and leaves at five o'clock. Finn spends another boring day watching and waiting. He phones in an empty report to Brown. Brown tells Finn the federal Cybersecurity and Infrastructure Security Agency based in Rosslyn, Virginia, learned about the plot through a national security briefing and asked to be copied on any new developments. Finn tells Brown about the boat trip with Ken on Saturday. Brown is amazed how quickly Finn has earned the man's trust.

Grace arrives on Friday afternoon. "I've never stayed in an Airstream before."

"It's kind of cozy. The campground has quiet hours starting at ten o'clock but before then it can be noisy."

They arrive at Merroir for dinner. Merrior is a tasting room for the Rappahannock Oyster Company. A national magazine rated Merrior the most popular restaurant in Virginia. With a spectacular view of the Chesapeake Bay, the restaurant offers small plates featuring oyster, crabs, fish, and other seafood delights. Finn orders a bottle of cabernet sauvignon. They sip while a full moon rises in the southeast and waves slosh against the multitude of boats docked in the waterway. The moonlight causes the waters of the Bay to reflect a soft red glow for a few moments. Grace orders ceviche with bay scallops, shrimp, cilantro, lime, tomatoes, and onions while Finn orders cobia, the fish of the day caught in the Bay that afternoon, with smoked corn, paprika, and local grown green beans.

"Wait," Finn says as the server starts to turn away. "Bring us some Old Salt clams to share as an appetizer." The server agrees.

When the server is far enough away from their table, Finn says in a low voice, "I met the man who manages the quantum computer in the bunker. His wife recently died, and he retired as head of a data processing center in northern Virginia. He seems clueless and harmless. He invited us to go out on his boat with him tomorrow."

"Sounds like fun," Grace says.

THIRTY-FOUR

"I think it's good we're hanging out with him, just in case something starts to happen."

On Saturday Finn and Grace arrive at the marina a few minutes before ten. Grace wears tight fitting white pants on her shapely legs and a white pullover shirt with broad blue strips. A tightly woven light brown straw hat sits perfectly on her head. Finn wears khaki cargo pants and a yellow beach shirt.

In white shorts and a green golf shirt, Ken makes ready the boat. The engine fires the first time, and air bubbles start popping at the surface behind the large outboard motor.

"Not starting is what you worry about when a boat has been sitting a long time. It must still have a strong battery."

"Is there anything I can do?" Finn asks. Ken tells them he has everything ready and to have a seat. Grace thanks Ken for the invitation.

Seeing the vast blue water, Grace asks, "I wonder how cold the water is?"

"This water has been warm for months," Ken answers.

"I'm from the mountains of North Carolina where the water doesn't get warm enough to swim until the middle of the summer. So, I always think about that." All three get a good laugh.

Ken backs the Grady White from the dock and moves the shifter forward. The boat passes slowly through the No Wake Zone. Passing the last buoy sign, Ken slams the shifter into full throttle and the boat lunges ahead with the bow of the boat rising into the air. Grace grabs her hat as it almost flies off her head. Grace rubs her face, arms, and legs with sunscreen and offers the same to the two men. Both insist they don't need it.

Ken, a wonderful host, packed cheese, crackers, pickles, and apples for all three. He offers them beer and bottled water. After successfully maneuvering through Hole In The Wall channel by keeping the red markers on the port side, they speed around the Bay, stopping or slowing down occasionally to view a lighthouse or historic building on the shore.

Back at the dock at three o'clock, Ken explains the summer sun saps his energy, and he needs to get back to the Kilmarnock Inn for a nap. Ken and Jonah exchange phone numbers and promise to stay in touch.

Back at the Airstream, Grace and Finn see a sailboat regatta on the Rappahannock.

"Wow, look at all those sailboats. Must be thirty or more," Grace says as they listen to waves slosh against the riprap stone on the steep shore.

"I heard a guy saying at the restaurant a few nights ago that Deltaville claims to have more sailboats than any place on the east coast," Finn adds.

"I bet Boston or Miami might have something to say about that," Grace says.

They shower and watch a PBS documentary on the Chesapeake Bay as their interest in the Bay area has been primed. With Grace in a yellow sundress and Finn wearing a light blue shirt with fish patterns front and back, they head for Prime Mediterranean, a new restaurant near the Rappahannock River. They have wine, Greek salads, and share a spanakopita appetizer. Both suggest they might not have room for the entrees they ordered. Finn's red snapper, roasted whole, arrives along with Grace's gorgonzola pasta with pear slices. They devour their entrees and laugh how hungry they got when the entrees arrived.

The next morning with steaming cups of coffee, Grace and Finn walk back to the shore. Deadrise oyster dredging boats are already dropping their nets. Crab-pot buoys bob on the surface.

"Some say this might be the oyster and crab capital of the world," Finn says as they walk back to the Airstream. They say hello to the adjoining camper. He raves about the brunch at The Local in Irvington.

With Finn driving, Grace goes across the narrow Norris Bridge for the first time but shrugs off any concerns. "That's a piece of cake compared to the swinging bridges I used to walk across over the South Toe River."

After Finn has a bagel with smoked salmon, onions, and capers and Grace has a creamy yogurt parfait with fresh blueberries and strawberries, they head back to the Airstream, make love, and then Grace departs for Richmond since she teaches on Monday. She plans on returning later in the week.

Finn phones Brown and tells him he will return to the bunker site for observation on Monday and invite Ken to lunch at the Vine in Irvington where he will press Ken for more information.

Ken responds to Finn's text, agreeing to meet at noon. They sit outside, under an umbrella, while soft warm winds blow across their faces. Both have tea. Finn has ahi tuna over mixed greens with ginger soy dressing. Ken orders a shrimp and mango salad topped with goat cheese.

Walking back to their cars, Finn tells Ken he needs to tell him something and asks him to sit in the car with him for a few minutes. Ken agrees. Car doors open and shut.

THIRTY-FOUR

"Ken, my name is not Jonah. I'm Finn Boone, FBI Special Agent. I need to ask you some very important questions. Is there anything else you are not telling me about your role here or anything else you can tell me about the organization behind the quantum computer?" Finn shows Ken his FBI badge.

"Oh my," Ken gasps. "I really don't know much more. I did think it was easy money. I thought this was a political organization, but I guess I should have asked."

"Is there anything you can tell me about G?"

"I don't know anything about him. Listen, it's boring as an empty plate in that bunker. I've read four novels and tons of magazines. The only thing I've done is put together several databases. I haven't sent them to him yet because he has not asked for them, but I suspect he could remotely pull them off Minotaur."

"Minotaur?"

"Yep, that's what he called the quantum."

"Our tech guys intercepted a message that said, 'minotaur is almost ready'. What could that mean?"

"I don't know, unless it has something to do with the databases."

"Listen, we need you to keep doing what you're doing. Don't change your routine or ask any suspicious questions of G. The FBI might raid the bunker at any time. You just need to cooperate and stay calm. We don't believe you're involved."

"Involved in what?"

"I can't tell you right now. Just be patient."

"Okay."

Finn returns to the Airstream and briefs Brown who will in turn brief the FBI brass and the agents at the Cybersecurity and Infrastructure Security Agency. Finn explains he thinks Ken is completely out of the loop on any threats and is simply babysitting Minotaur and assembling databases. Finn wonders if this location is simply a decoy, a diversion.

THIRTY-FIVE

Finn waits until almost seven on Sunday to call Grace. Grace does not answer. He calls again every thirty minutes until nine o'clock. With still no answer, he calls Brown. They discuss options. Brown will phone the state police and inquire about accidents between the Bay area and Richmond. Finn will ask a good friend in the FBI office who lives in the Fan District to check Grace's apartment. By ten o'clock, Finn knows there have not been any accidents requiring hospitalizations with patients fitting Grace's description. The friend checking the apartment reports there are no lights on in the apartment and no one answers the door.

Early the next morning, Finn is about to call the seminary when Brown calls. State Police found a car in the Wahrani Nature Park parking lot just off Route 33 near West Point. Route 33 is the most direct route to I-64 and Richmond. The license plate was issued to Grace Goins of Richmond.

Finn is baffled and anxious. In all his years with the Bureau, he has dealt with kidnappings, rapes, murders, white collar crime, and terrorist plots, but this is the first time it involves someone he loves. A love that eluded him for most of his life. His stomach twists into knots.

Brown calls. The forensic unit went over Grace's car and only found her DNA. Grace's electric car is autonomous, he tells Finn. The unit thinks someone might have tampered with her autonomous mode and directed the car to the Wahrani Nature Park lot. If she was kidnapped, she would have to be forced or coaxed out of her car, Finn thinks.

Grace does not show up for her classes, and the seminary has not received any communication from her. Finn knows the Bureau has missing person bulletins spread across the United States. Amtrak, bus companies, and airport securities have been notified. Still, Finn tosses and turns all night.

The search is made more difficult because Grace does not have any living relatives. Professors and colleagues at the seminary are interviewed, but no clues emerge. Officials at the Department of Homeland Security are contacted since Grace leads the workshops for them, but they have no information to share. According to the forensic unit, Grace's cell phone has not pinged since she left the Bay. Wednesday comes and goes and still no information on Grace's whereabouts.

At 4:30 P.M. Finn's cell phone buzzes. "Finn, we might have caught a break," Assistant Director Ben Carson shares. "I should say this does not have anything to do with Grace Goins, but we have more information on the shell company that bought the bunker in Irvington. It's complicated, but a mother-shell company was started. The problem, as you know, is that there is no identifying information on who started or owns a shell company. But here is where we got lucky. The mother-shell company started several worthless shell companies, and all of those shell companies started worthless shell companies. One anonymously bought the bunker property. Our business forensic experts found that a cousin shell company started by one of the second-generation shell companies bought another property in North Carolina. We still don't who owns them, but we now know there are two locations."

"Where's the property?" Finn demands.

"It's an old mining property on the South Toe River in Yancey County."

"What?! That's where I grew up, and that's where Grace Goins grew up!"

"We've already established that electricity has been reconnected to a cluster of buildings at the mine site."

"I think I know where that mine site is. They polluted the South Toe with flotation plant tailings from a mica mine. The river was like a floating mud hole. The EPA shut them down in the 1970s after Congress passed the Clean Water Act."

"Finn, there's something I need to talk to you about. There's some concern you're emotionally involved with the disappearance of Grace Goins and you might not give the Quantum Case your full attention."

"Ben, I am emotionally involved, but I'm the only person with a relationship with Ken in the bunker in Irvington. I can keep my personal and professional interests separate. In fact, I'm getting a call from Ken right now."

"All right, let's hang up and take that call."

"Hello."

"Hello, Finn, this is Ken. There's something I think you'll want to know."

"Okay, go ahead."

"I received a text from G. He's coming to the bunker tomorrow."

"What time?"

"10:00 o'clock."

"Ken, you just go in like you normally do. We'll have people in position. Just stay calm. Nobody will get hurt. We do this all the time, and we'll proceed with caution."

"Okay. But I haven't told you everything. I mean, I didn't tell you about all the databases G asked me to compile. I didn't think it was a big deal. But he asked me to compile a database of all AR-15 and assault style rifle owners in the U.S. And a database of all the executives of fossil fuel companies in the U.S. He wanted the heirs of a mining company in North Carolina. He especially wanted the phone numbers."

"How can you get all that information? Aren't their websites password protected?"

"It doesn't take long. G wrote a program, a complex algorithm, containing millions and millions of possible password combinations, letters, numbers, special characters, resulting in all the possible combinations of characters and their multiples. For processing, the quantum uses subatomic particles instead of electrical calculations, and it can sweep through websites entering all those possible passwords in seconds. It has not failed yet."

"Ken, some of those things might be illegal, but if you keep helping us, we'll make sure you are not prosecuted."

Resuming their conversation, Ben Carson asks Finn, "How many people do you need tomorrow?" Finn tells Ben he needs a team to stake out the bunker with him the next morning. They'll be three of them in the woods where Finn has been observing the bunker. Finn asks for a backup team to appear to be fishing on the creek down from the bunker. Brown will continue at the communication center in Urbanna.

The day passes without any news about Grace Goins. A team from the state bureau of investigation watches her apartment. Friends and neighbors continue to be interviewed. Her current and previous employers are interviewed. Did she make any enemies? Did she owe anyone money? Were there boyfriends? No leads emerge. Again, Finn tosses and turns all night.

THIRTY-SIX

Up early, Finn heads in the pale morning light to the stake out position in Irvington. With all the activity lately, he hasn't shaved and sports a thin gray beard to go along with his salt and pepper hair. By 7:30 Finn and his team are in place. In perfectly starched pants and shirt, Ken arrives at 9:00. The two fishermen arrive at 9:30. The wait is on.

In tactical camouflage gear, the agents with Finn are with the FBI SWAT (Special Weapons and Tactic Team) and are equipped with M4 carbines as well as their 17 Gen4 Glocks. Poised to respond at 11:00, the plan is to take G in for questioning at the Richmond FBI office. The agents hear the buzz of an FBI drone overhead, but there is hanging gray cloud cover. They wonder what the drone will be able to see.

At 10:41, Finn's cell phone buzzes.

"Finn, we got a problem," John, one of the backup team members fishing on the creek, says. "You've got a Lancaster County deputy sheriff headed your way."

Finn sees the Ford Explorer with sheriff department lettering coming up the road and worries their cover might be blown. He tells his team, "Hopefully, this is just a routine patrol. Everybody lay low."

The Explorer reaches the metal buildings, swings through the parking lot, and heads back down the road.

"All clear. Our guy, G, should be arriving soon," Finn says to his team.

At noon the agents continue to wait. The only afternoon excitement comes from a Great Blue Heron gliding just above the creek. Finn does not want to call or text Ken, thinking G might have a method to monitor Ken's calls. By five o'clock, not one car approached the metal buildings. The FBI fishermen have watched the tide come in and go out. Instructed to proceed as he normally does, Ken leaves the building, locking the door, enters his car, and drives away. Finn asks the tactical unit to stay in place while he follows Ken out of Irvington. As they approach the entrance to the Compass Entertainment Complex, Finn flashes his headlights. Ken turns into the theater parking lot. Finn pulls alongside and rolls down his window. Ken does the same.

"Did you hear anything from G?" Finn asks.

"Nothing. Not a word, not a text or an email."

Even though Ken previously did not share every detail of the operation, Finn trusts Ken's information.

"Listen, if you hear anything, please contact me immediately. I'll have to contact the boss, but I think we will have a unit watching the buildings tomorrow. I'll be in touch."

Finn calls the tactical units as he drives back toward Irvington. He tells them unless they hear otherwise to resume their observation the next morning. Finn calls Brown and fills him in. As per protocol, Brown will give a report to their superiors.

Finn's phone chimes indicating a text has arrived. It is an unknown number. The message is CROATAN.

Back in the Airstream, his primary phone compromised, Finn pulls out a secondary phone and starts a conference call between Brown, Ben Carson, and himself. As soon they say hello, Finn's primary phone chimes again with a text message: "You can have Minotaur. Centaur is much more powerful."

Finn tells them about the two texts. "I remember from high school history class, Croatan was about the Lost Colony. It was carved on a tree and the only clue they found after the Lost Colony disappeared. Historians think it was a message about moving on, maybe to a Croatan Native American village. I think G is trying to be clever and tell us he is moving on."

"I'll have the tactical squad move in on the metal buildings tomorrow. Don't tell Ken they are coming, just in case he might be inclined to tip off G. What's this Minotaur and Centaur shit about?" Ben Carson asks.

"G is using Greek mythology to taunt us. Minotaur is the quantum computer underground in Irvington. Centaur, he says, is more powerful and must be at the other location," Finn says.

"Does he still not know we know about the other location?" Brown asks.

"I don't think so," Finn replies.

"Okay, you two are headed to this location in North Carolina in the morning. Where is it again?" Carson asks.

"Near Burnsville. It's an old mining operation the EPA shut down in the early 1970's. It's very close to where Grace Goins and I grew up," Finn answers, hoping Carson might share news about Grace. Carson does not, so Finn assumes there is no new information. Finn does not want to ask directly since there is a concern he might be distracted from his mission.

"You'll fly out of Richmond International Airport in the morning. You'll land in Asheville. My assistant will have a car reserved for you and a place to stay near Burnsville. She'll get you all that information later today. Tactical units will be waiting for you in Asheville. Agents James Dooley and Bob Krauset will be dressed like they are hiking the Appalachian Trail and taking a few days break in Burnsville. Agent Turner will join you, Finn. You'll be a couple on vacation. Brown will set up his communications center in the hotel.

"We'll have people pick up that Airstream. Finn, I know you must be wondering about Grace Goins. We're doing everything we possibly can, but until we get a lead, as you know, there's not much we can do. But our offices all over the country and every state investigative unit are on the lookout."

"Thanks, Ben."

Back in Richmond, Finn opens the door and steps into what feels like a lonely condo. He repacks his bags for the mountains and orders a pizza delivery. His appetite suppressed with worry and anxiety, he eats one slice. He has a glass of Australian merlot and falls asleep on the sofa while watching the news and hoping for something about Grace.

After landing at Asheville airport in the late afternoon, Brown and Finn pick up their rental, a Jeep Wrangler. Finn thinks it is the perfect vehicle for the mountain roads. In Burnsville, they check into their rooms at the newly remodeled NuWray Hotel and dine at their Carriage House Sundries restaurant. They'll meet with Dooley, Krauset, and Turner the next morning to plan their next moves in the upstairs dining room of Appalachian Java, a favorite coffee and sandwich shop on Main Street in Burnsville.

THIRTY-SEVEN

Grace's head throbs as she opens her eyes. 'How long have I been asleep? Where am I?' she asks herself. Her dry eyes sting.

'This can't be! Must be a dream. I'm in the bedroom where I grew up! Have I gone back in time?' She pulls her hair around, sees the gray streaks, and realizes she is no time traveler. It's the same furniture from her childhood. The curtains are gone. She sees boards over the windows. Her bedroom door the same, but she eyes two new deadbolt locks. A knock at the door!

"May I come in?"

Grace hears keys jingling. The door swings open. A man, wearing thick eyeglasses and a baseball hat lettered with Mt Mitchell, holds food on a tray. She smells the aromas of buttered toast and scrambled eggs. "I thought you might be hungry," the man says.

"Who are you? Where am I?" Grace demands.

"You don't recognize me? You don't know where you are?"

"This is the house I grew up in! How did I get here? Who are you? You've kidnapped me!"

"You don't recognize me? I'll take the hat off," the man says and then gives Grace a clue. "My bedroom was across the hall."

"What! Grover! You're dead!"

"Well, everyone thinks I'm dead. But I'm alive and well. I faked my death."

"Why?"

"I have very valuable information inside my head. The Russians, the Iranians, the Chinese, and others want that information. So I thought it better for me to be dead.

"Some things came together for me. I left the DIII-D National Fusion Facility in San Diego. We were so close to making fusion energy possible, but the fossil fuel lobbyists wouldn't let congress allocate the money we needed to take the next step. I thought it might be different in Europe. So, I went to work as a research physicist for Tokamak Energy in Oxfordshire, but it is the same problem. The fossil fuel industry puts pressure on the politicians to drag their feet. Especially in the United States, the fossil fuel industry funds the political campaigns of so many of the Senators and Representatives. Then, I went on holiday to Turkey to do some genetic research and found out some interesting things about our ancestors."

"I don't care about all that right now. Why am I here?!" Grace demands.

"Grace, I brought you here to protect you. Some things are about to happen that will fundamentally change how our country is governed and what the priorities are. Since you are my cousin, I didn't want anything to happen to you. I'll always think of you as my twin sister, but we are cousins. Genetic research can bring painful information sometimes."

"I know. Aunt Linda told me when I was a teenager. Do you know who my father was?" Grace asks.

"Yes, Reuben Boone. You are not pure Melungeon, Grace. I am from a pure strain. My father descended from the dead Melungeon preacher who had not decayed although he had been in the ground almost a century. Remember when his body washed up during a flood in Lost Cove when we were teenagers?" Grover says. "And I found out why in Turkey."

"I want to hear all about it, but you need to let me go."

"I can't until I can trust you. We're very close to a world changing moment. I can't risk you alerting authorities."

"We, who are you talking about?" Grace demands.

"Eat your breakfast before it gets cold. " Grover says as he leaves the room, locking both dead bolt locks.

An hour later, Grover returns.

Before, Grover can say anything Grace demands, "How did you kidnap me?"

"Since your car was autonomous, I could tap into the computer and take control of the car."

"How did you drug me?"

"I didn't drug you. I've developed several technologies. I can send a signal to any cell phone. I sent a frequency to your phone that put you to sleep. The frequency slowed down the activity in your hypothalamus and made you fall asleep. I can send a frequency that will make people go blind. It damages the optic nerve."

"Are you G? Are you a madman?"

"I am not a madman. The madmen are the politicians, billionaires, and corporations that won't do what's best for the planet. But, yes, I am G, and I'm not alone. I can't give you their names, but several other physicists are working with me on this. We're not only going to save the world. We're going to make a better world, a much better world. We have the financial backing of one of the richest people in the world. Our paths crossed years ago, and he has kept in touch. He's as frustrated as we are with the way the politicians govern our country and the needless path of doom that we are on. We can still stop climate deterioration and save the planet."

"What in God's name does this have to do with Turkey?"

"It was the beginning of an empowering awakening for me. Remember how people made fun of us and looked down on us for being Melungeons. They made fun of us because we had six fingers and the Anatolian Bump. They laughed at our brown skin and oily hair. We had to live high up on the mountains. They called us Children of the Mist.

"As it turns out, we are a very special race. You're a theologian. You know Mary the mother of Jesus fled Jerusalem after Jesus was crucified. You know she went to Ephesus. Today, it is called Selcuk, near the coastal town of Kusadasi."

"Kusadasi! That's where you went off the cliff on a motorcycle! Well, supposedly!"

"The motorcycle went off the cliff. The Turkish authorities assumed I was dead and notified the U.S. Department of State. That's why you, as next of kin, got a letter that I was dead. I had to remain anonymous to do the work I've been called to do."

"I'm still confused. What does Ephesus have to do with what you're doing now?"

"According to the Synodal Letter of the Council of Ephesus in A.D. 431, Mary moved to Ephesus after the death of Jesus. It was certainly dangerous in Jerusalem for Mary and her sons. Mary's house still stands in Ephesus. Pilgrims visit the house where Mary lived and observe miracles, probably just excitement and adrenaline induced hallucinations. Mary remarried after Joseph died and had four more sons, James, Joseph, Jude, and Simon. All four are named in the Gospel of Mark and the Gospel of Matthew. James stayed in Jerusalem and was head of the church for a time. Jude, Joseph, and Simon went with their mother to Ephesus."

"I'm even more confused."

"Here's the thing. I got DNA samples from a fossilized excrement pit near Mary's house."

"But that was nearly two-thousand years ago."

THIRTY-SEVEN

"Under the right conditions, DNA can last a million years. Scientists use it all the time in dating fossils."

"What's that got to do with us?"

"It's a good thing you are seated on the bed. What I am about to tell you is rather shocking. I compared the DNA samples from Ephesus to my DNA and to several of our Melungeon relatives. Several strands match. We are the descendants of a brother of Jesus. We are descendants of the Holy Mother. I've traced . . . . I should say my quantum computer traced this DNA strand down through history."

"Grover, this is a fairy tale."

"Hold on. Keep an open mind. The software tracked this precise DNA strand. Jude married a Turkish woman in Ephesus and had children. When Spain rose to power, they notoriously captured Turks living on the coast and put them into slavery. Eventually, a male descendant of Jude became a slave on a Spanish ship headed to the New World.

"War broke out between Spain and England in 1585. Historical records tell us that Sir Francis Drake liberated a group of Turkish slaves at Cartegena de Indio in what is today Columbia, South America. Drake sailed up the east coast. He docked at Sir Walter Raleigh's settlement on Roanoke Island, what would become North Carolina. The Turkish slave remained on Roanoke Island after Drake sailed away. The slave is the ancestor of the Melungeons. The slave lived among Native Americans and escaped Africans. Their descendants migrated to the mountains of North Carolina. We are their descendants."

"You're making some big assumptive leaps in that chronology."

"Grace, you want some more proof. Count your fingers. Rub the back of your neck. Where do you find polydactyly and the unique Anatolian bump? Grace, Anatolia is Ephesus, Turkey!"

"But even if accurate, what has that got to do with what you are doing?"

"Remember the fortune-tellers among the Melungeons. They had mental and psychic gifts. I inherited these gifts. I wasn't sure what I was supposed to do with them. After what I uncovered at Ephesus, I've had this sense of calling. It is my job, as a descendant of the Holy Mother, to save the planet from extinction. I've recruited some of the best minds in the world to help me. I have a billionaire who is willing to put his entire fortune into this cause. He knows the fate of civilization is at stake."

"So, just how is it that you're going to do this?"

"I'm going to save the planet with benevolent algorithms," G says as he leaves the room again.

THIRTY-EIGHT

Gathered in the upstairs dining room at Appalachian Java, Finn and his team construct a plan to observe the abandoned mining plant on the South Toe River. Finn points to a map spread before them on the table.

"I've already talked to Ben Carlson this morning, and there's a slight change of plans. The road dead-ends at the plant. It's going to be very conspicuous if we just go driving in there. There are a few houses along the road to the plant. Lisa and I are going to pose as law enforcement officers looking for a woman with dementia who has wandered away from home. We'll go door to door and ask if anyone has seen this woman. Hopefully, we'll get some information on any recent activity around the plant.

"James and Bob go into the little village of Micaville. That's where Highway 80 starts up toward the South Toe River. Go into Maples, a coffee shop, and go into the Micaville Outpost, an arts and provisions store. Ask questions. Remember you are hikers, but you're also interested in minerals and gems. Ask about local mines. See if there is any new activity in any of the local mines."

Finn and Lisa hop into their silver Jeep Wrangler Sahara. They leave Burnsville and head east. At Micaville, they take Highway 80 toward South Toe River. Finn gives the Jeep more gas as the elevation starts to increase. Lisa eyes old farms with cows munching on green grass. Several of the brown and white cows raise their heads and peer through sagging fences at the roaring Jeep.

Finn turns on the side road that will take them to the mine and plant. A pair of dirty-white tennis shoes tied together hang over a power line that crosses over the road. An abandoned yellow school bus sits beside a small creek with white pines and hemlocks on the banks. Finn passes the first house but stops at the second house when he sees an elderly man cutting grass. Out of the Jeep, Finn and Lisa stand in the man's driveway lined with crabapple trees. The man pulls into the driveway and turns off his mower engine. Grease spots dot his overalls. His skin looks like hard bark from over sixty years spent farming in the sun. Hair, white as snow, gives him a ghost-like appearance. His mud-stained boots are untied.

"If you're from Jehovah's Witnesses, I'm a Bible believing Baptist. I want to be polite, but I'm already saved, me and my wife," the excited man says with spittle flying out of his mouth. "I ain't selling my truck neither," he points to an ancient looking pickup truck. "Everybody wants to buy my old truck, but I ain't selling Ole Bessy."

"No, none of that. We're law enforcement," Finn says as he and Lisa pull out fake state crime department badges. "We're with the missing persons department. We're looking for a woman with dementia who has wandered away from home. Her family thinks she might have come this way. Have you seen a woman wandering around?"

"Nobody comes up this road anymore. Well, they've started lately, but I haven't seen a woman. I've seen some electrical and plumbing trucks going down to the old mica plant on the river. Somebody must be getting ready to reopen that place. I hope not. When I was a boy, the air was filled with mica particles. I worried it might give us all lung diseases."

"My name is Finn, and here's my cell phone number. Call me if you see a woman wandering around."

"Sorry, my wife didn't come out and say hello. She's on the oxygen and carries that tank around."

"You tell her hello for us and don't worry."

Back in the Jeep, Finn phones Brown, in the situation suite at the Nu-Wray Hotel, with an update. Finn calls Dooley and fills him in.

"James, we are headed back to Micaville. Lisa will stay with you. Bob will go with me to Burnsville. I've got an idea on how we can get a look at the plant."

In Burnsville, Finn pulls into Stamey Electric Company. He asks the clerk if he can see the owner. The clerk points them down the hall, past the restrooms. Finn glances in the restrooms. The yellow stains on the sides of the toilets make him wonder if they've ever been cleaned.

"Come in," a voice says as Finn knocks on the open door. Finn and Bob close the office door behind them and show Elijah Stamey their FBI badges.

"We're trying to find out who did the electrical work at the old mica mine on South Toe River?"

"Yep, that was us. We put in a big generator and some new heavy-duty wiring."

"We need to rent one of your panel vans for a few hours," Finn says. "We can't tell you any details, but we need it for an operation. One of us will get an expense voucher from you later, and you'll be paid for our use of the company vehicle."

"Of course, of course, anything to help the FBI. Keep it as long as you need it."

"Just this afternoon, but we'll let you know if we need it longer. It's very important you keep our activity here strictly confidential."

"Of course. My lips are sealed. One of my electricians called in sick today. So, you can have his van. It's just about new."

"I see you have a Stamey Electrical baseball hat over there. Can we buy two of those?"

"I'll give them to you."

"How do you get into the plant? I imagine there's a gate or something?"

"Let's see. I got the code for the gate lock on my desk somewhere." Elijah sifts through several stacks of paper. "Here it is, centaur. Do you need me to write it down?"

"No thanks."

Eyebrows raised, Finn and Bob look at each other. They thank Elijah with handshakes and remind him not to tell anyone about what they are doing.

Finn and Bob leave Burnsville in the van but notice the fuel gauge shows near empty. They stop at an Exxon station and fill the tank. Soon, they are speeding up Highway 80 toward South Toe River.

The code opens the gate, and the Jeep moves toward the plant. A huge flock of black birds flutter out of a large oak tree, fly over the plant, and across the river. Finn doesn't see any vehicles. Normally, G would be at the plant during the day preparing Centaur for the assault on the government, but he has a house guest. The agents observe the buildings and their surroundings. Rust dots the tin roofs. As acorns crack under their feet, they approach the main building where a stack of rotten pallets has collapsed. An aged dump truck from the 1960s sits on four flat tires. A faded yellow forklift sits beside the truck with barely legible letters on the side, Hyster. Piles of mica dust look like forgotten graves. A storage shed is attached to the main building, and the door is open. The back of the shed is dark.

"Damn! Rats! Look at them! Might be hundreds! I see their eyes in the back of the shed, and they're chittering!" Bob blurts. "Wow, it doesn't look like this plant has been in operation for a long time."

THIRTY-EIGHT

"They were polluting the South Toe River last century. The EPA shut them down in the 1970s."

Bob spots a recently installed surveillance camera attached to a corner of the main building and another on a smaller building. Finn and Bob think they can avoid the cameras by circling toward the rear entrance of the main building. Steps lead up to a loading dock at the rear of the building. Mica dust covers the dock floor and the piles of discarded machine parts from another century.

Finn's eyes search the dock floor. "Look at the bottle," Finn suggests. "That flavor is new. Island Punch. I saw an advertisement for it a few days ago. Someone has been here recently."

"What do you think? Should we try to force our way in?" Bob asks.

"We can't let it look like someone has been here snooping around," Finn answers. "Get some listening devices out of your backpack. We'll put those around." The listening devices are in two forms. One looks like a little rock but has a microphone inside. The others with microphones inside look like round marbles and can be rolled under doors or through wall cracks.

"We'll put our cameras out near the gate." The cameras are embedded in small pieces of plastic made to look like weathered wood.

As they drive away in the borrowed electrical company van, Finn says, "Maybe we didn't need the van and the hats, but if we missed one of their surveillance cameras or if someone was at the plant, our cover would have come in handy."

Finn phones Brown and gives him an update. Brown says the microphones and cameras left at the plant are working, but only a Mr. Monk has been seen on a camera.

"Mr. Monk?" Finn puzzles.

"Chip Monk," Brown says.

"We need some humor, thanks. Lisa is coming to your room now to monitor the devices. Join us for dinner at the Garden Deli on the other side of the town square," Finn informs. "I hear the food is delicious."

Finn tries not to think about Grace but feels like his feelings are piling up, like an emotional junkyard filled with worry, hurt, anger, and sadness.

THIRTY-NINE

Grace hears the deadbolts retracting. G enters the room. Grace sees five phones attached to G's belt.

"That's a lot of phones!" Grace says.

"I've got a box of them and a box of SIM cards. I'm constantly destroying them. I don't want anyone to trace my calls."

"How long have you been working on fusion energy," Grace asks, trying to gain G's trust.

"Since the 1970s. I started at the Princeton Physics Laboratory. I spent some time at Chung-Ang University in South Korea. I learned quantum mechanics in Austria with the Austrian Academy of Sciences. Fusion research been going on since the 1930's. At the current pace, we won't have fusion energy until after the planet reaches its critical warming temperature and apocalyptic climate changes will sweep the globe. Grace, we are getting close to one-hundred years of research and development, and that's inexcusable. We could already have active sources of fusion energy. The coalition of fossil fuel companies and politicians continue to stand in the way.

"We've solved our biggest development problem. We created a record sixty-nine megajoules of fusion energy using 0.2 milligrams of tritium and deuterium. We're able to heat these elements to over one-hundred million degrees Celsius, seven times hotter than the core of the sun. The heat forces the two elements to fuse together into plasma releasing incredible heat. Hydrogen-boron has been even more promising and that's called aneutronic fusion. The tokamak in San Diego is lined with strong magnets that hold the heat in and produce pure, clean energy. Our problem has been that the plasma tears and escapes the magnetic field inside the tokamak."

"Wait, what's a tokamak?"

"A tokamak looks like a huge donut. They are very expensive to build since they must withstand incredible temperatures. And that's the problem. We need more funding to build more tokamaks. Recent AI algorithms can help us predict when the plasma will tear. We are on the doorstep of the most incredible discovery of all time, but we need funding. Democracy,

I'm afraid, is not working in this area. Politicians are beholden to the fossil fuel industry that pays for their campaigns and lines their pockets with millions. People are excited about AI and the big datacenters being built around the country. Those datacenters use a tremendous amount of energy and that energy comes from burning fossil fuels, and that amounts to more carbon in the atmosphere."

"So, what are you going to do?"

"Remember the technology I used to put you asleep and control your car. We're going to force the politicians to fund fusion technology. We're going to use cellphone technology and my algorithms to force politicians to act."

"Cellphone technology?"

"The same technology used by FEMA and the FCC to send Emergency Alerts. They send out an alert in October to every cellphone in the United States. Wireless carriers are required by law to send out these alerts, and cellular services are required to hand off the messages from one network to another in a process called peering. My algorithm can perform the exact same task. I can send a signal to any geographical area in the nation or to the entire nation. I had an assistant in Irvington, Virginia, compiling databases of target groups: Senators, Representatives, and others. He doesn't know what I plan to do with the databases. And I know you have been in that area with Finn Boone and the other FBI agents. They don't know about this operation, and by the time they find out, it will be too late."

"So, you're going to send a cell phone message to all the members of Congress?"

"We'll target just a few to begin with. The cell phone alert will contain a frequency variable that targets the optic nerves and renders the person blind. Then, we send another message demanding legislation be passed at once to increase funding to the necessary level for fusion energy development, or else more members will be struck blind. It's the same technology that put you to sleep, but it targets a different part of the neurological system. They won't know it, but blindness is temporary. If I must, I can increase the frequency to cause permanent blindness. Grace, wouldn't it be better to blind a few people in order to save the entire planet? It's situational ethics. Remember Joseph Fletcher? I'm sure you studied his ethical theories.

"And I'm sure you heard in the news about the acoustic attack on the U.S. Embassy in Cuba. Several embassy employees got sick. It's a non-lethal weapon the Russians have been using against us for years and not only in Cuba but in Europe as well. CIA agents are losing their sight and hearing.

"I also have the technology to send fake-robo calls to every citizen in the country with instructions coming from the President of the United States. I can have the President telling citizens to pressure members of Congress. With my AI technology, I can take over the computers on commercial ships and crash them into bridges. I can do a lot of things to force congressional compliance.

"And that's not all we'll do. Remember how our mother was refused hospitalization and treatment for her brain tumor because she did not have insurance or money?"

"Of course, but she was my mother . . . . and your aunt," Grace says.

"I know, but I will always think of her as my mother. Nevertheless, we will force Congress to provide Medicare type coverage for all so that no one ever again goes through what we did. We spend more money on healthcare than any country in the world and a lot of other countries have better health care systems. We'll cut out the companies that are getting filthy rich off our healthcare system and donating large sums to politicians.

"We'll demand common sense gun control legislation.

"We'll demand term limits for the Supreme Court. It's simply ridiculous these people have lifetime appointments. A lifetime appointment in the late 1700's was okay. There were very few people with a legal education then, and they did not live very long. We have lots of brilliant legal minds today. We'll demand the court be expanded. The justices are so incredibly slow. There will be more justices. They can focus on different areas of the law, and court cases will be solved much quicker.

"And there's much more we can do. We'll dismiss Congress eventually. Think of all the money that's spent on political campaigns and how little gets done. We'll put that money to better use. Lobbyists will be put out of business. That money can be used to fund more fusion development and human development."

"So, who is going to govern the country and make the laws?"

"Benevolent algorithms! We have the technology. AI can determine what is best for the country. There'll be no political campaigns. No bribery, that's often what political campaign donations amount to. We can write the algorithms, input the necessary information, and AI can calculate all the variables and possible outcomes and give the best outcome. For example, AI can calculate where highways and bridges really need to be built, instead of in a particular Senator's state who is up for reelection. We'll need national administrators with limited terms, and people will get to vote on them."

"Grover, and I am not going to call you G anymore. You'll always be Grover to me. I like your goals. I don't agree with the method. We should use our democratic principles to make these changes."

Grover makes a fist and releases it. "You need to understand! It's going to take too long! The planet is going to overheat and cause the greatest suffering in the history of the world. When the polar ice caps start to melt, huge deposits of methane gas will be released into the atmosphere. Methane gas multiplies the greenhouse effect more than any source of pollution. The greenhouse effect means the sun's heat can come into the atmosphere but can't escape. Deadly changes in the atmosphere could happen in months. Living on earth will be like living in a zip-lock bag and could quickly get so hot skin slides off peoples' faces. It will be an apocalypse of pain. Perhaps the wealthy will make special arrangements for themselves and stay in safe areas, but the common people of the world will have to endure physical and mental agony like never seen before.

"Grace, we'll not only save civilization, but we'll also make a better world. There comes a time in human history when bold people must do bold things. It's time for a Second American Revolution."

"You're really going to do this, aren't you? You're going to inflict blindness on people! What if people are in their cars when they go blind? They'll crash into other cars. People will die! You're going to kill people!"

"I don't want to kill people, but hopefully only a few people will die. Think about the ethics of this. If I do nothing, many millions of people will die from climate catastrophe. A few people might die when we take our action, but millions will be saved. We sacrificed hundreds of thousands of soldiers to save the world from the madness of Hitler."

"There's got to be a better way," Grace pleads.

"Grace, I need you to trust me. And I think you need to expand your mind. You need to see the possibilities. I'm tripping tonight, that helps me put things in perspective."

"What? Tripping? LSD?"

"Yes. I've been dropping since the 70s. I knew Timothy Leary. Our paths crossed at Harvard. He was a psychologist and recommended LSD for my Generalized Anxiety Disorder. The medical field is just now admitting LSD is a viable treatment approach. I like it because it helps me see things more clearly. I'll bring your dinner, and we'll talk about it."

"Okay, but I don't want to drop acid."

"Grace, it's deeply introspective. You'll appreciate the experience," Grover starts to leave the room.

"Grover, what's that hump on your back?"

"My G-Pack. I made it, and it's the only one in the world. My billionaire backer gets the next one. It's a mini-quantum computer inserted next to my spine. It constantly monitors my blood pressure and cardiovascular system. It destroys malignant cells as soon as they are created. It can detect viruses that enter my body and send messages to my pharmacy if I need any medications. If Congress will make the wealthy pay their fair share of taxes, we can make one for every citizen. We can make a better world."

Grover leaves the room and returns minutes later with a microwaved eggplant parmesan dinner and a bottle of water. "The eggplant was frozen, but I like it. I don't eat meat. I don't want to support the very cruel animal meat industry."

One of Grover's cellphones chimes. He leaves the room, not wanting Grace to hear the conversation. Grace remembers seeing friends in Durham using an eyedropper to place tiny drops of LSD on their tongues. She wonders if Grover might have put LSD drops in her food. She goes into the bathroom and flushes her dinner down the toilet. She checks the bottle of water and sees the seal has not been broken. She feels dehydrated and takes a few sips. Grover returns to the room.

"The eggplant was good, but I'm feeling a little lightheaded," Grace giggles as she sees if Grover will tip his hand. "Did you put something in the eggplant? Maybe LSD?"

"Yes, and I took mine just before I came in the door. I want us to have this experience together. I often find myself floating over Yancey County. The best experience is lying down. Do you mind if I get on the bed with you?"

"No problem," Grace fakes another giggle.

In an hour Grover, with a narrow grin on his face, mumbles and occasionally laughs. "Grace, you see any colors?"

"Yes, bright colors. It feels like time has stopped."

Grover laughs and moans for almost five hours. Grace notices Grover sleeps. The bedroom door is unlocked. She gently rises from the bed and takes soft steps toward the door. Outside, she walks quickly on grass slick with heavy dew.

FORTY

Finn's phone alarm is set for 6:15 A.M. His phone rings at 5:47 A.M.

"Hello."

"Are you that Finn feller with the law looking for a missing person?"

"Yeah, that's me," Finn says as he hears a dog barking in the background.

"I just went outside to feed my chickens. I don't know if it's the same person, but a woman I've never seen before just come walking down the road."

"Okay. Thanks! I'm headed that way."

Finn jerks on his pants, pulls an Atlanta Braves t-shirt over his head, and puts his arms through a dark blue windbreaker. He phones Ken, who meets him at the Jeep. They speed down 19-E and up Highway 80 to South Toe River. They meet a few cars with workers headed for the fabric mill in Burnsville. A half-mile from the turn to the mining plant, they see a figure walking down the road toward them. As they get closer, they can tell it is a woman. Finn rolls down the window and stops alongside the woman. The curve of her face is familiar.

Finn's head jerks to the left when he realizes it is Grace. "Grace, jump in the backseat!"

Back at the NuWray Hotel, Finn introduces Grace to Lisa, Bob, and Brown. She feels like she already knows Brown because Finn has talked about him so much.

Grace tells them everything Grover has told her.

"Wow! This guy is really going to try this!" Brown exclaims as he nervously pops his neck to the left and then to the right.

"We knew growing up he was a genius," Finn says. "And now he thinks he is going to save the planet."

"He's a polymath who wants to change how we all live. I like what he wants to accomplish, but he sounds like he's lost touch with reality. It's like he thinks he is a Melungeon High Priest or something," Grace says. "But he has the skills and the technology to carry this out."

"The way Grace has described him he's like a roaring lion about to spring into action," Finn adds.

Finn calls Carson and shares everything Grace learned about Grover's plans. Carson tells the agents to stay put and go have breakfast. In the Nu-Wray Hotel restaurant, Grace orders oatmeal with fruit and avocado toast while the others order various forms of cooked eggs and meats. They all enjoy coffee. Finn tells the others he will pay the bill on his FBI issued credit card.

While waiting to sign the credit card receipt, they hear a couple enter the restaurant. They appear to know one of the servers.

"Julie, there's been a big explosion up on South Toe River, not far from where you live, near the old mica mining plant. Windows shook at our house."

Finn's phone rings. It's Carson.

"Finn, the problem's over. The threat was taken out this morning. The director explained the situation to the Secretary of the Air Force. He sent a fighter jet from Shaw Air Force base near Columbia, South Carolina. A couple of small missiles took care of the Lord of the Quantum, that was the code name. Your team gave us the information we needed. Thank the other team members for us. And listen, take a couple days off and enjoy the area before you head back."

Finn asks the team to meet him on the front porch of the hotel where they sit in rockers. A soft rain falls and a gray mist hangs in the air. He tells them what Carson told him. Grace puts a hand over her mouth as tears form in her eyes.

"I'm not surprised about the missile. When we were searching for the Atlanta Centennial Park bomber, and we thought Eric Rudolph was hiding out in western North Carolina, they had a military jet on alert at Shaw," Bob says.

"Folks, Carson said to take a few days here to rest and enjoy the area. So, let's meet for dinner at Carriage House Sundries. I'll be in touch."

Finn realizes Grace is in a tough position. "Grace, let's go somewhere where we can talk." They go to Finn's room.

"Grace, you must have a flurry of feelings right now. Grover is dead."

"A part of me is sad, and another part relieved. When he told me his plan, I thought he was psychotic, but he was really going to do it. And I think he could have done it, at least part of it."

FORTY

Finn left the television on in his room. He always does so others will think someone is in the room and so no one can overhear his conversations from the hall. An Asheville station broadcasts a regional news report. Finn and Grace turn their attention to the broadcast.

"We have a report of an explosion near Burnsville at a dormant mica plant. Officials say old tanks of LP gas are to blame. A rusty tank was apparently struck by lightning, triggering explosions. Officials say their investigation will continue."

"I'm guessing the public will never know the real story. I've been part of a few of these, nothing this serious. The Bureau does not want to alarm the public or give bad guys any ideas," Finn says.

On the desk, a phone vibrates, a text message. It's Finn's original phone that was compromised in Irvington, but Finn thought it might be a good idea to bring it along.

Finn picks the phone up and cannot believe his eyes. CROATAN. He shows Grace. "That's the same message Grover gave me when he gave up the bunker in Irvington."

"My God! He's alive!" Grace blurts.

Grace's phone pings. She has a message. "I'll find another way to do this. Something must be done soon."

Finn and Grace both try to respond to the texts, but it's clear the sending phone has been destroyed.

FORTY-ONE

After enjoying tasty and nutritious Sweet Melissa Salads at Pig and Grits, the couple spends the day walking the streets of Burnsville and visiting the antique shops.

Over afternoon coffee at Appalachian Java, Finn says, "I'm retiring for good. I'm not coming out of retirement for any more special assignments. I'll just go back and clean out my desk."

"I'm supposed to go on sabbatical this academic year. The seminary has a visiting professor lined up to teach my classes. I'll retire. Let's move back here. Buy a place on the South Toe River. I want a vegetable garden. Sit on the porch. Listen to the water rush through the rapids, the owls hoot, the tree frogs chirp. See the fireflies in the night sky. And Grover has inspired me. I want to do all I can about the climate crisis."

"Legally?"

"Yes!"

"Deal! We'll start finalizing our plans tomorrow. Maybe, if we have enough money, we'll get a small place in Irvington, too. I really like the area and the Bay. I want to get a dog. One like Ole Blue I had as a boy. But I want to go see my mother this afternoon."

"Finn, she's so proud of you. I can hear her now, 'Finn, you are a good man!'"

"Grace, they made fun of you growing up, but what you've accomplished in the theological world and beyond is incredible! You've empowered lots of minorities to claim their God given equality!"

"Finn, I love you, always have."

"Grace, I'll love you as long as my heart beats!"

APPENDIX A

Thanks to Barbara Kingsolver and her Pulitzer winning book *Demon Copperhead*, more people are aware of the term Melungeon. It is a controversial race classification and used in this book for descriptive purposes. Even the root for Melungeon is debated: the French word *mélange* (mixed) or m*elunjinn* from Arabic translated "abandoned by God" or "a cursed soul"?

Controversy swirls as well around recent DNA testing. Some people contend Melungeons are simply the result of African and Northern European ancestors brought together in the New World (1500-1600s). Others insist on a more complicated ancestry and claim Melungeons descended from Turkish (Moors) slaves brought to the New World by Portuguese or Spanish sailors.

For this novel, we went with the Turkish explanation. War broke out between England and Spain in 1585. Sir Francis Drake raided Spanish settlements, settlements using Turkish slaves, in the New World in 1586. At Cartegena de Indias (present day Columbia), Sir Francis liberated several Turkish slaves who went with him on his journey up the coast of the New World. He sailed to Sir Walter Raleigh's settlement at Roanoke (on the coast of present-day North Carolina). At Roanoke (later to be The Lost Colony), a Turkish male slave was released. The Turk became the genealogical ancestor of the Melungeons in the mid-Atlantic. Eventually, the descendants of the Turkish slave intermarry with escaped Africans, Native Americans, and some suggest survivors of the Lost Colony. This would account for the mixed DNA results of those who claim to be Melungeons today.

In this novel, the Turk came from Ephesus in Turkey. The Anatolian Bump (also known as the Central Asian Cranial Ridge and in the United States as the "Melungeon Bump") is found only on the people from the Anatolian region of Turkey (Ephesus) and Central Asia. People claiming to be of Melungeon descent in the United States often have a distinct bump at the top of the neck just where the skull begins. In addition, inhabitants of the Anatolian region and Melungeon descendants in the U.S. have unique dental configurations called "Asian shovel teeth."

Also unique to the Efes (Ephesus) region of Turkey is polydactyly (usually six digits/fingers). People claiming to be of Melungeon descent in the U.S. sometimes exhibit six fingers. Furthermore, people of Melungeon descent in the U.S. often come down with diseases that are unique to people of Mediterranean descent: *erythema nodosum sarcoidosis* for example.

English explorers as early as 1654 reported seeing very small communities of "mixed race" people living in remote areas of western North Carolina.

As a child growing up in the Appalachian Mountains of North Carolina in the 1950s, a person would occasionally be pointed out to me and identified as a Melungeon. Typically, the person would have brown or olive skin, oily dark hair, and blue (or occasionally green) eyes. I sat beside a young boy in elementary school with all those characteristics who was routinely identified as a Melungeon. See my first book *Tethered to an Appalachian Curse*, published by Wipf and Stock in 2021.

An internet search will reveal famous people thought to be Melungeon descendants. This book is a work of fiction and only uses the term Melungeon for descriptive purposes and does not claim to be an authoritative source on the history of the Melungeons or anyone's DNA.

According to ancient church documents (Synodal Letter of the Council of Ephesus, A.D. 431), Mary, the mother of Jesus, moved to Ephesus, Turkey, after the death of Jesus. If you have traveled to Ephesus, you might have visited the house where Mary lived (according to some accounts). One can imagine being the mother of Jesus in Palestine after his death might be a difficult situation, perhaps even a dangerous one. So, moving across the Mediterranean might be a solution for Mary. It might not be unreasonable to think at least one of Jesus' younger brothers, Joseph, Jude, or Simon, went with his mother and perhaps married a Turk who bore him children.

APPENDIX B

Our protagonists, controversial Presbyterian theologian Grace Goins, PhD, and FBI Special Agent Finn Boone, grew up on the banks of the South Toe River, in a tiny community nestled between Burnsville and Spruce Pine, small towns between Asheville and Boone, North Carolina.

Many of the Boones are descendants of Daniel Boone, the 1700's explorer. Daniel's family were Quakers in England, but, like the Scots and the Irish, they were persecuted by the English for not following the religion of the King of England. These minority religious groups fled England, and many arrived at the harbor near Philadelphia. Seeking lands of their own, these fiercely independent souls migrated down the Great Wagon Road of the Shenandoah Valley with some settling there, but many journeying on through the Maggoty Gap (near Big Lick, Virginia, now called Roanoke) of the Appalachian Mountains and into North Carolina. Avoiding the coastal and piedmont areas where the hated English have already settled, they made their way into the Toe River Valleys of Western North Carolina. Daniel Boone is one of the first to explore the area.

During the 1700-1800's, the settlers sustained themselves with vegetable crops and protein from pigs and cows on their small farms located beside small creeks where flooding over the centuries washed out small areas of relatively flat grass land. In the early 1900's, the Industrial Revolution, hungry for raw materials, found resources in the North Carolina mountains. The coal gods left coal deposits mostly in Kentucky while western North Carolina had veins of pegmatite minerals: mica, feldspar, and quartz.

Mica was needed for paints, drywall, and insulation. Mica was used in radar wiring systems, and mica-mining became a "necessary war industry" in World War II. Our protagonists attend elementary school in a small village named Micaville. A single block of mica was used in the mirror for the Mount Palomar Telescope lens.

Feldspar is processed into ceramics, chinaware, glazes, and enamels. Rather than the "black lung" diseases of coal mines, workers in North Carolina mountain mines and processing plants suffer from "white lung", typically silicosis. The community of Kona, where a large feldspar processing plant once thrived, is named after the chemical composition of feldspar: K for potassium, O for oxygen, Na for Sodium.

Quartz was once viewed as a nuisance and disposed of when found in feldspar or mica ore. However, in an incredible turn of fortunes, the computer age brought a hunger for high purity quartz that is an essential component in semiconductor chips. High purity quartz is only found in one place in the entire world. Today, every computer in the world that uses a silicon chip has a little piece of this part of Appalachia in it. The fate of the world's economies hinge on two mines near Spruce Pine, North Carolina, according to Ethan Mollick, associate professor at the Wharton School (University of Pennsylvania). In an article in the March 2024, edition of *TechSpot* journal, he says, "If they were to stop operating, it would mean a few years of catastrophic disruption . . . ."

In the early twentieth century, the mines and processing plants provide opportunities for employment, but they were very low paying, non-union jobs. Industrialists in the northeastern United States saw the opportunities for cheap, non-union labor in the mountains and moved hosiery, thread, and garment factories into the area.

Unless one becomes a supervisor, the jobs barely pay enough to survive. Great scarcity forces people to use birch tree twigs frayed at the end for toothbrushes. Children play with hog bladders filled with grains of corn. In winter, snow blows through cracks in the siding of houses. Many live on the edge of malnutrition especially during winter months when vegetable gardens are dormant. Salt-pickled vegetables in jars and pots of pinto beans provide essential vittles and nourishment. Rather than going to unaffordable doctors, ailments and diseases are treated with sassafras tea made from sassafras leaves picked from trees in the woods. Yellowroot tonic, made from roots dug from creekbanks, treats several disorders. Young teenagers are forced to quit school and work in the factories or mines to supplement the family income. It is a hard life for most.

When The Great Depression hit the United States in 1929, folks in the Appalachian Mountains did not notice. Their lives were already extremely hard as most lived below the poverty level. The Great Depression lifted for most of the United States prior to World War II but hung on in the Appalachian Mountains of North Carolina until the 1980's. To this day, pockets of poverty, hopelessness, and opioid addiction sprinkle the mountain areas.

www.ingramcontent.com/pod-product-compliance
Lightning Source LLC
Chambersburg PA
CBHW070629310726
48982CB00001B/214

* 9 7 9 8 3 8 5 2 2 5 3 2 3 *